X-TROT FOXRAY

Bill Arnold

HOBART BOOKS

X-TROT FOXRAY

ISBN 978-1-914322-03-7

First Published in 2021
by
Hobart Books, Oxfordshire, England
hobartbooks.com

Printed and bound in Great Britain by Clays Ltd, Elcograf S.p.A.

X-Trot Foxray

By Bill Arnold

Technical adviser: Mick Corrin,

the finest corporal in the army

Prologue

These were the days when I could crouch without my knees aching. I crouched now, the doorway giving me cover as I watched our corporal gently questioning a lady with an empty pushchair. I say *empty* but it was filled with shopping in plastic carrier bags from many different retailers. One was from Boots. Her hair was tied back to reveal striking cheekbones like those of a model, although in every other respect she apparently lacked the grace, deportment and composure required for that profession. She wasn't ugly but rather unkempt and worn down by life. Sallow skin made her look a tiny bit unclean and her cheaply made clothes fitted badly.

She was being civil enough, but I could tell that she wanted to get away from him. It didn't pay to look like you were being too friendly with the soldiers – the Brits. Not round here.

I was a little bit dismayed to see a tiny patch of rust forming on the flash eliminator of my rifle. I wondered if I could wipe it away with a piece of oily flannel without anyone noticing. It could wait, I decided.

The rain continued to fall. In my mind, it rained every day we were there. Every day, it rained in my mind.

The Funeral

The truth is I only went to his funeral because I had nothing better to do. I had a charity shop suit and a white shirt that I kept for interviews and which I wore with a blue tie. The tie had stripes in a darker shade of blue which gave it a vaguely regimental air, although it had come from Next. I wore black Oxfords which I had owned since school. They were as stiff as boards now and made a sound like some sort of crude percussion instrument being played with a languorous rhythm in an old church hall with a parquet floor and those huge metal chairs covered in cracked red vinyl.

But it was a funeral, and my clothes were adequate. No one could see that the suit had developed the satin lustre of well-worn fabric or that my laces were frayed. The stain on my tie was hidden by my buttoned-up jacket. No one noticed these things at a funeral.

I was having a bad time myself but at least I was still alive. That's what I told myself. Life was better than whatever followed it.

Strangely, I had actually written in my diary, 'never forget how unhappy you are right now', and yet that is precisely what I have done. I can't remember what prompted me to put those words down. I mean, obviously I wrote them because I wanted a reminder of my mental state, but I can't recall any specific event that had led to me feeling that way. For that, I blame the onset of middle-age and the realisation that the best part of my life is over and that I have had my one great adventure, and not even recognised it for what it was until it was too late.

I think I hated the whole thing – every last moment of it – and yet now I yearn to be young again and to go back there, do it again, do it slightly differently, and most of all appreciate the whole experience. I want a fresh reminder of what I gave up when I left the army. I want to taste that freedom all over again – the freedom of not having to do it, that is. I want to relive every precious moment and to do it in such a way that I truly understand where the past lay and what the future really held.

All of which is impossible. Instead, I have let everything slip through my fingers like the dry sands of a desert. It took over twenty years before the last of those grains landed on the ground at my feet and now here I am at Alan's funeral, which also feels like a chapter of my life coming to an end. He was the first of us to die.

I should thank my employer for giving me the time off to be here. But I won't. I'm actually suspended and being investigated for a crime I did not commit – as if those bastards care about minor details such as guilt and innocence. I really am innocent, by the way, but I won't bother you with the details, not in this book anyway. If I write a sequel that will be time enough...

The thing is, I lived close to Alan and I saw his obituary in the paper quite by chance. I was shocked at first, and then less so as it became obvious that his death was, in a way, overdue. He'd never been quite right. Thinking about him now, people would say he had ASD or something like that and was probably depressed too. Back then I had just thought he was weird, the sort of person you avoided if you could. Of course, we were all crammed together in a foetid room, so there was no avoiding anyone unless you planned to spend long periods of time sitting on the toilet or wandering about like a homeless sheep.

When I think about Alan it is clear that he never fitted in. What's less clear is whether *I* fitted in. The army is just a collection of misfits thrown together and made to get along under the banner of camaraderie. Our section in particular was the biggest bunch of misfits ever to wear a uniform. There was nothing that linked us at all apart from the fact that we worked, ate, drank and slept together for those four months. We shared the same fears, discomforts and privations, but for all that we had nothing in common. Take those things away and you are left with nothing. We breathed the same air, I suppose. God knows what we found to talk about. Well, you'll see what I mean as I relate my story to you.

You might think you know what goes on in the army, but you don't know the half of it. This is a story from recent history, and it is *just* a story unless you choose to believe it.

The Coffin

Alan's coffin was just a regular pine thing with fake brass handles and very little apparent workmanship involved in its production. I suppose he would have liked that. He wasn't a man for superfluous detail, emotional involvement, colour, cheer or compassion. He had virtually no character, and now that I know what ailed him – his autism or Asperger's – I feel guilty about describing him in those terms. But it was true. There was no human warmth in his character. In fact, he didn't really *have* a character. He was impossible to like. Trying to like Alan was like trying to make an emotional connection with a bag of cement.

The positive side of this character attribute is that you couldn't really hate him either. There was nothing to like or to hate.

He only spoke humorously in error. His smiles were the nervous sort. Alan couldn't make eye contact and never even attempted to be friendly or kind. Things like that – emotions and so on – were anathema to him. Such was the dearth of personality he displayed that he never even earned himself a nickname. He was plain old Alan, or behind his back, *Boring Alan*. There was nothing about his personality to which a cheery epithet could be attached. I try to convince myself that I regret not being a better friend, but it isn't true for I didn't really enjoy his company. My one consolation is the knowledge that he probably didn't really want a friend, me or anyone else. What was the point of friends?

So even in the company of misfits he was too far out to fit in. It wasn't the case that people made fun of him – although many disparaging remarks were made behind his back – it was just that people avoided him. He wasn't exploited or ridiculed. He was just more or less ignored. It helped that he was good at his job.

I knew that he would never make it as an NCO because he lacked both initiative and the respect of his peers. But as an ordinary soldier he was good enough and better than some, for he always did his job – slavishly, if anything.

But the story isn't just about him, it is about all of us from that time and place, it's just that Alan happened to pop his clogs first. Nowadays, it would be fashionable to call us a *band of brothers* or some other phoney aphorism, but back then we were a mismatched collection of soldiers from all over the country, thrown together and made to do a particular job, the necessity for which we didn't fully understand. For much of the time I didn't really feel like I was part of a close-knit team. I didn't feel that we *had each other's back* to use the modern term, although we probably did to some extent when I think about it now.

I also knew that we would never keep in touch when it was all over. Even with the advent of Facebook, I haven't managed to get in touch. Haven't managed? Haven't tried, more like.

You can't go back. We have all changed.

'D' Company

The rest of the company had been there about a week when I turned up, and that put me at a disadvantage straightaway, for even those soldiers on their first tour of Belfast felt as if they were grizzled veterans compared to me. They had been on patrol, stagged on at the gate, slumped in their beds seven times, whereas I had just turned up in a civilian Metro, fresh from my NIRTT course and, before that, fresh from training. I had been told that I was lucky to be sent out to the province rather than being kept in Germany as part of the rear party, but as I stood there, with my sausage bag at my feet, wearing my best jeans and sweatshirt, I didn't feel lucky. I felt sick with apprehension. Four months of this...

It was all going on around me. Everything was busy, purposeful. Everyone had their uniform on. Everyone had a job to do and a place to be. And everyone had a place to *go*, somewhere they belonged.

Except me. I was new. I was green. I was a sprog in common parlance. When our tour ended we would go to Germany, me for the first time, where I would become a NIG (New In Germany), which if anything sounded worse than sprog, and suspiciously racist. No

7

one knew me. No one cared about me. This was the army. The army was my mother and my father, and I was its unloved son.

My driver, a gap-toothed Brummie with a Browning pistol in a shoulder holster, pointed to company HQ and advised me to report in. As he sped out of the gates I was on my way with a heavy heart and heavier bags of kit.

HQ was a long, low, concrete building with small, reinforced-glass windows and a series of antennae reaching into the sky. These, I would subsequently learn, belonged to the Ops room, the inhabitants of which spoke to us (via earpieces) like God when we were out on patrol. They were a shady bunch who lived in near darkness, spoke in whispers, and never mixed with the rest of us. For some reason that is how I remember them: creatures of the night with grey, papery skin, thick glasses, and the faint odour of stale coffee. In truth I don't know if I ever saw one of these secretive creatures, but I formed this negative opinion of them nevertheless.

One of the jobs given to the soldiers on QRF – the quick reaction force, who generally were nothing of the sort – was to bring the Ops room staff their meals from the cookhouse since they were far too busy directing the war to go there in person. The first time I performed this task, in the company of another soldier called Johnno, I was puzzled by the fact that he piled their foil trays with vegetables, mainly turnip, peas and sprouts, with perhaps a token potato and maybe a pale, under-cooked sausage.

The result was a distinctly unappetizing meal and certainly not a balanced diet. I asked why he had done this, and he told me that he hated them, without explaining any further. His hatred struck a chord with me and from that moment on I hated them too.

I still hate them.

As for Johnno, I don't know what happened to him. He was not with us at the end of our tour, but his departure went unremarked. Some people just fade away.

I trudged to the company lines and the first person I bumped into was the company clerk, the exceedingly tall Corporal Harvey, who looked like a pole-vaulter but would later find a modicum of fame as a failed bank robber. Failed, as in *got caught*.

Harvey looked at me from on high and without expression. I timidly explained who I was, feeling unloved and useless, and he told me to dump my stuff, get some uniform on and follow him down to the sergeant major's office. I got changed in a side room, my heart thumping in my chest, anxiety high.

When I was ready, I sought him out and waited while he made his way to the CSM's office. He explained who I was. I heard only his voice, as if he was speaking to an empty room, but I was summoned and then stood nervously in the doorway as he slipped out.

The company sergeant major was at his desk. He told me to come in. I marched in and halted, slamming my foot to the floor in a display of perfect drill. The few objects in the room vibrated as if Belfast was suffering an earth tremor, and the CSM rolled his eyes in despair.

'Fuck's sake', he cursed quietly, his ire directed at the shaky wooden floor rather than my dramatic drill movements. He looked at me and then said, 'in a moment I am going to ask you to stand at ease, but I want you to do so without stamping your feet.' I nodded. 'Do you understand?' I nodded again and added a 'yessir'.

'Stand at ease', he said and with an effort of will I did so, sliding my foot out gently and putting my hands behind my back. If you had had to perform drill whilst on a night-time recce patrol behind enemy lines, then it would be done this way. I felt more than faintly ridiculous but the CSM was satisfied with my efforts and bade me sit down, which I didn't do because there was no chair. He looked at me quizzically when I didn't respond as he had expected.

'There is no chair, sir', I ventured.

'That bastard Patterson', he said, standing and sweeping out of the room. He was gone for over a minute, giving me the chance to wonder what the hell was going on, but he returned with the chair, plonked it on the floor and indicated once more that I should sit. This time I complied.

He asked me if I was Private Dickson and I replied that I wasn't. He looked at a list and mentioned a few other names until he hit upon mine, the ownership of which I eagerly grabbed. I was surprised that the army posted its newly-trained soldiers in such a haphazard fashion. I mean, how could he not know who he was expecting? And where was Private Dickson if I was not he? Had they lost him? Did he ever turn up? Did he even exist?

'Okay then, welcome to D Company', he said. 'Just out of training?'

'Yessir', I said nervously. The CSM wasn't unfriendly or forbidding. Rather he was matter-of-fact, slightly jaded perhaps, as if biding his time until retirement. His attitude was quite unexpected. Unlike the psychotic loon from my training company at the depot, he seemed happy to display common humanity, almost as though he cared about the young soldiers in his care.

'Well, this is a good time to start. You get a bit of service under your belt and the army even gives you a medal for it, although you might be a hundred and three before you ever get it'.

I nodded and smiled, although I didn't feel like I deserved a medal. At that precise moment I think I would have swapped the medal for an immediate discharge. I couldn't picture myself doing this job, working in this place, meeting these people and doing the right thing. I felt completely out of my depth. I felt that I might make a terrible mistake that would result in somebody dying.

'I dare say you feel a bit nervous', he said, hitting the metaphorical nail on its actual head.

'A bit, sir', I admitted.

'You'll soon get into the swing of it'. He looked at his list again as if I might become the person he had originally been expecting. 'You are going into three platoon, in foxtrot three one alpha', he said, tracing his finger along a line like an accountant reading from a ledger. 'Corporal Spencer', he added. There was no particular inflection in the way he said the corporal's name, but I still detected what I thought was a note of distaste in his voice, although I could easily have been mistaken. What he didn't do, which I thought was very noticeable, was tell me that Spencer would *look after me* or that I *would be okay there* and the omission made me suspect that I *wouldn't* be okay and that he *wouldn't* look after me. Nevertheless, his overall tone was encouraging.

'The best thing to do is to listen to some of the advice you are given, keep your head down, do what you're told and say nothing – at least to start with. Try to remember that you are the new boy, and it takes time to fit in'.

Some of the advice? Which bits? How could I tell good advice from bad?

He nodded at me and smiled. I nodded and smiled back. Then he looked at his list again and said, 'you've got Lance Corporal Murphy in that section. He's a good bloke'. This last statement I took as further proof that Spencer was not to his personal liking; Murphy was a *good bloke*; Spencer was a corporal and nothing more. He made no mention of my sergeant or platoon commander but took me down the corridor to meet the OC, the unfortunately named Major Raper.

'When you are called in, you march in and salute', he said.

I presumed that I was now free to perform drill in the normal manner and so when I was called in, I marched in, halted… and that was where I came unstuck because Raper had his back to me and was searching for something in a filing cabinet. I didn't salute.

'Salute' hissed the CSM and I did so at once although Raper would not see me do so and would not therefore respond with one of his own. It seemed like a pointless gesture; why salute when the person to whom the salute is directed doesn't even know whether or not you have bothered? I was still at attention when he finally turned around with a manila folder in his hand. Now that he was actually facing in my direction, I felt like saluting again, but I fought the inclination and stood there like an anxious statue instead.

'Take a seat', he said, and I complied at once because this time there was a chair in place.

'So, Private Dickson, welcome to 'A' company', he said.

I frowned. The sergeant major had only just welcomed me to 'D' company, yet now I was in 'A' company according to the OC. What was going on? Had I been transferred in the brief moments between marching out of one office and into the one next to it?

But he quickly corrected himself.

'So sorry. Meant to say 'D' company. Just taken over', he added.

'This isn't Private Dickson, sir', added the CSM, tonelessly. I was beginning to think it would be easier if I just *became* Private Dickson – did it really matter who I was? But once my identity was established the interview continued.

Raper was actually fairly young but his grey hair and large glasses aged him somewhat. He looked like an owl. The uniform aside, he did not resemble a soldier.

He talked about the same things as the CSM, gave me the same advice, and then dismissed me. I saluted, about-turned and marched out.

****

Alan's coffin was laid on two trestles and it was at that moment that I felt my first genuine twinge of regret. He was what age, forty-eight or forty-nine? No age at all. Could someone have helped Alan before he got to this point? Wasn't it someone's job to stop him from killing himself?

But thinking of it now, I wasn't sure what sort of help he might have needed. *I* hadn't spoken to him for over twenty years and we had *never* been friends, so it wasn't as if he would ever have turned to me for help. And if he had, what could I have done?

Hopefully, I'd have done something had I known the dire straits in which he found himself, but in reality it's all too easy to under-estimate or dismiss other people's worries and fears. For a man, particularly an ex-soldier, it is natural to try to hide these things anyway, putting on a brave face and brushing the dust of despair under the rug. You have an obligation to be a real man right to the end. After all you've been through worse times, haven't you? You're tough, so get a grip…

How did he feel on that last day, the day when he had decided to kill himself? Did he experience a burst of elation knowing that his release was imminent or was he crushed by one final wave of despair? I tried to put myself in his place, but I couldn't. I had never felt *that* low. Had anyone known how bad things were? Was there any human contact in those last days? He'd always been a loner and, fittingly, his final act was something that he did alone. Suicide was an anti-social thing.

The church was compact, with a handful of crooked gravestones out the front, a short path to the door and gate with a wooden archway that looked like some sort of garden building from Homebase, the purpose for which was hard to define. The nave was small, with two sparsely filled bays of pews. The service was suitably low-key and poorly attended, the lack of mourners somehow mirroring the tragedy of Alan's life.

An empty church spoke of an empty life.

Of course, it made no difference to him who was there and who wasn't, but maybe, had we paid him more attention in life, this day might have been postponed for thirty or forty years.

This depressing train of thought had one advantage for me – it brought with it a genuine twinge of regret. Perhaps I *did* care.

Meet the Gang

After speaking to the OC, I was given a quick tour of the place by the CQMS, the man who looked after the stores and sometimes deputised for the CSM. Unlike a great many soldiers of that era, the CQMS was clean shaven but I was startled when he removed his beret to reveal a bald head. He aged immediately, seeming to gain ten years.

My assessment of him was that he was *okay*. He was neither pleased, nor displeased to see me and my newness was a fact of life rather than a handicap. Perhaps he was bored by army life or at least with the job of issuing oily things to sullen soldiers in queues but he treated me entirely... neutrally.

He pointed out the cookhouse, indicating its squat form with a languid finger and saying, 'cookhouse.' He favoured brevity. He pointed to the gate and the sangar and told me that they were, respectively, the gate and the sangar and so it went on. We passed a row of armoured Land Rovers, which went unmentioned and then up a short flight of steps. Halfway up, he paused and turned, pointing at a wooden hut.

'Chogie wallahs', he said. I nodded as if familiar with the term but in reality, I had no idea what he meant. We carried on up the steps and came, surprisingly, to a cricket pavilion. He pointed at the cricket pitch and, using the wonderfully flowery language that seemed to typify the man, said, 'helicopters.' There were no helicopters, not even one, but I got the message.

We continued walking on a tarmacked path littered with potholes. He pointed at a grand-looking redbrick building to our front and said 'TA.' That was all he said. We carried on, weaving through the potholes until we came to a sparsely occupied car park – two Metros, a soft top Land Rover and a Vauxhall Cavalier – and then cut across to the right. We came upon a little camp within a camp and he uttered the single word, 'Felix.'

I was able to deduce that Felix was the name given to the Royal Engineers bomb disposal team. Three Ford Transits and a couple of Land Rovers with the Felix the Cat symbol on their side gave the game away. One of the soldiers was operating their tracked robot, making it turn this way and that with the aid of a remote control like the ones used to fly model aeroplanes into trees on ultimately disappointing father and son trips to the park.

We didn't stop until we came to a second guardroom and another sangar, this one in the form of a tower.

'Guardroom, sangar', he said pointing. I nodded but he wasn't quite finished. With a literary flourish he added, 'Outside – bandit territory.'

I understood that too.

***

Naturally, given the fact that I was living on a little military island, allegedly surrounded by bandits, I was taken away to be issued with my personal weapon, a self-loading rifle, or SLR, by now quite an old design. It was a long, black, menacing and carried twenty large calibre bullets in its magazine. Not that accurate, it could nevertheless kill at six hundred yards in the hands of a skilled rifleman. Few soldiers could shoot with the necessary skill to hit a target at such ranges. Furthermore, the chances of hitting an enemy on the streets of Northern Ireland from such a distance were remote unless they decided to stand absolutely still and give you at least twenty attempts on their life.

The minute I took it into my hands I felt like a proper soldier. I experienced no immediate compulsion to shoot someone, but it was nice to know that I could defend myself. I mean that's part of the deal when you join up, isn't it? You are signing yourself over to the Queen for a minimum of three years and agreeing to shoot the enemies of our country on her behalf. You accept the reciprocal of that i.e. being shot yourself.

You might ask if soldiers actually think about such things? But of course, they do. I certainly did, although not with blood-thirsty relish. I merely considered the chance of mortal combat as a possibility. Even here, in Northern Ireland, where an armed enemy existed and operated against us, I thought it unlikely that I would have to fire my rifle in anger.

What was I doing here? What was this *thing* in which I was now involved? It wasn't quite war… but it wasn't peace either.

I took my rifle and cleared it in the approved manner, checking the safety catch and pulling the cocking handle to the rear to look inside the breech, making sure it was devoid of bullets. The storeman made me sign a chit. He exuded boredom.

'Don't lose it', he said, unimaginatively. I signed for ammunition and magazines and then I followed the CQMS back out into the daylight.

'Don't lose it', he said nodding at my rifle.

For the remainder of the day, I completed a myriad of small tasks, collecting kit and signing forms. My heart sank by increments at the thought of this new alien life I was now leading. I would have crawled back into the womb had I been able.

I felt lonely and isolated. I felt inadequate. No one gave a shit about me.

Shortly before tea I was finally shown my room and was able to dump my bags off. I was alone but my bed space was easily identified as the one with a pile of blankets and general bedding on the green piss-proof mattress. The other beds had duvets with football themes, cars or superheroes. One soldier had a Noddy duvet cover but for now I would have to make do with blankets and sheets until I discovered where to buy this singular luxury item – the coveted duvet.

I was making my bed, feeling unloved and weary when my new comrades traipsed in following a long foot patrol in and around the Falls Road area of Belfast.

'Who the fuck are you?', said one, his face a grimace of extreme distaste. The remainder didn't speak and barely looked in my direction. They dumped their kit and left the room again before I got the chance to explain who the fuck I was. I wondered disconsolately where they had gone and if I should go there too and I was still wondering this when a head poked round the door. On the head was the usual array of human features including a mouth from which the following words came, 'you'd better come and get some scran.'

I took my rifle and followed them to the cookhouse.

***

The person who had spoken was not Alan. I had no idea who it was at the time, but I was grateful for the acknowledgement of my existence and that I might have some basic human needs such as the need to salve my hunger occasionally. Alan would never have made the suggestion simply because it would never have occurred to him to help. It wasn't ignorance, it was his condition, but I didn't know that at the time. He was aloof, unfunny and couldn't make eye contact when he spoke. He found socialising difficult and the people who might otherwise have been his friend just found him difficult to be around. He claimed to like his own company, which was just as well because it was the only company he ever had, but looking back on those times as an older and wiser man I can see that was a defence mechanism. I think he might have enjoyed being one of the lads had it been possible for him. I think he was lonely.

Sadly, he had no idea how to become the person he wanted to be. He was like a dog which had never been around other dogs. Sociability isn't something you can teach, well not to someone who had Asperger's, my own diagnosis for his condition. I do think he studied the other men and tried to emulate them, copying their mannerisms and speech but his jokes always fell flat, his banter was unfathomable and his attempts at general wackiness came across as crass and embarrassing.

There was one thing that he got right, however, and that was to pay me no heed at all. Thinking of it now, it was a brilliant move. I must have seemed like a gift from heaven, arriving like that, not because I offered the chance of a new friendship but because I took away the pressure. Being new was worse than being weird, so straightaway he had me trumped. Despite my youth and my green-ness, I recognised this essential truth almost at once. Being new was unforgivable.

The others had set their rifles on the floor next to two tables which they were claiming as their own and so I followed suit, setting my rifle on the smaller pile of two. They were queued already, edging towards the hotplate like condemned men teetering towards the gallows. The hotplate was a mass of hot swirling steam, clattering crescendos of sliding stainless steel, clouds of odour, shouts and yells. The noise emanated from the kitchen and when I drew level, I was able to peer into this culinary cauldron. It was a glimpse of hell. I was glad I wasn't a cook.

I was the last man in the queue, the last man in my section, none of whom were bothering to look at me or make me feel welcome but as I stood there patiently, I was at least able to identify Lance Corporal Murphy with a single chevron on his combat jacket sleeve and Corporal Spencer with two. Murphy was tall and dark with a spectacular scar beneath his right eye which was visible when he turned his head. Spencer was smaller with red hair and thin, pale features. He was handsome but thin in the faced as if starved. He looked like a man under pressure. I don't know how to describe him other than to say that.

At some point one of the other soldiers, whom I later discovered was called Stoker, told Murphy a joke and the two men dissolved into laughter, falling about helplessly with tears running down their faces. They slapped their thighs and found difficulty in speaking although both men tried to relive the joke over and over to extract maximum mirth from it. Spencer looked on as if they were mad, but the remainder joined in laughing without having the original joke to give the situation some sort of context. Even I smiled, although I wished I knew what they were laughing at and wished that I was part of the gang.

By the time they reached the hotplate they could only point at the food they wanted and hope for the best. This was to be my first encounter with Sergeant Crotus, a man with a huge red nose, marked with enormous pores and greasy hair poking out from beneath his hat. Ugly and unkempt in the manner of someone with poor hygiene, it was unfortunate that it was his job to cook our food. He looked angry at the laughing soldiers' antics and his ire had not dissipated by the time I got to him. Nevertheless, I collected my lamb chops and mashed potato without incident although he looked rather startled when I thanked him; manners are not a big deal in the army. Apologies are *verboten*, a sign of weakness.

I saw Crotus every day on my trips to the cookhouse and strangely his face is one of the few that I can remember in detail. He had piggy eyes and looked at the world through cataracts of disdain. Everything about him was the wrong shape or slightly out of place. His hair was too long, his moustache too straggly. He was probably in his mid-thirties and yet his ears had already begun to sprout the thick grey hairs of old age. He was fascinatingly ugly.

For some reason I am sure that he was married but I simply couldn't picture the woman who might have chosen him to reproduce with. How terrible must she have looked if she had found him attractive?

I sat at a table with three soldiers who I gradually came to realise, through the use of their names, were Rockets, Chip and Dinger. Rockets had a broad face and an equally broad smile. He had Dracula black hair and pale skin and yet he was a cheery sort, saying little and laughing often. He was hard to dislike and no one did. He was the first one to really speak to me.

As we ate, Rockets pulled a little card from his pocket and showed it to me.

'This is my chuff chart', he said and indicated that I should look at it. As I spooned a forkful of tepid mash into my mouth, I perused his double-sided chart which detailed the number of days he had left to serve in the Army, currently standing at a total of 238, which seemed rather a lot, too many for it to be worth his time in counting them down. I smiled and returned the card to him.

'So, when do you sign off?', I asked politely. Rockets dabbed his chin with a serviette, mopping up some gravy. It was a surprisingly refined gesture.

'Already done it', he said, proudly. 'You sign off when you have a year to go.'

I made a note of this information and did a quick calculation; my own chuff chart, where I to construct one, would have something like 900 days on it. It might as well have been 900 years; I would never make it to the end. On the next table Stoker and Lance Corporal Murphy were finally bringing their laughter under control.

Rockets shook his head and gave a wry smile, 'Spud and Stoker are fucking nutters', he said. There wasn't much I could say. I was new. I couldn't agree or disagree, so I just smiled and that was okay for now.

The blokes were tired, the patrol had been a long one and it had been cold, boring, uneventful, all the things which sap a soldier's energy. After tea they would have showers and watch some TV and then get some well-deserved sleep. I supposed that I would do the same, although I would have an ordinary sleep rather than a well-deserved one. At the minute I didn't deserve anything, and I felt this lack of worth acutely as if I had already been labelled a second-class citizen. Suddenly I thought of something to say and I directed my words to Rockets, who clearly accepted my presence.

'Is this your first tour?', I asked him.

'Second', he said. I don't think he meant to be brusque, but the conversation did wither on the vine.

***

The few mourners looked as if they had been hired for the day; there was a palpable lack of genuine sorrow in the air. The exceptions were two elderly people whom I took to be his Mum and Dad, who sat right at the front and did not look around as the congregation filtered in. Looking at them, their grey hair, their stout overcoats, made me feel profoundly sad for the first time. That emotion was almost welcome. Up to now, I had felt anxious and guilty but not sad.

Alan and I had not been friends and we hadn't seen each other in so long that it would have been unnatural for me to feel great sorrow at his passing but now I had a vicarious emotion to fall back on claim as my own. Here, I supposed, lay the true tragedy. Alan was at peace now, or as he would probably have put it, *dead*. He didn't dress things up.

It was the living who suffered in the form of the only two people who had ever really felt anything for this strange man – his mother and father.

With my mind otherwise blank, I tried to imagine what it must have felt like to hear the news that not only was their son dead, but that he had killed himself. Some deaths are worse than others, but to find out that someone you had loved like no other had ended his own life – had seen no alternative – must be the worst possible news. How had he seemed the last time they had spoken? They must have re-played this final encounter in their heads many times since, looking for signs that he was thinking of exiting the world they shared. Was there anything from which they took comfort other than their own proximity to the afterlife?

Surely life had nothing good in store for them now. Growing old must be hard enough without the additional pain of outliving your child.

I wondered if Alan had any brothers or sisters – they didn't seem to be present if that was the case – and this thought reinforced the fact that I didn't know him at all.

The Patrol

Someone mentioned that we would be on patrol the next morning, setting out at zero eight hundred hours. Everyone went to bed early, including me.

Spencer took me to one side for a quick chat.

'You know what you're doing, don't you?', he asked, and I nodded, but not too eagerly because I wanted to give the impression that going on patrol was just a run of the mill event in my life. I waited for him to say something else, maybe along the lines of some sort of terse, grudging welcome, but he turned away at once and that was that. I wasn't tired and I wasn't excited, but I took some comfort from the fact that this time tomorrow I would at least have been on patrol with my new comrades and might have something to actually talk to them about. My shared experience had to begin somewhere and this business of being in Northern Ireland was the real thing – the only war that we had at the time. I vowed to keep my head down, to watch how the others behaved, and to learn the ropes as quietly and discreetly as I could. My opinions and experiences had no value to them at the minute, but this was the point at which I began to learn the ropes as it were.

And for now, I just had to relax somehow and then go to sleep.

The others chatted quietly as I finished making my bed, feeling very self-conscious as I arranged blankets and sheets in the absence of a duvet. I felt like a recruit. One of the soldiers had brought a ghetto-blaster with him, a huge silver monolith with bulging speakers and lights. It looked like a prop from Terminator, some sort of portable bomb of incredible destructive power. Currently it was blasting our ghetto with a tape of recent US soft rock classics – an album called *American Heartbeat* – most of which were unfamiliar to me at the time, but which would forever be burnt into my consciousness when I left Belfast a few months later. It was a sort of musical awakening for me: Blue Oyster Cult, Boston, Kansas, groups I came to love.

There were other tapes too, but not very many, and they did not all get an equal amount of play. *American Heartbeat* was the absolute favourite but there was also a mix tape of *Uriah Heep* songs that got played once, *Dark Side of the Moon* which got played two or three times, and various other mix tapes made from that year's chart music.

Another 'favourite' was a pirated copy of 'Bat Out of Hell' which was played incessantly, until one day Stoker could take no more. Without any fuss or show of anger he rose from his bed and padded over to the ghetto-blaster, flicked open the tape drawer, extracted the offending article, and then placed it on the floor, where he proceeded to smash it with his rifle butt. Not one word was uttered by anyone in the room, and Stoker returned to his bunk. The remainder of the evening was spent in near silence.

These songs were the soundtrack to our tour in Northern Ireland, much as Motown and Jefferson Airplane supplied the soundtrack to the film *Platoon* which came out around this time. It was near the end of our tour that we finally got to see that picture on a pirated video. In retrospect I am glad that we didn't see it at the beginning, but we are not at that point in the story.

Other popular music at the time was delivered to us by the Friday Rock Show. Even then I thought it strange that men with short hair liked music created by men with long hair; not just long but ludicrously long, and in some cases permed. The soldier's psyche is not easy to explain. I would rather have listened to a bit of Led Zeppelin or Deep Purple, the latter having recently reformed, but it wasn't the right music for that time and place. This was the era of Bon Jovi, Guns 'n' Roses, Skid Row. Besides, I had no say in what music we listened to. I was new so I kept my mouth shut on that and every other matter.

Of course, there was long hair and there was *long hair*. Iron Maiden had long hair and that was okay. Kajagoogoo had long hair and it wasn't. It would be hard to explain to a visitor from another planet, but somehow Iron Maiden wrote and performed songs you could fight a war to and Kajagoogoo really did not. The camp barber who turned up on Tuesdays and Thursdays in his Fiat 126, and who was completely *homosexualised* according to Stoker (he really was the *camp* barber), had the wrong sort of long hair, but we were forbidden from mentioning this to him since he at least had the courage to drive into an army base and do his job.

He was a pretty good barber too, if I recall. I don't doubt that he received threats on his life but in my time there he never missed a day and never turned anyone away even when he was packing up to go. He was okay really.

An alarm clock went off at five, and we all rose from our beds like wraiths to begin a sort of routine that would characterise the whole tour. Lightweights and boots on, towel round your neck, wash kit and rifle, pad over to the ablutions block, ablute, then return freshly shaved and smelling of Pears soap or similar. All of this was done in near silence, for although soldiers are disciplined and can get themselves up and ready in almost any situation, that doesn't mean they can always display enthusiasm. Five o'clock was too early for anyone, especially me.

I hadn't slept well, my mind alive to all the things I could do wrong in front of these men who didn't care about me. For some reason I could think of a dozen ways to make them like me less but no ways to make them like me more. If I slept at all it was from about 04.45 to 05.00, or at least that's how it felt. There was nothing I could do about it, but it felt like a bad way to fight a war if that's what I was being called upon to do.

The others paid me no attention, even when I followed them to the cookhouse where the duty cook slopped out some bacon, fried bread, beans, egg and sausage onto a plate. Again, I sat with my new mates and poked my food around the plate, until I noticed that I was being watched by Alan who was ready to pounce on any uneaten portion of food that attracted his attention. As a result, I forced myself to eat, ignoring the yellowy grease that ran over the plate's pristine white surface. This was *my* breakfast, and I might not get to eat for some time, so Alan and his worms, or whatever ailed him, would have to forego the remains of my meal.

I could almost feel his disappointment, but he said nothing. To have done so would have been to acknowledge my existence of course. The food wasn't that bad. Looking back, I might actually rate it 'okay'.

Ten minutes later, at five minutes to six, or 05.55, we were standing at the loading bay, pointing our rifles in the sand as we cleared them and then fitted our magazine of twenty rounds. I could kill twenty people, or double that number if they stood in rows two deep and not too far from the muzzle of my rifle. Now it felt real. This wasn't just going for a walk round a regional UK city, this was... well, it felt a bit like war. If someone shot at me then I was going to shoot back, and if that wasn't war, then what was it?

We lined up at the gate in our half-sections, which had once been called 'bricks', a term the army was moving away from on the grounds that bricks weren't very clever and to call four soldiers such was unflattering. Fair enough. I was with Spencer, Alan and Chip and we would take the lead, *bomb bursting* out onto the street and then providing cover while the second brick did the same. Spencer's briefing had been short and not really informative; after just a week, the job of patrolling was becoming routine to them. Most of the section had served in Ulster previously, so I supposed that they knew the ropes, but I hadn't and would have liked a little bit more gen on what I was expected to do. It felt like on-the-job training and on-the-job training always felt like a cop out.

So, one day after arriving I was out of the camp and onto the street, feeling brave and baffled in equal measure. I knew what I was supposed to do thanks to my Northern Ireland training course, but for some reason I was not completely convinced that the others would respond in any given situation in the same way that I did. I had assumed that they would cut corners.

Obviously in the event of being fired upon you took cover and tried to locate the shooter as the section commander sent a contact report through to the Ops room. Well that was the theory, but people reacted differently in different situations, and not always in accordance with the rule book. I had already figured out that the big flaw with the procedure lies in the bit about locating the shooter, who is likely to fire one or two rounds and then leg it.

It seemed to me that the best we could hope for in the event of a contact was to not get hit. Our enemies the IRA now knew, from bitter experience, that gun battles were a waste of time – *very early seventies* – and had developed tactics which gave them the initiative. The British Army, by contrast, was there simply to display that the rule of law still held on the streets of Ulster, even if this meant us being on the back foot for much of the time. We didn't exactly go on the offensive. Rather we patrolled in the hope that *they* were unable to go on the offensive.

So, we bomb burst out of camp, running like hell, appearing dramatically in the midst of the street.

It was just a British street after all that.

The eight of us took cover in doorways and behind whatever we could find, kneeling and watching, getting our breath back and assessing our surroundings before we carried on. My pulse was racing and not just from the brief exertion involved in running out of the gates; this was what all the training had been for, this was the only war I would ever get. Even after just one day this escape from the camp's confines felt like coming up for air, and the street looked fresh and clean as if it had been washed by the rain, despite the graffiti and litter. I think it was just the openness I liked.

But here I was in the dark heart of Belfast which must have been one of the most violent cities in the world back then. Two thousand people had already died as a result of the troubles, including a few hundred soldiers. By the standards of the Second World War, for instance, that was a tiny number, but for supposed peacetime it was an awful lot, particularly when you dropped that figure into the context of Northern Ireland being the UK's smallest and least populous country by some margin.

The street was more like a boulevard, but where exotic life might be found there was instead squalor. No trees grew, the sun did not shine, and the people did not stroll about in straw hats and shorts like boulevardiers of old. The people did not stroll about at all, and that was the first thing that struck me. To my left and to my right there were houses, but to my front there was nothing but cleared space, the sort of thing that you might have found in the nineteen fifties, when war damaged houses had been cleared but not replaced. But this was the nineteen eighties and there was no war. The *Blitz* was a distant memory. I had to remind myself of that fact.

Graffiti was popular but not very imaginative in its application. *Brits out* was self-explanatory, as was *IRA,* but I had to ask later what was meant by the initials *FTQ.* The Q stood for Queen.

We remained crouched for about fifteen seconds and then stood. The rifle felt good in my hands and I was fairly relaxed about our tiny mission. Only with a conscious effort would I maintain my alertness for the duration of the patrol; human nature dictated that my mind would wander. I had heard someone say, *that's when they get you,* but the threat of someone getting me seemed to recede quickly, much more quickly than I would have thought possible. We began to move towards the end of the road, two hundred yards distant.

I was the third man along. Spen took the lead, his head moving from side to side as he surveyed the ground before him and to either side with practised eyes. He was not someone I had warmed to yet, but in this situation I trusted him fully. For the first time I had the sense that he was the real soldier and I was just pretending.

I had never felt this way before, but up until now I hadn't had much time to think about my place in the world. I think I envied him his rank and his self-assurance. He was probably just five years older than me and yet a gulf lay between us in terms of respect and experience, those important things which make a soldier.

A police car, a Cortina with myopic, bullet-proof glass, drove past slowly, the driver giving us a little wave which was returned by Spen. We were on the same side of the conflict, allies, I suppose.

These men were unlike the usual British bobby with his bicycle, whistle and funny helmet. For one thing they were armed, and for another they had to police a country torn apart by something like a civil war. They got it in the neck from all sides – Protestant and Catholic, Loyalist and Republican – and a lot of crime went unreported simply because to tell the police seemed like collusion. They were well paid, or so it was said, but I didn't begrudge them their wages. If you want a policeman's wage, then join the police. If you choose to join the army instead then you'll get paid as a soldier. It was simple enough.

In a moment they were gone, the saloon car turning the corner to the left and disappearing from view. We were going in the same direction but first of all we paused, kneeling behind cover as Spen sent the other brick across the road first. When they were in position we followed and so it went.

We found ourselves on a busier road now, the eerie silence and desolation left behind as if we had left one world to enter another.

The row of red-brick, terraced houses, was punctuated by local shops: butchers, bakers but no candle-stick makers. I saw a tattoo parlour and next to it a barber. Further along I spotted a doctor's surgery, pharmacy and undertakers in that order, a neat arrangement, a statement about the ultimate futility of life. Dead-eyed shoppers thronged this street and at first I thought we might have to battle our way through an unyielding morass of humanity. In fact, they really didn't impede our progress at all, although their combined hostility was plain enough even when left unspoken.

These people were Catholics, something which I knew simply because this was their area and the two opposing sides thoughtfully remained within their own demarcated districts in a sort of self-apartheid. I had learned all this during my NIRRT course lectures and had been fascinated to discover just how different one part of the UK could be from all the rest. The Catholics and the Protestants went, for the most part, to separate schools, and it seemed logical that many of the country's problems must start there simply because they would see each other as different types of beings almost from birth. I wondered how such a situation could be tolerated, but that was just how it was. The history of Northern Ireland was complex and its social structure totally unique.

On one level this could have been any street; I could have been walking through Burnley, Dagenham or Perth, and yet on another level this was a place apart. Was that the effect that our presence had, or was it something that could be blamed on my heightened awareness? You could walk through Bedford on a busy day without feeling intimidated or under threat, but the same could not be said of Belfast.

The whole thing was surreal of course. We were dressed as soldiers and armed for combat, and yet our battlefield was this street with these shops and these people. We continued our patrol through this battlefield of outward normality. We passed a greengrocer's shop, a bookies, a TV repair shop and a newsagent. A hoarding outside the last of these had a Sun newspaper headline about Mrs Thatcher. A sign next to the newsagent's door told me that there was a watchmaker situated above the shop. Further up, there was a chip shop and a café, the latter open and doing good business already. *Didn't they know there was a war on?* Obviously not.

***

Next to Mr and Mrs Boring Alan was a man who looked like Alan, right down to the limp moustache and slightly gaping mouth. I was shocked when he turned briefly until I realised that this had to be Alan's brother and not the deceased haunting his own funeral service.

Had I known about this brother? No.

I had known nothing about Alan, and I suspected that was the case for the rest of us in the section. Alan had been a closed book. He never really talked about himself or his family. When he spoke at all it was about inconsequential things or matters of military importance (to him), such as what setting you had put your rifle sight on. His conversations were superficial. It was an effort for him to speak and, sadly, an effort to listen to him. Boring Alan.

I could still feel a vestige of annoyance about Alan after all these years, which in the circumstances was poor timing, when I was supposed to be mourning him. I was thinking in particular of his attitude to me during that tour, when he more or less decided that I was below him in the pecking order and that, as a result, I could safely be ignored. I suppose it had something to do with pack mentality and that he had identified a weakness in me which could be exploited and which would keep him one place above me. But what irked me – and as I sat there at his funeral these feelings came galloping back with renewed intensity – was the fact that he might have been better seeking me out as a friend.

37

I didn't *want* to be his friend, and the lack of mutual regard never became a source of regret, yet I couldn't quite understand why he didn't at least make the attempt. It was a bit like not being invited to a party that you didn't want to go to anyway; your relief was tinged with regret. What had you done to sleight the person whose party you didn't want to go to?

I looked again at the brother and wondered if he also suffered from Asperger's syndrome. Did it run in families? Back in the 1980s, when my life had intersected with that of Alan, I don't know if the condition was ever talked about or diagnosed. In those days, some people were just weird, but *no one* had Asperger's. I pulled a face as I thought back and then flicked at the corner of the tatty blue hymnbook as if some answers might fall out. They didn't.

***

So, as to the point of the patrol, I had to remind myself that we were there to be visible and to show that the Queen ruled on the streets of Northern Ireland despite the wishes of a large, vocal minority. Apart from their scowling faces these were ordinary people, and I supposed that some of the scowls were simply there as the result of the early morning blues rather than a deliberate display of hatred for the British oppressor.

Hatred is tiring and can have a greater negative impact on the hater than on the hated. Nelson Mandela probably had something wise to say on the subject, but he wasn't as widely quoted in those days, his wisdom much more widespread after his release from prison, which was still years away. But the point is that some of these people were just on their way to work and didn't have the energy or concentration span to hate us in particular. Besides there is only so much hate to go around, and sometimes you have to hate your job or your boss. Sometimes you have to hate your spouse or your parents. Sometimes your hatred is directed at a complaining neighbour or a grumpy bus driver, or someone who cuts you up in traffic. There were times when hatred for the British had to take a back seat, times when it had to be conserved for more pressing needs.

I didn't know who hated us, who tolerated us and who liked us. They all looked the same to me, friends and foes. I was wading through a human soup some of which was hostile and some of which was probably neutral. Who was who? Our enemies moved among us disguised as shopworkers, lorry drivers, teachers...

By this point, the 'Troubles', as they were called, had ground everyone down. Idealism wasn't quite dead but idealistic fervour was on its deathbed. Some of my new comrades saw all of these people as the enemy and made little attempt to distinguish between friend and foe, but I could never quite believe that they all hated us, even round here in bandit country. I certainly never subscribed to the view that all the Catholics were bad, and all the Protestants were good either, although a number of allegedly well-read soldiers held this to be true, thinking that they understood the situation with much greater clarity than the rest of us.

We didn't do battle with the shoppers for long, diverting to the right and taking ourselves down Parfitt Street, a residential area with the usual rows of red-brick houses. The street was clean, spotless in fact, and the puddles offered bright reflections of the heavens as if reminding us all that hope remained. It seemed as if no

39

one was about, that everyone was shopping or on their way to work or hiding. A few cars remained on the street and as I eyed the broken line of Vauxhall Cavaliers, VW Golfs and Toyotas, I could have been anywhere in Britain. This could have been Liverpool or Derby, not that I had been to either, but they seemed to fit the bill for ordinary middle-sized cities. There was nothing of Beirut or Saigon here, just the outward trappings of routine domestic misery. As I paced the slabs, I felt more in danger of an encounter with some curler-wearing harridan than a team of urban guerrillas. It would have been easy to switch off. The enemy was out there somewhere and, if I did enough patrols, I would meet them one day, or so I imagined.

The threat of rain became actual rain, as the clouds began to break up high over our heads. This was a place which suited grim weather. We kept walking.

Now and again, I looked behind me and saw the rest of the patrol following on, concentrating on concentrating. No one had fired at us and we had fired at no one. Was this the pattern? I wasn't worried and I wasn't bored, but I still felt mildly puzzled by the whole thing. I was patrolling British streets, looking out for an enemy that spoke the same language, that wore the uniform of the man in the street and that paid his taxes to the same Queen. That enemy could be anywhere. He could be driving a Renault 19 or an Austin Montego. He might have hair like Nik Kershaw and listen to mixtapes of the Chart Show recorded from the radio on a Sunday night. This wasn't an enemy like any other. They were as deadly as the Germans, more ruthless than the Japanese and yet they looked like our big brothers or our unwanted cousins. But to be honest, after a while, it became an effort of will to believe they were there at all.

Maybe not on this patrol though. This was my first and I could make myself believe that they were watching me over the sights of their Armalite rifle. And that was another peculiarity of the IRA; they were armed by our friends the Americans rather than by our enemies the Russians. *They certainly bucked that trend!* But who were the enemy and where were they hiding? I could be walking down their street right now and I wouldn't know it. So, for now, I had to be suspicious of everyone.

From behind those lace curtains I felt eyes watching me, and yet there was probably no one watching me at all, a possibility which I always acknowledged. I scanned the street looking for open windows from which a sniper's rifle might poke, or for attractive items which might be booby traps waiting to blow my hand off, and yet I felt secure being part of a group. I tried not to think it, but that would make no difference if a bullet hit me.

My training all made sense. I stayed alert and retained my positioning within the section, checking around me. So, I was looking for snipers. I was looking for booby traps. But for all I knew, the next bomb attack wasn't planned to go ahead until next month in a different part of the country, miles from here. I was braced for situations that were not even scheduled to happen.

The patrol became nothing more than a leisurely armed walk, almost pleasurable in a sense, and I started to feel part of this little group, as if they needed me. Maybe I was simply plugging a hole in their numbers but, if that was the case, then I could at least claim that as my role. It made me think about my predecessor though. *What had happened to the man I'd replaced and was I attempting to fill unfillable shoes?*.

By the time we came to the end of the street two things had happened, the first being that the rain had stopped, although a solid mass of grey cloud still barrelled along above our heads. The second thing was that the terrain had changed, the plain terraced houses giving way to low-rise flats which must have looked great on the architects' drawings in 1961 or whenever. The solid and relatively salubrious terraces, which at a stretch could have been symbolic of an Englishman's castle, however inappropriate that might be on a socio-political level, were replaced by white-painted fortresses with balconies, exterior steps and sine curve piss stains. Flat roofs, and peeling paint on cheap façades gave an air of functional disposability.

I was reminded of pensioner's bungalows laid one on top of the other and then hastily pushed into a hollow square shape. The resulting courtyard was home to a rusty swing and the remains of a Nissan Bluebird which had been stolen, returned and burned out. We seemed to slow our pace a little as we proceeded, and I became aware of hostile eyes in hostile heads on hostile bodies standing on one of the most distant balconies. The eyes, and the other bits too, belonged to a family of gum-chewing thugs who shared a look of chip shop despondency.

Bad skin and bad haircuts, they looked on in disgust. Mother and father, both overweight, glowered in silence. The children, two boys, laughed and smirked at some unheard insult and then clammed up as we drew level. Their silence unnerved me more than any spoken words. From the corner of my eye, I saw one of the children take a swig of beer from a blue can. We continued our patrol without breaking stride.

When we had passed, I heard the father say, 'look at this fucking lot'. We kept walking regardless of their patent hostility; there was no crime against hating the army. The family continued to watch us as we passed, but no words were exchanged. They were menacing but utterly harmless. For them to be otherwise would have required more effort than they looked capable of. It made me think about my enemies again. The real enemy, the one who would turn up with a gun or a bomb, was cunning and stealthy, and didn't waste time giving the troops hard looks.

Although we always called their crimes cowardly, I supposed it took a certain amount of courage to take on an army patrol; eight rifles against one. I never said anything to that effect of course. We never flattered this foe and certainly never acknowledged the legitimacy they had bestowed upon themselves. They weren't soldiers. They were murderers, terrorists, scum. We might have admired the Germans for their soldiering ability in both wars, if not for their ethics, but no one admired or respected the IRA. They were worse than animals.

The Belfast hillbillies behind us now, we crossed the road as a section, the traffic slowing slightly to let us reach the other side safely. This was still bandit country so the drivers' restraint could be put down to two factors: the drivers might not be local and had merely found themselves on this road as a function of getting to work, or they simply didn't hate us enough to damage their cars by running one of us over. It would take time to get the hang of this lark.

43

***

After about two hours, during which the rain had started up again, we found ourselves at the gate of a police station which swung open as we approached. The cop shop was like a Wild West fort, with high walls, sentry towers and all manner of antennae projecting into the sky. These were no ordinary police of course. This was a police force at war, more or less. I doubted if there were many comparable situations in the world at that time. With their bottle green uniforms and revolvers on hips, they looked the part too. They often patrolled in armoured Land Rovers, and carried heavier weapons such as sub machine guns and carbines. In the course of the Troubles they had lost a lot of men, and a few female officers too.

We unloaded our rifles and traipsed inside the main building, exchanging nods with the weary cops we met. They didn't know I was the new boy, unless that status somehow shone out from my camouflaged body. The atmosphere inside was peculiar, perhaps best described as purposeful hubbub. There was something which suggested impending doom, over-ridden by forced good humour, as if they were only just keeping the peace, struggling against the odds but succeeding time after time regardless of the obstacles they encountered. The *Blitz* spirit was alive and well here and after just a few hours on patrol I felt a part of it.

We joined a queue which snaked out of a pastel painted door. I didn't know what I was queueing for, but I supposed that there would be some form of food on offer if I stayed long enough and made it to the front. My abiding memory is of discomfort, being too hot and not even slightly hungry. I felt dizzy and sick but that passed. I stayed in the queue because no alternative course was open to me.

I was at the back to begin with although a female police officer joined soon after. No one asked if I wanted food or not and no one suggested an alternative course of action such as simply sitting in the canteen or watching TV. So, I stayed put and edged forwards until I was within sight of the hotplate. A sudden fear gripped me, greater than anything I had experienced on the patrol; did I have to pay for the meal I was about to receive? I felt in my pockets for some change but there was nothing and I could tell without even checking that I had left my wallet behind in my locker.

That discovery caused another wave of fear like the aftershock from an earthquake. *An emotional aftershock*. I would use that phrase if I ever wrote a book on the subject of my time in Northern Ireland. My new fear was based on the realisation that my MOD90 – my ID card – was inside my wallet and therefore not on my person. In a sense I could not prove that I was really a soldier, although the uniform, rifle, ammunition and body armour might provide a clue as to my occupation. Nevertheless, to step out without one's MOD90 – nothing more than a pink plastic card – was a chargeable offence. I wondered if I would get away with my crime, and then I wondered how I could possibly get caught.

I was frowning.

By the time I was at the front of the queue the others had gone, presumably tucking into their lunch in an adjoining room. I had chickened out of asking about how the food was paid for, but this was the point of no return. The serving wench was about two hundred years old, with puffy eyes and grey hair which sprang out in every direction from beneath her grubby cap.

'Do I have to pay for this?', I asked but she appeared not to hear and shuffled off to a back room to do her make-up or to fry more chips. My salvation came from the female police officer who was now standing to my right as we waited to be served.

'Your corporal has an agency card', she said smiling. She was very pretty in a tough way.

'Oh', I said, although I didn't really know what she meant, other than that I personally was not expected to hand over cash for my meal.

'First time over here?', she asked. I fell in love with her right there. I fell in love with voice, her blonde hair pushed up into her cap, with her uniform which did not drown out her figure. I even liked her boots and could imagine her kicking in some IRA man's head wearing them. It was a strange fantasy I grant you.

'Yeah. First patrol, in fact.'

'Not easy being the new boy. Or the new girl for that matter. But we've all got to start somewhere.' She smiled again and I felt devastated that this could never be the start of a beautiful friendship. I think that had she had suggested we run away together to a remote island and spent our days gazing into each other's eyes until we died or got bored, that I would have gone there and then, leaving my melamine tray next to the beefburgers and my rifle propped against the soft drinks fridge. But as I thought these things, and probably some other things as well, the serving lady returned with a huge metal canister of chips which she promptly dumped into its allocated space on the hotplate. Only then did she look at me, challenging me to ask for some food.

I'd just been on armed patrol in a hostile environment, but the biggest threat to my well-being and safety came from this soup dragon. In the face of such intimidation, I took the easy option and opted for burger and chips. As I moved away to rejoin my comrades, who more than likely hadn't missed me, I said goodbye to the police officer and she replied with the words, 'see you around', which I could easily have taken literally. I narrowly avoided saying anything crass like, 'I hope so', and took my tray through to the dining room or canteen or whatever it was. Or so I thought.

I pushed the door open to be confronted with the bin store. Immediately all the blood in my body rushed to my cheeks but I was saved once again.

'It's through here', she said nodding to her right. I followed her to the canteen which was through a door unambiguously marked 'canteen'.

'Thanks', I said. 'It's been a long day'. She laughed graciously.

'The canteen is slightly nicer than the bin store', she said, wryly. 'But only slightly.'

I took my tray to a table with Rockets, Spencer and Alan and joined them.

'You don't hang around', said Spencer. 'Gettin' in with the local totty.'

I shrugged modestly and smirked, although I disliked the comment. Any other sort of reaction would have invited disdain, for real men liked totty, they didn't like *women*.

I picked at my food until I became aware of Alan eying up the greasy burgers that slopped around my plate as I chased chips with my fork. From that point onwards, I pledged to eat all my meals with greater determination. Alan was a gannet, but he wasn't getting my scraps on this occasion or any other. His greed annoyed me.

The others chatted about inconsequential things and I zoned out rather, although the phrase had yet to be coined.

From somewhere behind me I heard a broad Northern Irish voice say, 'hey, Debbie! Didn't think you were on duty today.' I turned slightly to confirm what I thought I knew: that the police officer was named Debbie.

Spencer looked at me from his forkful of sausage and said, 'someone's tryin' it on with your woman.' I laughed and shook my head like a man of the world, and yet I did indeed feel a pang of jealousy. Whoever had spoken stood a chance of forming the relationship I wanted. I, on the other hand, stood no chance.

Not that there was any realistic chance of anything happening between us, but maybe at that time I just needed to cling onto something that might seem like hope if I screwed up my mind's eye and squinted at it for long enough. Debbie – and I was very pleased to know her name for it would flesh out my daydreams somewhat – represented an escape from the grind I had let myself fall into. If I had her waiting for me then everything would be okay. It was pie in the sky of course.

When we had finished eating, we sat around for a while and one or two of the blokes smoked. It is funny to think of it now in the smoke-sterile world we inhabit, but that was just a fact of life. You could just light up wherever and whenever and everyone else had to enjoy the toxic fumes you released whether they wanted to or not. I listened to the conversation and smiled or chuckled as appropriate without offering any opinions or observations of my own; I hadn't even completed a full patrol yet, so what did I know? But I yearned to turn round and make eye contact with Debbie and to fuel my modest fantasy that she might have been watching me as I sat with my soldier mates. Instead, I played it cool and, when finally we stood and gathered up our plates, cups and trays, I noticed that she had gone. My disappointment must have been apparent for Spencer said to me, 'she didn't even say goodbye. What a bitch.'

***

The second half of the patrol was the same as the first, but we paused a few times for Spen to put car registrations through the radio. The idea behind this was that the watch keeper in the Ops room could check if the car was stolen or belonged to an IRA suspect – a player as they were called. None of the cars we checked that day through our Cougar Net radio raised any alarm bells. So, my first patrol went off without a hitch, and I flattered myself into thinking that the first step in my acceptance into Foxtrot 31 Alpha had been a success. It was when we stepped through the gates of the camp that the metaphorical shit hit the fan. It happened so fast that I really didn't know what to do. Luckily no one else did either.

***

Every aspect of the ceremony seemed to deepen the dearth of understanding I had for the man whose body was about to be interred; I hadn't known him at all. These days it is a growing trend for the dead person's favourite music to be played at their funeral, the funeral director and attendant clergy no doubt hoping that it would be something with a vestige of good taste and not selected highlights from *Never Mind the Bollocks* by the Sex Pistols, but with Alan it was plain old sterile, safe church music, played on an organ.

I had been dragged to church as a child but I recognised none of these tunes. Perhaps they were calculated to offer some sort of comfort to the parents and friends, but for the deceased of course, well, what did he care now? He had needed help before events came to this particular point, so a bit of organ music wasn't much use to him.

There was something of a hiatus as the church filled up. The delay just heightened my sense of dread and dismay – there was nothing good about a funeral, no 'upside'. Not for the first time I felt like a fraud, for Alan and I had not been friends and I didn't really grieve for him.

I took the opportunity to observe and assess my fellow mourners, none of whom was known to me. I mentally savaged them for their poor dress sense and uncaring attitude. This was a social occasion for some of these people or a mere stop off on the way to something more important – they just 'quickly nipped in' to pay their respects…

They were bloody hypocrites, I decided. Like me.

It seemed obvious that some of them were here to be seen and had spent their morning getting 'dolled up' for the big event. Fake tan, hair gel and false nails were much in evidence, and that was just the men.

I wondered where these hideous people had come from and why they had chosen a funeral to put on their finery. Maybe this was their way of showing respect, but some of them could easily have finished the service and made their way straight out to a nightclub for an evening and early morning of drunken debauchery.

You can probably tell that I wasn't in a good mood or well disposed towards my fellow mourners. I had my own troubles of course, none of which were comparable to those that Alan had experienced, but I was still around to face them. I remembered with great clarity the day I had finally left the army after three years of service and how I had felt. My life from that point would be *gravy*, to quote a character from the film *Platoon*. How wrong I had been.

Pasta

We heard the bang just as we had come in through the gates and Spen was telling the Ops room of our return. We took cover at once, finding places to crouch in and amongst the various objects that sat around the guard room, the sangar and the gates. I was no expert on these things, and I am not sure if anyone else was either, but it sounded like a mortar to me, one of the IRA's favourite and most indiscriminate weapons. The bang was louder than a mere shot but sounded hollow and flat as if whatever projectile they had hurled our way had failed to explode. If I remembered correctly, these homemade munitions fired converted gas cylinders at their target which then exploded, but they were inaccurate, and only suitable for use against large targets such as army bases and police stations.

From my cover behind a series of metal drums filled with concrete and intended to be part of a barricade, I watched Spen in action as he listened to his instructions through the radio, nodding his head and giving concise responses. I admired his coolness.

He stood and called us in. There had been no further bangs since the first one, but I could hear shouts from the main part of the camp, which was some way from our present location. Spen was referring to his map and gestured that we should close in, which we did at the double.

'Right. We're going to bomb burst out of the gates and take a left turn. Follow my lead but we are going to do a quick tour of the base from the outside. If you see anything suspicious, it's the usual script but we are looking for flatbed lorries or any Paddies acting weirder than normal.' We nodded collectively and I heard Rockets say something which I couldn't make out. The lads were very calm, and this calmness emanated from Spencer who acted as if he was in complete control of the situation.

Northern Ireland had been described as a corporal's war and Spen was our corporal, the centre of our little world on those patrols. I had complete and unwavering faith in his courage and judgement.

We doubled up to the gate, automatically falling into our patrol order, and when the huge gate swung open we ran out and took cover. I don't know how the others felt but I have to admit to a bit of schoolboy excitement. This felt like the real thing. The enemy was nearby and had attacked us. We weren't looking for phantoms. We were after a genuine quarry who had tried and possibly succeeded in killing our comrades. We stood and then began to run towards the end of the road where we would turn left again, stopping the traffic so that half our number could proceed on the other side of the road. It was rush hour now, but they would stop when we told them to. The L1A1 Self Loading Rifle was too big to argue with; I would never wield such power again.

We continued at a trot, but this became a fast walk as we merged with the traffic. We were looking out for our enemy now. My pulse raced as I looked down at my rifle and briefly imagined bringing it into action, lining up the sights on some scrawny Provo as he darted between the stationary cars, feeling the first pressure of the trigger... It occurred to me then that nothing would happen in that little scenario – no bullet would come spinning from the muzzle since the rifle wasn't cocked. Only in the movies did you simply pull the trigger and spray the area with bullets. I would be lucky to get one shot off, if the opportunity came my way.

We were looking primarily for flat-bed lorries, the IRA's chosen transport system for their homemade mortars. They might already have abandoned this vehicle and taken off in a car, or even on a motorbike, leaving the stolen truck behind and quite possibly on fire. As ever it was impossible to know what we were looking for.

I watched the faces of the drivers and their passengers as we wove our way down the street. They studiously looked at anything other than me. Not all of these people felt great antipathy towards the army; the traffic at this time and place was heading for all parts of the city and many towns way beyond. Some of them were supporters and glad to have us and the protection we brought, and some would have seen us dead in a ditch, but I couldn't tell which was which. I never could.

This was my first proper day on the job, but a lot of things never became any clearer to me. I did not subscribe to the view that we should treat them all as the enemy. Nevertheless, telling the two tribes apart was impossible.

Ahead, I saw Spen flag a car down and the rest of us automatically took up defensive positions, taking cover where we could. The driver of the car, a Fiat 127, wound his window down and the two men chatted like old friends before Spen waved him on. He wasn't our mortar man obviously. How did Spen know that? We walked on, watching, listening, observing, each sense stretched to its limit. It would be easy to see enemies everywhere, to see each gesture, each scratch of an arse as the beginning of some offensive action, but I reined in my imagination. If someone looked like they were returning home after a long day at work then that is probably exactly what they were doing. All the same, there was an enemy out there.

We walked for another two or three minutes, the next junction coming into view. In the distance I heard a police siren and then I heard the unmistakable whine of two Land Rovers speeding down the road behind us. This was the QRF – the Quick Reaction Force – who despite their name and its suggestion of haste, were fated to only ever turn up after the event.

The last of the daylight was petering out and the streetlights flickered into life. Spen flagged down a truck and called me forwards to assist him as he checked the back for... I wasn't sure what, but my childish heart swelled with pride that I was selected to help him. The rest of the traffic backed up now, but they would have to wait. There was nothing else for it and no recourse to complaint. We were in charge of the situation: friend and foe alike did what we dictated. Their immediate destiny was being controlled by a twenty-four-year-old Englishman, who, had he not joined the army, might have worked in a shop or a factory. I found time to be astonished at the power he held and the responsibility he shouldered so lightly.

The truck was a Bedford with canvas sides that could be pulled back for loading and unloading. I couldn't picture this being the vehicle we sought, simply because firing a mortar from such a platform would probably have blown it to bits. But I deferred to Spen's greater experience and the truth was that I found the whole sequence quite exciting. A recurring thought hit me: *this is the real thing*. Before we climbed up, he told Murphy to call in the truck's registration number. That would tell us if the wagon was reported stolen or not, but we were going to search it regardless.

I heard Spud shouting and realised that he was getting the cars moving again as we searched. He was trying to keep the travelling public at least partly on our side, engendering a little bit of goodwill perhaps. Spen and I clambered up once the nearside curtain on the truck had been pulled back. I caught a quick glimpse of the driver's face in the gathering gloom and sensed that this was a minor inconvenience for him and that he certainly wasn't concerned about what we might find, which turned out to be boxes of crisps.

'I take 'em round the pubs', he explained. 'I'd give youse a box, but I don't know whose watchin', he added with a sheepish shrug. His speech was thick with Belfast idiom, starved of vowels, deep and sonorous. There was nothing remotely suspicious on board his truck and we dismounted after a few moments.

Spencer surprised me then by apologising for the delay, and with that we let the driver go. Belfast's pubs would be replete with crisps tonight.

As the truck drove off, leaving a cloud of fumes behind, we gathered ourselves. A message came through the radio instructing us to return to camp. I was slightly disappointed. It was an anti-climax, but what had I hoped for? Did I want someone to be shot or blown to pieces just so that I had a war story to tell when I was older? Be careful what you wish for...

***

I noticed that Alan's coffin had cheap looking handles, and I took a moment to think about my own funeral and about who might make the decision about how much to spend on the casket in which I would take my final journey. Did cheap handles signify a wasted life, in which no lasting bonds of friendship were made? It was nicer to think that the cost cutting had been brought about for some other reason to do with one's legacy, like a huge cheque being sent to a charity, or from a desire to put memory above all else.

I pictured someone picking out my coffin from a catalogue and saying, 'that'll do.' This in turn led me to wonder whether the handles were made from something which burned, or did the incinerator maintenance man have to retrieve them during his routine cleaning operations, brushing them out and then throwing them into the recycling bin?

As I get older, I think about death more often, having shrugged off the arrogance of youth which made me feel invincible. It is a peculiar side effect of army service that this sense is heightened; it is after all one of the few jobs where the risk of death is just part of the overall package – written explicitly in the terms and conditions almost. If you're a soldier you can't reasonably argue against being put in danger.

The invincibility aspect must stem from training in which you charge down pretend enemies, firing blank ammunition and always surviving. No one ever lost a firefight in training, but it wasn't mirrored by real life. Perhaps it is worse with the *PlayStation generation* who can simply unplug themselves from injury and death whenever they choose, say when their mum calls them for tea. Real soldiers can't break off from the battle to eat fish fingers and crinkle cut chips.

I looked at the coffin again, gaining some perspective; Alan was dead, I was alive. In that sense I had the upper hand, but I still couldn't quite believe that it was him in the box and that he was gone for good. It had been so many years and yet he came back into my life as a corpse...

***

We unloaded under the supervision of Spud Murphy. Spen immediately made his way to the Ops room for a quick de-briefing, which turned out to be quite unnecessary. There were jeers and cat calls as we returned to our hut, but none of us knew why.

'Did you get 'em?', he asked laughing at us and pointing. 'Did you get the ravioli bombers?' It was Ray Nulty who spoke. He was from another section of our platoon.

'What are you on about?', asked Rockets. I got the impression that he didn't like Nulty. Had I to predict the outcome of a fight I would have picked Rockets any time. Nulty looked too small and thin to be a soldier. He resembled some sort of large insect, with a big brown head, prominent teeth and straggly hair. He could have been anywhere between twenty-five and forty, but he was still a private. There was something of the Victorian underclass about him, a modern-day Fagin.

'The bomb?', he said cackling. 'It was a tin of ravioli. Someone was heating it up in a kettle but forgot to dent the sides and it exploded. Tomato sauce everywhere.'

Behind me I heard someone swear in dismay. We had been attacked by one of the Heinz 57 gang. Rockets shook his head in wonder.

Nulty continued to delight in our discomfiture. We had wasted our time reacting to a home-made pasta bomb. He made no mention of how he had reacted when the explosion occurred.

'I bet you shit your pants, Nulty', said Dinger.

Chip clapped me on the shoulder, sighed and said, 'let's get some scran.' It was a modest acknowledgement of my existence and the fact that we had been on patrol together. I was part of the gang. Well, maybe. If I kept my head down then things might be okay. I felt encouraged but not complacent; I was still *so* new that my uniform had a factory fresh sheen to it, but I had begun the process of acceptance.

After tea we retired to the hut and were joined by Spen who looked angry.

'Fucking bollocks', he said. It was hard to disagree.

'I'm going to punch that twat Nulty one of these days', said Dinger. 'He really grips my shit'.

The others grumbled their agreement and Dinger told us a story about Ray Nulty which the others may or may not have heard before.

'I was in training with Nulty, you know. All the way through he told us that he was an orphan. Then, when it came to the passing out parade, his parents turned up'.

'Dead?', asked Spud, smirking.

'Alive'.

'That must have been a bit embarrassing', suggested Chip.

'I don't know. He looked really disappointed as if they had let him down. He's such a prick.'

I allowed myself a smile and cast a furtive glance around the hut, taking in my new mates almost for the first time and enjoying the fact that I wasn't Ray Nulty. It was good to know that there was someone held in less regard than me. That was the first time that I saw them as human beings rather than soldiers. They were individuals with personalities who could work with robotic precision when required. But they weren't robots.

For the first time I felt comfortable in the presence of these men.

Rockets was lying back on his bed staring at the bed springs of the bunk above his head. He wasn't speaking as if it had all been said. Chip was on his bed too but propped up on one elbow like he was reading a magazine. Dinger sat on the edge of his bed reading an actual magazine.

With great profundity he said, 'that bird Samantha Fox is a hunch front', but no one seemed to listen.

Alan was at the table cleaning his rifle, his face fixed with a strange intensity, a frown locked in place. With hindsight, I can see that there was something wrong with him, but we just accepted, uncharitably, that he was a bit of a weirdo.

For a moment or two I was transfixed as he pulled a piece of four by two through the barrel of his rifle with an energy and passion the task hardly warranted. I remember a mad glint in his eye and could picture him fixing bayonets and charging at the enemy. There was a hero in there, but one without the right sort of war to fight. There would be no bayonet charges on the streets of Belfast, and maybe that would be a source of regret for him in the years to come. His activity was noted by Spencer too who looked annoyed and seemed unable to keep his ire to himself.

'For fuck's sake Alan, you'll wear that friggin' rifle out.'

Alan laughed gormlessly and carried on. He had the rifle's working parts laid out in a neat row on the table. After another couple of *pull-throughs* he laid the main part of the rifle down and lavished his attention on the gas plug, cleaning it with the end of match. This was something we normally did after firing the rifle; it was a quick way to dislodge encrusted carbon from this vital part.

Spen, irritated, felt the need to speak out on this matter.

'Alan', he began with forced patience. Alan put down the gas plug and looked at him. 'Why are you doing that?'

'I'm just cleaning my rifle, Spen', he answered. I noticed the rest of the section had tuned into this discourse. There was a certain peculiar tension in the air as if some form of emotional explosion was likely but they, of course, knew the two protagonists far better than I did. Perhaps this was a scene that was played out regularly.

'Okay, okay', he said, his tone placatory. I was witnessing a supreme display of patience from our long-suffering NCO. 'But have you actually fired the rifle today?', he asked, continuing to draw from a rapidly emptying well of tolerance.

'No.'

'Did you fire it yesterday?'

'No.'

'The day before or the day before that?'

Alan shook his head and gave a gormless smile which even I found a little bit irritating. Spen nodded, a decision made. He was reaching the point where he could draw this matter to a close.

'So why the fuck are you bothering to clean your gas plug?'

Alan's gormless smile remained fixed to his dopey face, wavering for the briefest of moments. Spen was not ready to let the matter drop. It is plain to me now that he just needed a way to let off steam, and the easiest way to do that was to tackle Alan about his over-zealous application of elbow grease.

'Just stop cleaning the fucking rifle, Alan', he said. I saw Spud turn away from the ugly scene. Maybe that was the best way to deal with these situations; let him have his moment and hope it blew over.

Alan put down the gas plug, his face creased with childish confusion; he was doing a good thing as far as he was concerned, but being told off for it. It didn't make sense to him. Good soldiers cleaned their rifles, and he was a good soldier.

'Now put the rifle back together again', said Spencer, finally beginning to regain his composure. Alan blinked rapidly but did as he was told; good soldiers also did as they were told.

Some sort of unpleasant scene was averted because of Alan's acquiescent nature, but I was a little bit puzzled by the fact that it had occurred at all. I lay back on my bunk, thinking about what I had witnessed with my eyes fixed on the steel bed springs of the bunk over my head. The green mattress bulged in the shape of the recumbent figure of its occupant whose name I tried to remember. I could picture his face, swarthy skin, a round face and dark eyes. He was a typical cheeky chappy Londoner, but his name...

Stoker! He was called Stoker and someday I would ask why, but not now. I was too new to ask questions. I lay there feeling as if my newness might be a permanent state.

I could never be someone like Stoker or Chip or Dinger. They were only privates, but they had experience, and with that experience came some vague authority which they did not exercise. No one spoke for some time, but I could hear Dinger flicking over the pages of his magazine. Was this what they did in the evenings? Was this it? Was this all there was?

I had a couple of Ed McBain books tucked into my bag and I wondered what sort of reception I would get if I produced one and began reading it. I didn't want to seem like some sort of intellectual. As it turned out there was no comment at all as I retrieved one of my books and began reading about Detective Steve Carella.

At 1900 hours Spencer and Murphy gathered their kit and made their way to company HQ to be briefed for the following day. They returned after about fifteen minutes with a map and a few pages of scribbled notes.

'Gather round girlies', said Spud.

When suddenly, nothing happened....

Breakfast was breakfast was breakfast. It wasn't just a meal in the army, but the first parade of the day, and it was an offence to miss it. Perspiring Sergeant Crotus was there ready to dish it up for us like some cruel workhouse lackey. Behind me I overheard Dinger describe him as a *miserable twat* and it was hard to take issue with that assessment. He was the archetype for that particular genus of human being, his very flesh oozing unpleasantness. Crotus was at war with humanity and the preparation of food was his weapon.

Nevertheless, despite the fact that my morning stomach was ill suited to the task of eating fried food, I bravely accepted my ration of murdered pig intestine packed with scraps of alleged meat, beans in tomato sauce, egg and fried bread. I already knew that to eat this was to gradually reveal a small lake of grease left behind on the plate, but I got stuck in with gusto, washing it down with coffee that tasted rather like... well, coffee actually. It wasn't bad. None of it was. In the long term it would probably take years off my life but in the short term it set me up for the day's hostilities. The others ate as if they'd been starved for days. Soldiers always ate quickly, a habit learned in basic training.

I was remotely aware of Alan's disappointment upon seeing my steadily emptying plate. He wanted a share of my food but that was not going to happen. There was only one explanation for his incredible appetite and the fact that it did not leave him encumbered by rolls of fat – worms. Parasites in his guts must have been eating his food for him. I was too new to suggest this to him.

Breakfast didn't take long, just long enough to hear two songs emerge from the kitchen radio, one by Culture Club and the other by Simple Minds. When I hear either song now – and I hate both – my mind snaps back to that morning and I feel the new boy's dread all over again as though for the first time.

We left Crotus and his little gang of cooks, making the short journey on foot to the loading bay as our two drivers brought up the Land Rovers they had signed for earlier. The rain fell as drizzle as we attached twenty-round magazines onto our rifles, muzzles pointed towards the darkening sand. I overheard someone muttering that the CSM was watching our preparations from a distance.

'Better get it right boys', said Spud.

As we waited for the Rovers to join us, Spen chatted as if he was giving us an extra briefing.

'Footie on the radio tonight', he said. 'Spurs v QPR.'

I came to realise that most of the lads supported one of the London clubs, with the exception of Alan, who didn't like football, and myself who, through a strange twist of fate, supported Aston Villa. I wasn't ready to share this information with anyone.

'Who do you support, mate?', asked Dinger – Private Bell, of course.

'Villa', I said, embarrassed.

'Fuckin 'ell', he said. The conversation ended at that point. He might never have met a Villa fan before for he certainly did not know what to say to one. For him, supporting Aston Villa was an affliction.

***

You could always hear a Land Rover approach long before you could see it. The whine of its transmission or its cross-country tyres – I was never sure which – was unmistakable, and of great benefit to enemies who might spring an impromptu ambush upon hearing it. Our drivers were Rockets and Chip. The NCOs would sit up front with them and the remaining soldiers would sit in the back with their rifles pointing out into the traffic.

The vehicles were covered with a special armour called Macralon, which added crippling weight to the vehicles despite the fact that no additional modifications had been made to compensate for it, like a better state of tune in the engine, or improved brakes. Thus the wagons were slow and ponderous, easy to overturn, and awkward to use. They would have been hopeless in a hot pursuit unless chasing down some fleeing terrorists on mobility scooters.

In so many respects they were far from ideal as patrol vehicles. A shin-cracking towing hook made entry and exit awkward. A silent exhaust leaked deadly fumes into the load area. For sunny days, of which there were few, a crude hatch in the roof allowed the troops to stand. This was called giving *top cover*, which was cold and boring. Once the novelty wore off no one bothered.

'Let's go', said Spen as we mounted up. He sent a message to the Ops room and that was it – we were off. This was the beginning of my second full day, so I was more than happy to see the sights. The thought that someone might shoot me or blow me up receded quickly as it always did. It felt like a phoney war, both sides edgy, unwilling to give full vent to the fury within. The IRA wanted to kill us soldiers to make the British vacate their country. The British soldiers wanted to shoot and kill an IRA man, but the odds were always stacked against us in that respect. We didn't set ambushes often. It was far more common for us to drive into them.

And yet neither side would just declare war and have done with it. It was all about brinkmanship, mind games. No one wanted to take the blame. I was reminded of an account of a WW2 bombing mission in which the author, a gunner in an RAF Lancaster, had spotted a German night fighter but not opened fire simply because his opponent had not spotted him. To open fire and possibly miss would give the German the chance to shoot them down. The risk was too great. It felt like that now: peaceful co-existence between bouts of extreme violence.

Later I would wonder if the two sides were fighting the same war. We would patrol, keeping an eye on our foes, letting them know we were watching and still in charge. They would hide from us and plan attacks using bombs and guns. We never met on the field of battle, we just edged around, watching and waiting for someone to make the first move like two old pros in the ring.

But it didn't make for much of a spectacle. I mean, today we were driving out of the city, up onto the mountain which overlooked the urban sprawl of Belfast. We would set up vehicle checkpoints (VCPs) at various pre-ordained locations and search an arbitrary selection of vehicles which came our way. That was fair enough but did our leaders actually know something we didn't? Did they know that a certain player might pass through, or that a certain piece of hardware was being moved from its hide in preparation for an attack? Sometimes we did get these titbits of intelligence, but very often we did not, and when that was the case it all felt a bit unplanned, as if we were being used simply to keep us from getting bored. That was just my lowly perspective on it of course. For all I knew I was the linchpin in a grand strategic plan, but I suspected otherwise.

The gate swung open under the guidance of a small, round, bespectacled soldier, the antithesis, in appearance at least, of the modern warrior caste who served to keep us safe from foreign enslavement and that sort of thing. We swung out at speed, turning right and heading for the looming mass that was Black Mountain where we would begin our operations for the day. I knew what was expected of me generally, but not in any detail, and as usual I would just take my lead from the others, hopefully without making it too obvious.

I was in the back with Alan, feeling very much as if I had drawn the short straw. I wonder how he felt about it. Up in the front, with the heater going full blast, sat

Chip and Corporal Spencer who chatted animatedly throughout our journey. When we were part way there Spen shouted into the back, asking if we were okay. Alan nodded which wasn't very helpful and I shouted back that we were. I watched as Spen made some crack to his driver which I guessed was directed at us. Chip nodded and laughed his unheard reply.

There should have been a good distance between us and the second Rover, but such was the traffic density that we had to keep closed up to stay together. I have to admit that it was exhilarating to sit there, even if I only had Boring Alan for company. For the first time in my life I felt like someone, which was odd given my lowly status within the organisation for which I worked. But the point was that to an outsider – a civvy – I must have looked like a tough killer, and who didn't want to look like that when they were a teenager?

Aptly enough for me at least, Paul Hardcastle's hit *Nineteen* was in the charts around this time, and although written about the Vietnam War it resonated in my head. I was *n.. n.. n.. nineteen* after all and serving my country in some far-off land. The IRA were every bit as dedicated and deadly as the Vietcong, if not as prolific. And, okay, Northern Ireland wasn't that far removed from our homeland, but for all its similarities to the rest of the UK, it still felt remarkably alien at times. There were no jungles, and the streets could have been those of Burnley or Bristol, but in those places you didn't have to take a rifle with you when you left the house.

It was cold, and the spray from the rain somehow curled itself into spirals that wrapped themselves round our vehicle and drifted inwards through the gaping back door, leaving Alan and me increasingly wet. Alan did not complain of course, not even to comment on the weather we were enduring. He just peered out the back, seemingly alert to danger, and yet I wondered if he was really seeing anything at all. Something about his face, its deadness and lack of expression led me to believe that his brain processed information differently to the rest of us, that perhaps there was a time lag or a filter which subtly altered the images taken in. Well, I suppose I was right, but I would never have called it Asperger's Syndrome. Asperger's still sounds to me more like a brand of West Country cider than a medical complaint.

Perhaps the idea was to at least *look* alert and, that being the case, we managed it pretty well, Alan scanning the left rear and I the right rear portion of the road. Had we been attacked from both sides at once we would have got in each other's way, but our vehicles were not bespoke fighting machines, designed for optimum defence. They were just agricultural trucks really, modified for a role and not really suited to it. The Ministry of Defence did everything on the cheap in those days, and nothing has really changed in that respect from what I read in the papers. It became increasingly apparent to me that our equipment was either utterly ancient or seriously compromised in terms of its design. The army wanted its Land Rovers to operate as personnel carriers, gun limbers, command posts and ambulances, when really they were designed to move distraught sheep around bleak Welsh hills in the depths of winter. Our rifles were of the elderly variety and due for replacement, the problem being teething difficulties with the new weapon. But the old rifle – the SLR, designed in Belgium, not long after WW11 – was actually much better than its replacement.

Our webbing dated back about twenty-five years, it soaked up rainwater like a sponge, took years to dry out and shrank in the process. Having said all that, our radios were new and functioned remarkably well. We were expected to perform without lavish sums of money being spent on our equipment. I suppose it has always been that way and remains so to this day; if the British soldier didn't have a sense of humour then nothing would ever get done. Laughter is the only way to get over the lamentable state of the army. Reading accounts of the British Expeditionary Force sent to France in 1939/40, it's clear that it was as true then as it is now.

The road was the usual seething mass of Renaults, Nissans and Vauxhalls, each of them buzzing around as we lumbered towards the mountain. Nearly all the drivers avoided eye contact with us but some waved or flashed their lights in support. Children waved too, but children were presumably oblivious to the political aspect of appearing to support our presence. Nevertheless, we made good progress, sweeping through the city on an internal dual carriageway, which I would later learn was called the Westlink. We left this road eventually and then took our chances at traversing a broad junction, the motoring equivalent of Russian roulette. Sitting in a box junction at the apex of so many potential fields of fire felt plain wrong, and we edged forwards until the rest of the traffic relented and let us through.

I heard Spen say something to Dinger and then make a radio message to the Ops room. The only bit I could make out was his use of our callsign – Foxtrot Three One Alpha – and I felt my chest swell with immature pride; I belonged to that call sign. Presumably no one else gave it a thought.

On the other side of the junction, we were once again in the thick of the traffic, weaving our way past parked cars, vans and lorries doing deliveries to shops We came at once to a police roadblock, but the coppers waved us through and shouted some words of encouragement as we passed. I thought they looked exceptionally smart in their uniforms, but soon they were lost to view.

As ever, this could have been any street in any part of the country – the only difference was us. No other corner of the UK had armed soldiers on patrol.

Some of the shops had Union Jack flags flying above their doors, and on the gable end of one row of houses could be seen a huge mural of King Billy on his white horse. I tried to remember who King Billy was.

'Protestants', I said to Alan above the noise of the transmission and the general traffic. He looked at me with his dead eyes and gave an imperceptible nod; him speaking to the new boy was not on the cards. I gave a mental shrug and let it pass, concentrating on looking for snipers and other unspecified do-badders.

A gang of truanting boys, cigarettes clamped in their lips, cheered us as we drove past. Alan returned their exultant waves with a lifeless one of his own. I felt like a GI liberating some French town in 1944. Alan felt like someone commuting to Bognor on a train at seven on a Monday morning in January. If the IRA didn't shoot him, I thought I might. Frankly, he was ruining my war.

But that was how I felt then, of course. I was young and could afford to be flippant or to suck the emotional juice from every strained moment. But I am young no longer and I see the whole thing differently.

**

The singing was poor; self-conscious rather than up-lifting, dreary rather than joyous. It made me think of the purpose of hymns, not just at funerals but on any occasion. What did God care if you sang songs about him? What precisely was the point? If God was really such a great bloke, he'd be a bit embarrassed at the hyperbole, wouldn't he? Or was the real reason for singing to provide comfort to the earthbound masses who had yet to die and take advantage of the wonderful opportunities afforded their forebears in heaven? One thing was certain: none of it helped Alan. I stood with the rest of them and even opened the hymn book as if I was providing a service for some infirm person standing next to me, but my lips uttered not one syllable. They didn't move at all except to permit a yawn.

I wasn't too sure of the etiquette. I was in a church so perhaps I should have been adhering to a basic set of Christian rules concerning behaviour, but I thought that an omnipotent God would see through that particular ruse and might actually appreciate someone who made his feelings on the matter of divinity quite unambiguous. When I thought about it why *shouldn't* I go to heaven anyway? It wasn't my fault that I didn't believe in God. I was made in his image, so therefore my credulousness was just part of the deal.

Nevertheless, the singing reached as high as the vaulted church roof, if no higher, and singing was the decent thing to do in the circumstances. What would I have thought if they had just stuck him in a box in the ground with no sort of farewell? Suicide was a sin, though – one of the worst in fact – and that made me think of the practicalities of Alan getting into heaven, which was surely the point of having a church service. Would the merciful God we are told about view Alan's transgression as something forgivable in the circumstances or was that it – had Alan crossed a sacred line? If my personal theories on religion were correct then no one would ever find out. No one was going to heaven; not me, not Alan, not even the poor old vicar who had led a miserable life in the hope of eternal joy.

***

One of the most peculiar aspects of the conflict was how the two warring communities lived almost cheek by jowl. No sooner had we left that obviously Protestant area with its patriotic addenda than we were in the parallel universe of deep-seated Republicanism. This was enemy territory, and although we were merely transiting through, we were on our guard. It was probably just my imagination, but it seemed as if hatred hung in the air like an oppressive cloud. No one waved. If they could be bothered to look in our direction at all people just scowled.

I just about saw the half brick that came through the air and hit the armoured flanks of the second Rover, but the occupants did not, and consequently they screeched to a halt thinking that they were under a more serious attack than might be expedited with a piece of masonry.

Boring Alan came to life unexpectedly and called upon Dinger to stop.

Spen turned angrily in his seat.

'What the fuck?', he said.

'They've been hit by a brick', explained Alan. Our vehicle had stopped too, and I got a great view of Foxtrot Three One Bravo debussing, ready to take on their unseen enemies. Spud's breathless contact report came over the radio.

'Zero, this is Foxtrot Three One Bravo, contact, wait out!' That short phrase, oft-practised in training, seldom used in operations, galvanised us all, cleared the airwaves of other traffic, had the Ops room staff bolt upright in their chairs, awaiting the next instalment...*when, where, what it is, what it's doing, what you're doing about it.* Everybody knew the drill, everybody knew what was to come.

Even I, who understood what had happened, felt a surge of adrenaline as if Spud's blood was merging with mine.

I had seen the brick, briefly, but I really had no idea what to do. The noise had been enough to make them think of a bullet strike.

Spud and his little crew were taking up fire positions, still thinking they'd been fired upon. They scanned the streets looking for snipers, a flickering curtain, a movement of some sort as a rifle's muzzle was withdrawn from a window.

By comparison we were rather tardy, the fog of war, the uncertainty holding us back.

'Are you sure, Al?', asked Spen.

'Sure, Spen. It was a brick', replied Alan, seriously.

Corporal Spencer looked at me for confirmation and I nodded.

'Come with me', he said. 'Alan and Dinger guard the wagon.'

I followed him down the road to the second vehicle. It was a short journey, maybe fifty yards or so, and as he closed in the other half of his section he called out.

'It was a brick', he said. Around us, shoppers shopped and truants – Catholic ones – jeered at us. Rockets began to divert the traffic round the Land Rover, already sensing that the emergency had ended before it had begun.

I was some way behind when Spen stopped and I drew myself into the doorway of a house converted into flats to give cover. I noted four separate letter boxes screwed to the wall with occupant names made from those brass-coloured adhesive letters that you used to get from Woolworths. At some point, one of these must have read STEWART until a local wit had prised off the letters S,E and R to leave the word TWAT behind. Most amusing. I heard Spud question Spen.

'You sure? It sounded like a friggin' bullet to me.' They were standing in front of the vehicle now.

'Let's look for a bullet hole', suggested Spen, logically, but as they rounded the front bumper Spen accidentally kicked the half brick in question. He pointed down and said, 'There's your bullet, Spudly.' They still checked the side of the armour. There was no bullet hole. A gang of boys in school uniform came down from a side street, drew level with and then passed the men of Foxtrot Three One Bravo, before shouting abuse and running up the street.

'Brit wankers!'

They were shocked – but only for an instant – when I suddenly stepped into their path, emerging from concealment like I was part of a deliberate trap.

'Fucking bastard Brit!', shouted one as they deviated momentarily in their flight from the scene. His voice cracked, robbing his words of conviction, and his bravado leached from his tiny frame with this unexpected proximity to the enemy. Two of the lads wore Celtic scarves, more of an identity badge than practical clothing. They all had ragged haircuts and the scowl of the oppressed.

In another time and another place their antipathy would have been incomprehensible. In this time and place, it made perfect sense. They were vessels filled with hate.

Only a few more moments passed before we rejoined our wagons and set off again for the mountain.

I heard Spen radio the Ops room to explain the situation and I could visualise the relief on the watchkeeper's face as the news came through. Or was it disappointment? In the weeks and months ahead, there would be moments where I craved excitement – was it the same for everyone else? This was a long, drawn-out war – a war of attrition almost – in which interminable periods of seeming inactivity were punctuated with brief moments of high drama and danger. It was almost a cliché; the same could probably be said of all wars, but this one in particular took the idea to its ultimate expression. When we did our training for Northern Ireland – me and a load of cooks and bottle washers from other regiments – they assured us that the biggest service we provided was simply that of public reassurance. We were 'a presence' they said, keeping everyone safe, and doing so very visibly.

I would remind myself of their words when I stood on some freezing roadside or other, with rain attacking me sideways and queues of irate motorists who hated me, and the delay I was causing, snaking back up the road. I'm a reassuring presence.

Once we hit what I supposed was the foot of the mountain and began our long climb to near the top, the Land Rovers, weighed down with their armour, slowed alarmingly. This only served to frustrate the drivers behind us. These were the most gutless vehicles this side of a milk float, and it showed. Eventually we turned off the main road and onto a broad street lined with 1930s council style houses that seemed well kept and in private ownership. This had the beneficial effect of releasing the rest of the traffic, but it did mean that we were confronted with a hill steeper than any I could remember seeing before in my entire life. I wondered if we could possibly make it to the top, but Dinger changed into a low gear and we screamed past the parked cars, hell bent for the summit where we turned left.

We zig-zagged through an area of middle-class housing, the roads lined with Ford Cortinas and Vauxhall Cavaliers, and then quite suddenly we were driving into the countryside, the city dropping away like a discarded blanket. On our left a forest straggled down to the roadside, seemingly contained by the combination of a fence and a dry-stone wall, and on our right the vast panoply of the city was visible. From my vantage point I could make out the runway at Sydenham and the nearby shipyard, where, about seventy years earlier, the Titanic had slipped into the sea for the first time. Belfast looked huge, but from here the signs of conflict were shrunken and impossible to see.

We drove on for about two miles more, and then set up our impromptu vehicle check point using the vehicles as a chicane to control the traffic. The drivers assisted the NCOs in guiding the traffic up to a point where the occupants could be questioned, and the car searched if necessary. The soldiers in the back provided cover and controlled the traffic further down the queue, taking instructions from the NCO about who to stop and who to wave through. We'd blocked the road with the VCP, and we had caltrops, spiked steel chains that could be dragged across the road to puncture tyres should a vehicle try to drive through without permission.

From my training I understood how all this worked, and I was mildly surprised to find that we operated in a textbook manner, no shortcuts taken at all, or none that I could see. The idea was to filter the traffic, looking out for suspicious drivers or passengers, or cars that were stolen or known to be used by players. It wasn't as simple as just that, of course: our enemies had become adept at moving themselves and their weapons from one place to another. We weren't fighting an enemy in uniform who identified themselves and said *here I am, let's slug it out*. Everything was much more subtle, and the battle was fought in the context of 'normal life' which still went on around us. We were there to maintain normality and defeat the enemy – no mean feat and something which could easily come undone with a split second's inattention.

It was common for a terrorist to drive through a VCP, knowing that they would invariably be stopped and questioned. Somewhere behind them in a second vehicle would be the bomb or gun that was being transported for a future attack. As the player was being questioned and/or searched, the rest of the traffic was usually waved through, meaning that the weapon went undiscovered. What should have happened was that the known player was waved through – they would *never* be in possession of anything incriminating – and another vehicle, maybe three or four cars behind, stopped and searched.

The army had some clever counter tactics, but there were times when they failed simply because letting a known terrorist go without questioning just seemed wrong and illogical. We would fall into our enemy's trap time and again.

Another tactic used by the terrorists was to move weapons on buses, these being rarely searched. Some days we would be tasked with stopping only buses as a result. We never found anything.

It is impossible to say if our VCPs ever did much good. We made life awkward for the IRA, but did we stop them? Did we foil many attacks? In our lowly position it was impossible to say if an attack had been prevented if there was no evidence that it had even been planned! It was hard to validate events that didn't happen.

So, caught between the big city and the bleak mountainside, we began our task. I provided cover from a damp ditch, my rifle clutched in both hands, looking over the iron sights at enemies I couldn't distinguish.

This wasn't a hard job, just uncomfortable, and I was glad that no one challenged me about what I was actually doing in that ditch, as my answer might have been vague. I was also glad that no one fired at us because a mist was coming our way, and I would have been hard pressed to accurately return fire.

A small queue of vehicles quickly formed, the first three being, in order, red, white and blue, which signified nothing. I kept my eyes fixed on the road beyond, but I heard Alan talking to the drivers as they waited, his voice robotic, devoid of intonation and warmth. He did however look immaculate and professional, and in that respect, I couldn't fault him. He was a good soldier and would probably be courageous if the situation ever required. It simply wouldn't occur to him to be anything else.

I was at just the right height to be poisoned by exhaust fumes and I adjusted my position so that I was slightly clearly of the car's noxious emissions. In doing so I broke my cover, but I had to make a choice, would

I rather be poisoned or shot? The latter was the less likely prospect.

Before much time had passed, I was soaked through with rain and dew, the latter absorbed from the grass through the seat of my pants. I had rising damp. My beret was a sodden lump and little drips of water lined up on the leather headband like pearls which occasionally dropped off onto my nose and cheeks. I began to shiver as cold seeped into my young, unprotected bones. Before long, mist enveloped the whole scene, and it became too dangerous to stop traffic.

I heard Spen calling us all back in, and so the whole operation was folded up and packed away once again, like a market stall at the end of a day's trading. My stiff knees protested as I climbed back aboard. The effects of the cold were a feature of my time in Ulster.

Mobile again and taking it slowly, we climbed a bit further up the mountain until we came to a layby. We pulled in so that Spen could rethink our mission.

Rockets and I patrolled listlessly, both frozen to the core, as Spen and Spud had a conflab – one of Spen's words. The traffic sped by on the main road, seemingly heedless to the mist which should have slowed it. I could hear the engines and see outlines and flashes of colour but little else.

'Have you been here before?', I asked Rockets.

'In this layby?'

'In Northern Ireland?'

'Did a tour in Fermanagh, down near the border. Bandit country', he said. He spoke without passion, the experience leaving him unmoved.

'How was that?'

He looked at me and shrugged.

'Okay. Most of the time nothing happens. You don't realise that on your first tour. You think you're going to get shot at every day and then when you do, you shit yourself and you don't know what to do.'

'Were you shot at?'

'I don't know', he answered. I wanted to hear more on the subject, but we were called back by Spen. We remounted our wagons so that we could maintain a mobile patrol with no VCPs unless the mist cleared, but the unspoken question remained with me. *How could he not know if he had been shot at?*

***

The streetlights had just flickered into yellowy life as we finally pulled into our base. The clouds were gathering again, their predecessors having divested themselves of moisture on the drive back. I felt as if we were entering the set of a horror film, the weather giving events a grey, terrifying sheen. In the movies bad things never happen on a sunny day, and I certainly had the feeling that something dramatic and dangerous was about to happen. In my imagination it might be some terrorist attack. What else?

We unloaded our rifles and our drivers took the wagons back to the garage. We gathered around the cookhouse, where a small group of off-duty soldiers from another platoon hung about smoking and chatting, looking bored. Out of uniform, they suddenly looked like a bunch of delinquents who might otherwise hang about outside their local Spar shop waiting for some irresponsible adult to buy them cans of cheap lager; they weren't the obvious choice to be armed and sent onto the streets to keep the peace. Spen had gone to the Ops room to give a debrief on our abortive patrol, and when he returned he confirmed that we would be stood down.

'Chogies', said Dinger rubbing his hands together with childish glee. I wasn't asked if I wanted to join them, perhaps it was assumed that I would, but either way I followed Dinger, Rockets, Alan and Stoker to the hut run by an Asian chap who cooked burgers and sold sweets, chocolates and cans of fizzy drinks. It was said that he lived in the back of his shop, but I didn't think there was room as I stood in the queue. The lads ordered their food in short order and within moments the shop was filled with the aroma of fried onions and hamburgers.

'What would you like pal?', asked the Asian man looking over the heads of his little queue and pointing at me. I didn't want anything; my stomach was tied in knots.

'Plain hamburger and a can of coke, please', I replied. Another burger joined the sizzling mass. Dinger turned to me, smiling. 'Best burgers in Northern Ireland'. I took comfort from these rare moments in which my existence was acknowledged. My stomach settled just slightly, allowing me a tentative hunger pang. The queue continued to grow behind me, mainly troops from other regiments and some of the sappers on the bomb disposal team in camp. As the food was prepared, I heard a helicopter clattering in, clearly making a landing on the cricket pitch. The noise was deafening but somehow exhilarating as if the energy from its huge engine and rotors was transmitted directly into my bones. I wanted to run outside and watch the spectacle, but everyone else was utterly unmoved by its arrival, and I didn't want to advertise my newness by gawping like a tourist in Manhattan.

We had paid for our food and were taking delivery when the air shook with the sound of a distant explosion.

'Somebody's copped it', said Dinger, and behind me the sappers cursed and ran back to their hut without getting their burgers. I wondered why they would bother to attend to a bomb that had clearly exploded but I supposed that this was their normal procedure – their SOP – or maybe they felt it was the correct thing to do. Whatever, we did nothing and made our way back to the hut to consume our food. The bomb did not concern us; the war was being fought by someone else as we consumed fatty discs of mechanically recovered cow bits. It wasn't the Somme, but it was the only war we had. I wasn't complaining.

Sport

The main sport on offer seemed to be pitch and toss, in which the competitors, trained to a high level of competency, threw coins against the wall in an effort to see whose money would finish up closest. The winner took all. We played this sporadically throughout our tour, and fortunes of up to a pound were regularly made and lost. As far as I recall it was classed as gambling, and the army didn't really permit gambling, but as with many other things a blind eye was turned. How bad could it really get? And, if it kept the troops entertained, then surely it was worth letting them play unhindered?

I soon found that I had the knack of winning, and although this was never going to make me a gambling fortune in the style of Omar Sharif, it did provide me with a party piece and a reputation of sorts. It wasn't a skill I had sought, or even tried to develop, and before joining the army I had never played the game, but I had been born with the gift. I became some sort of Ninja master at this most arcane and useless of sports. Rarely has anyone been so good at something quite so pointless.

Twenty years and more have passed since I last pitched (or was it tossed?). I am sure I have the knack still, but in those olden times my skill served me well, making me somebody other than just the new boy. It may be hard to believe but in the midst of that odd conflict my pitching became the stuff of near legend. I never considered the amount of money I made but it can't have been much. The legend became greater than any actual match, but I took on all comers and rarely lost. Much of my off-duty time was spent defending my title. The great Pitch and Toss Tournament – it was really a loose collection of individual matches – was peculiar to that tour and to those particular soldiers. Its time would never come again, but I milked my notoriety to its fullest extent.

'How do you think he does it?', they asked. *What makes him so good?'* I was the Pinball Wizard for a new generation.

The knack was to use a flick of the wrist that dropped the coin on its edge near to the wall and made it roll in slowly. More than that, I cannot say. I doubt if I could coach someone in the skills required; it was more akin to Zen Buddhism than mere sporting prowess. Sadly, it was a sporting dead end.

There was a squalid gym on the base in which a few overdeveloped lugs built their biceps. There was a running machine and a rowing machine upon which men could expend their excess energy. Few did. There was a makeshift running track which took in the Chogies' steps, both car parks, the back of the TA centre, and went past the guard room, the Felix detachment and back down to company lines. A few organised runs took place, but it was an unsatisfactory arrangement with choke points, potholes and mud patches, all of which could cause injury.

Other than that, sport was of the spectator variety, mainly via the TV or radio, and mainly football. I was never that fascinated by football, but the rest were fanatical supporters of West Ham, Spurs, QPR or Arsenal. Only this seemed to break the bond they felt for each other. I was never sure where football fitted into their hierarchy of loyalty; it was not a straightforward matter. Did they value their team above their regiment, or their regiment above their team? Did they value their family above their team or their platoon or section? At times I felt like an outsider just visiting their world and not being permitted full access. That they seemed like proper soldiers and I did not was a recurring theme of my army service.

***

When we had completed the first hymn and only the last lingering notes of the organ were left to reverberate around the church's high ceiling, we all sat, and the minister began his hearsay appraisal of Alan's life. He could have been talking about anyone; his description matched that of no one I knew, and it served as a reminder that Alan had been an enduring enigma. There had never been much of a link between his face and his mind. He never looked happy or sad, bored or thrilled. The nearest he got to expressing emotion was when he looked confused, which he did often. But the thing is, I had no idea what went on in his head or how he viewed the world around him. He had a robot-like intellect, acting in a manner which was conditioned rather than instinctive or perceptive. In this respect he was an ideal soldier, although he would never make a leader. A leader must be reflexive and sensitive. Alan was neither.

The vicar was in late middle-age and no doubt attractive to the opposite sex of a similar age. He was neither fat nor bald, but he did drone on rather to the point where I felt my mind slipping away from the matter at hand – the life of Alan. Against my will I found myself back in that moment when the army and I had parted company: returning to the depot, handing in my ID card, signing various forms, picking up travel warrants to get me home and receiving a huge wodge of cash from the pay office. This was before internet banking or anything like that. I'm surprised that there weren't gangs of muggers waiting outside the gates to prey on newly discharged soldiers. I had waited so long for this day and yet when it finally came it was a monumental anti-climax.

Rather than being smothered in a cosseting blanket of relief and elation, I found that no longer being a soldier consisted of numerous things which you *no longer* had to do, such as guard duty and PT. It brought with it no additional benefits and you could only enjoy your new status if you actively reminded yourself of how life had changed for the better.

I would soon discover that being an ex-soldier brought no real entitlement with it. I wasn't owed a living. No one said, *'you've done your bit son. Why don't you spend the rest of your life sitting on your fat arse drinking beer?'*. At least they didn't say it to me.

The minister was still talking when that train of thought pulled out of the station and was replaced by another. I was thinking of my life from that moment to the present day and of how it had been a clichéd rollercoaster ride. Everything had seemed possible when I left the army. I had a month's terminal leave during which I was still being paid, and for that month I could afford to do nothing. But the money didn't last, and I found work washing dishes in a café. It paid enough to cover the rent on my bedsit and for me to eat reasonably well. I had no social life, and so my expenditure on alcohol came right down, although I sometimes bought myself a four pack of cheap lager to dull the edges of my mind.

The bedsit was pretty terrible, with no heating apart from an electric fire which smelled of burning dust when it was switched on. It wasn't much of a life, but I was young and optimistic. Things would pick up. I had no specifics, but I was just starting out on life really. It might have been easier had I been released from prison instead of the army – I think things were done to help ex-prisoners – but my situation would undoubtedly improve.

And of course it did, although it took some time.

***

We were dropped off in the city centre by Saracen, a six-wheeled APC driven by a soldier from the Royal Corps of Transport. It was cramped and noisy. We took a few hits from accurately thrown half-bricks but arrived ready for duty, protecting the civilian searchers who manned the gates leading to Royal Avenue and Donegall Street, where all the big department stores were situated. Belfast at this time had gates through which the city's shoppers had to pass if they wanted access to the city centre. To pass through they had to subject themselves to a search, a search for bombs to ensure no one tried to target one of the boutiques. Bombing shops was one of the IRA's favourite tactics at this time, so the searchers, dressed in a uniform rather like that of a prison officer, were given the task of ensuring that no bombs came through. By and large I think they were successful, although it must have been hard to maintain their vigilance for hour after hour, day after day, week after week. But that was the nature of this conflict; it was a grind, and the winner would be the one who didn't give up.

There was something about the city which I liked. In better times it could have been a cheery place, and many of the worn-down residents displayed a friendly acceptance of their lot – the ones who didn't hate us, that was. But Protestant or Catholic, Jew, Hindu, Muslim, terrorist, clergyman, off duty policeman, off duty soldier, everyone submitted to the search. There was no other way in. At peak times there was a permanent queue of shoppers and workers, standing with their arms held away from their sides in readiness for the frisk. It was as natural as breathing after so many years. No one complained – there was no point.

Our job was simple. We just had to stand there and look alert, keeping the searchers safe to do their job. It was boring, but there are worse things than boredom. When our transport came to take us away, I could strike off another day of my tour and of my army service. Time was not exactly flying by and I didn't yet know enough about the world to look upon it as the greatest adventure I would ever have. My life would eventually become humdrum, and only then could I view those strange months with anything like satisfaction.

I tried to remain alert, but it really isn't easy when nothing much seems to be happening. The civilians paid me no heed. They knew nothing except soldiers on the street and I was only one of the latest young Englishmen to stand here, slightly bewildered.

I thought about Debbie, the beautiful policewoman and looked out for her in case she came through on her day off. But she didn't and even if she had it would have been unwise for her to acknowledge me in any way... if she remembered me at all.

***

We were off duty, the following day and I looked forward to the occasion with no eagerness at all. When I was on duty I had a job to do and a place to be. When someone spoke to me it was generally to give me an order. I knew what I was supposed to be doing when I was on duty. A rest day by comparison was unstructured. I had my washing and ironing to do. I thought that I might go for a run round the camp – four circuits should be enough. I could read or listen to some music, and we were allowed to drink two beers each. And yet the thought of being left to my own devices did not appeal. Supposing the others decided that they did not like me? For all I knew I had only been tolerated up to this point. It was an irrational fear, but for the meantime I was stuck with it.

I woke at 0730 and tried to get back to sleep, but that proved impossible. I read for a while, but eventually I got dressed in a tracksuit, and with my rifle in tow like an extra shadow, I shuffled over to the laundrette with my bag of washing. I was the first one there, a fact that I found oddly satisfying. I read a large chunk of my book as I waited for the huge machine to do its thing, but when I wasn't reading, I just let my head rest against the wall and thought about my situation. Knowing that I had another two and a half years of military purgatory left did not cheer me, so I forced my thoughts off in another direction, thinking ahead to the time when I had maybe six months left and I could spend my day in warm anticipation of discharge into the land of milk and honey where I would be a *bona fide* hero, both blessed and cursed with the horrors of war.

Strangely I always dreamed of that time – the months before I finally left, rather than the day of my actual discharge – as if I was already preparing myself for the disappointment of a return to civvy street. Did I already know that it was going to be a let-down? Was my mind reining in my emotions to protect me from harsh realisation? The anticipation always seemed so much better than the fulfilment of any modest ambition. To be in uniform knowing that the end was in sight was better than actually handing the uniform over. It was odd.

Every now and again I thought that I might sign on for another three years, or maybe nine in total. These thoughts usually came to me when I was waiting to go on leave, or after I'd had a few drinks, when the world seemed like a rosier place. These same thoughts swiftly departed every morning when I had a few moments to coldly assess what another three years in the army could be like.

My mind led me on its own journey as the clothes revolved in the machine. I hummed a Pretenders song, *Watching the Clothes Go Round* and then mouthed the lyrics. *Oh, Saturday night. Everyone's having fun. Me, I'm at the laundromat. Trying to get my washing done.* I made no sound, and it would have been drowned out by the mechanical, cyclical roar of the great machine had I tried to.

From there my mind returned to the RUC station where I had briefly met Debbie. I wondered if I would see her again, or if we could go out together. What a difference to my morale that would make! But then I began to worry that if I did see her again, she might not even remember me. I would be crushed. I decided that I would expunge her from my mind. It was much easier to do that.

But she wouldn't go. Debbie stayed in my mind, lodged there. I pictured us hand in hand, walking over the mountain, pausing to gaze down over the city, my arms round her waist as we made plans for the time when I could leave the army and be with her forever. I was an optimist back then...

When I returned to the hut, my arms filled with clean uniform, I found that half of the section had risen and the other half still slumbered. Stoker was quietly playing one of his tapes – it sounded like The Carpenters – and Spud was reading a magazine about motorbikes. Alan was dressed casually in jeans and regimental sweatshirt. He had a towel round his neck and was preparing for the trip to the washrooms, seemingly by putting himself into a trance. For someone with so little going on in their head a trance-like state should have been easy to achieve, but the look on his face was troubling, so blank as to render him inhuman. There was no warmth about the man at all. Where the rest of the men had human flaws, Alan was just empty, neither good nor bad, he felt nothing. He had no intuition. He was a robot.

I set up the ironing board quietly and began to press my uniform for the week ahead. Stoker lay on his bed still in his Union Jack boxer shorts, singing quietly, plaintively. *Why do birds often disappear, every time you are near?* I smiled at his bastardised lyrics. What sort of soldier liked The Carpenters? When that song had finished, he scratched his groin and waited for the next one to come on. Stoker was at peace with the world. Alan finally raised himself and, rifle in hand, slipped out to the ablutions.

'Are you going to ablute?', asked Stoker as he passed. Alan nodded without humour. I smiled to myself as I ran the iron over my lightweights. Like wraiths, the remainder of the section slowly came alive, and our day off began in earnest.

The big event was watching a video of *Blade Runner*, a soldier's favourite for some reason. That men who lived an ostensibly violent life should seek their escapism in yet more violence was a puzzle to me. Nevertheless, the TV was brought in, perched on a chair and attached up to a video player. We spent the next couple of hours watching Harrison Ford take on all manner of robotic criminals in a dystopian city of the future. No one spoke. We watched in perfect silence. We were rapt. Was it the act of watching a film or was it the film itself which engendered this state? Could Stoker, who was after all a fan of the Carpenters, have happily watched Mary Poppins with the same degree of fascination? Would the others have watched it too? Whatever. For two hours we were some*where* else, doing some*thing* else.

From a hidden stash, Rockets produced a box of Nutty bars and we each munched happily, except Alan who didn't like nuts.

'If you put one of these in someone's pint it looks like someone has done a shit in it', Rockets proudly proclaimed.

'I would still drink it', said Spud.

'Even if it was a real shit?'

Spud thought about this for a moment. Clearly, he was gathering an image in his mind. Finally, he answered.

'Yes', he said.

The tension I had felt earlier in the day, eased. I was still the new boy of course, but my presence was being tolerated and my comrades had got used to my being there. When the film finished, they got on with their cleaning and tidying. Boots were polished, rifles pulled through and oiled. It was tedious but the room was warm, and a sort of calm reigned over us, even when Rockets put his new Iron Maiden tape on.

***

For three weeks we patrolled on foot or in vehicles. Mostly we patrolled the city but now and again we ventured out into the countryside, braving the weather which ranged from wet and cold to wet and really, really cold. I made various mundane discoveries around this time. For instance, putting on two pairs of socks did not make my feet any warmer. If anything, two pairs of socks reduced blood circulation and exacerbated the problem. I learnt that the leather gloves we were issued did nothing to keep your hands warm. I learnt that the infantry company in residence before us had disabled the heaters in the Land Rovers. It didn't matter to me, since

I was always in the back and never felt the benefits anyway.

I learnt that Chip was on his first tour in Northern Ireland and that all the others had been here at least once. Spen had two previous tours under his webbing belt and was planning to leave the army in two years to work for his dad who was an electrician in Dagenham. Spen had never quite got over the disappointment of not being sent to the Falklands War. The army had begun to lose its sheen from that moment on.

I learnt that Spud, for all his relaxed demeanour, was planning to be a career soldier and wanted eventually to become RSM of the battalion. The others scoffed when he mentioned this, but he took it in good heart. For my part I found it astonishing that anyone could contemplate staying in the army longer than was strictly necessary. It wasn't that I had anything spectacular to get back to, but even still...

The patrols comprised long periods of boredom interspersed with more boredom. The novelty of being a young warrior in his prime soon paled with each frozen day. We drove from one isolated road to another, trying to catch out an enemy who ran the war according to their rules. Transposing *our* rules onto the game didn't seem to work, although it was hard to tell of course. I had to remind myself that we might have foiled a shooting or a bombing just by being in the right place at the right time. If a shooting didn't happen, for instance, then we would never know that it was us who had been the critical factor in its prevention. We were stoned now and again but that was all. Stoned, as in having stones thrown at us, not toking on a big communal pipe.

One of our main tactics was to set up a VCP with one vehicle, on a long road from which we were extremely visible. Our second vehicle was off on a side road, similarly set up. The logic was that we would catch the drivers who turned off to avoid us and that this gave us a better chance of intercepting someone who was up to no good: after all, why else would they turn off?

Except of course people turn off for all sorts of reasons. Some of them were due to turn off anyway, either to go home, or go to work, or to make a delivery. Others turned off to avoid a delay in their journey. None of these reasons necessarily made them terrorists. But we questioned people and searched their cars. Some of them liked us and were grateful for the efforts we made, some were unmoved, and some clearly despised us. They all, however, complied. To do anything else was a waste of time. The Republicans weren't going to force the British out of their country by being surly at checkpoints, and the Loyalists sought every opportunity to confirm their support for the British by being open and friendly. Come rain or shine, mainly the former, we patrolled, searched, questioned. This was the war we fought. We fought it by stealth and by following our own rules and, in this way, we hoped to prevent the enemy from attacking. Attacking what? We never knew until it happened.

The Troubles continued for years after our departure. Over a period of thirty years, three and a half thousand people lost their lives as a result of this prolonged battle, and this was from a population of just one and half million. But although this sounds a lot, it equates to very few people killed per week. Thirty years is about ten thousand days, therefore on average a third of a person was killed each day. At times, when the rain pelted down on the roof of the Land Rover and the radio was loud, busy with traffic, and when someone shouted abuse or lobbed a brick at us, it seemed worse than it was. But in reality, it was a low-key war.

The amount of danger faced on an individual patrol was tiny, but you never knew when or where the enemy would strike, and that meant that you had to be prepared at all times.

We talked about this phenomenon and it was Spud who made the most salient point on the subject.

'We might not see much of them but don't forget that if the IRA take you prisoner, they will kill you. There are no POWs round here.'

***

I suppose our leaders did try to break things up for us a bit by introducing some variety into the tasks we were given. On a couple of occasions, we were given heli-ops and one of these provided me with a tour highlight. It was a rare fine day when the Wessex helicopter dropped in on us, falling from the cold blue sky like a noisy angel. It was an old thing with a whale's profile, developed by Westland from a Vietnam-era Sikorsky. It would take us, four at a time, to a pre-designated spot where we would de-bus, set up a snap checkpoint and then await its return. In the meantime, it would return to camp and pick up the other brick, taking them somewhere, dumping them off and then picking us up. In this way we would leapfrog around the roads leading into the city, catching unawares those who might try to smuggle weapons.

The system worked surprisingly well, so well in fact that Spen, in communication with RAF loadmaster, was able to stop the same vehicle twice after its occupant had shouted obscenities at us when they had driven off, having been stopped for the first time. The vehicle in question was a brand-new Nissan pick-up truck and the occupants were two brothers from the O'Rourke family who plainly sided with the IRA. Spen had been courteous and professional as he had questioned them about their cargo and their destination, but this had not been reciprocated; as they drove off they called us *Brit wankers* and gave us the fingers. When we stopped them further down the road, got them to unload their cargo, made a show of searching through it and then left them to repack just as the Wessex appeared to take us away, they had time to rue their bad manners.

It was a tale which was told many times subsequently, and I was glad to have been there to take part. That we could mete out justice with such apparent ease and with such justification made my time in the province seem worthwhile. We were avenging angels.

'We showed them, the bastards', as Spen had it. And he was right. We really did.

***

That wasn't the only thing that worked out with marvellous serendipity. On another patrol we returned to the police station for our break, and I once again bumped into Debbie.

'We must stop meeting like this', she said, which saved me the bother. I was relieved that she at least remembered me. Maybe I had made some sort of impression on her. Maybe even a good one. To look at her she was obviously out of my league and yet she did seem taken with me...

Or was I reading too much into it?

I realised that this was probably my last chance. By rights we were ships that passed in the night, possibly not even on the same waterway. She spent little of her time actually at the station and I spent even less time there. There was no guarantee that I would ever return.

'Do you fancy a drink, Debbie?', I asked her. I was under pressure of time, but I think I managed to sound casual as if it didn't really matter to me whether she said yes or no. Of course, my heart was pounding. I was in the lunch queue, just behind Chip who turned to look at me with a sly grin on his face. I knew what he was thinking and feared he might be right.

'What, now?', she quipped before frowning and asking me another question before I could answer. 'How do you know my name?'

We edged towards the hotplate.

'I heard someone call you Debbie last time we were here.'

'Oh, did you now?', she said archly. With each provocative word I was falling deeper in love, losing myself in that languid way of speaking. Hers was not the short syllable-light Ulster accent but something much more... creamy. Can that be right?

I nodded and even managed a smile.

'Where would we go for this drink?'

I had no idea. Where was there to go? It was Chips who saved the day.

'Bangor', he said. 'We have R and R next week. Meet in Bangor.'

I sat at a table with Rockets, Chip and Spud. As I tucked into my sausage roll and chips, Debbie sidled over and dropped a piece of paper next to my plate.

'My number', she said.

My heart leapt and a rousing cheer went up from the assembled soldiers. Spud slapped the table with the palm of his hand.

'How the fuck did you manage that?', he asked me incredulously. I gave a modest shrug because I couldn't really explain it.

'Who Dares Wins', I said.

Which was as close to being in the SAS as I ever got.

***

But there was a war to be fought before we went on R and R. My new comrades looked at me with a hint of admiration, apart from Alan who had been born without the admiration gene. Not only was I a pitch and toss champion but I was the company's number one (and only) lady killer. I could explain neither phenomenon; I was suddenly being visited with hitherto unknown gifts. My new fledgling relationship with the beautiful creature that was Debbie coloured things for me, especially once I was able to ring her and arrange our meeting in Bangor the following Wednesday. I spoke to her dad first –

103

which told me she lived at home – but he quickly passed me over to her.

The payphone was attached to the side of the Ops room and had a Perspex dome over it upon which the rain drummed. Despite the percussive effect of the falling water, I was able to communicate and I was relieved that she hadn't gone cold on the idea. The rain fell from the dome in a steady trickle and I had to press my body fully inside to avoid getting soaked.

We quickly sorted the details out and when we were finished, I said, 'I'm really looking forward to this.'

'Me too', she replied and suddenly I was overawed by the romance of it. I was the young soldier far from home, she was the local beauty who saw something special in me. It could have been nauseating but it wasn't, not for me.

I dashed back through the rain – this had to be the wettest winter on record anywhere in the world – and made it to the warmth of the hut where the lads were sitting round a borrowed TV watching an FA Cup match between two London clubs. Spen looked up from the screen.

'Did you get through?', he asked.

'Yep. All organised for next Wednesday.'

He shook his head in wonderment.

'You're a jammy bastard', he said.

I watched fifteen minutes of football before retiring to my bed to read. Against a backdrop of groans and complaints about missed shots and bad decisions I read about Steve Carella solving crimes in the fictional US city of Isola. I was drawn into that world more easily than that depicted by Blade Runner. Real life had always attracted me. Even fictional real life.

***

The following day a policeman was shot dead on some waste ground on the outskirts of the city and two sections of troops were helicoptered out to search for evidence in the form of spent cases or even cigarette butts. Once again, our transport was the ungainly Wessex, two of them this time. Both sections were lined up, kneeling and ready to board as the great beasts clattered into view, a sight which I always found impressive. Climbing aboard, one always had to be wary of the gigantic exhaust mounted beneath the pilot and next to the door; why it had to be sited there I could not say, but it seemed like a design flaw to me.

It took only seconds for us to clamber aboard and for the helicopters to lift off again, quicker than it would take the IRA to mount an impromptu attack.

Speaking was impossible so we sat dumbly and admired the fantastic view of the city, before leaving the concrete mass behind for the super-green fields of the lush countryside. From my seat I could see the other Wessex and I couldn't help but be awed. This was like living a scene from Apocalypse Now. Naturally I had to look bored... This had to seem commonplace, if I was to look like a hard-bitten veteran.

The long grass flattened as we came into land, the rotors' downwash pressing an immense disc of vegetation flat to the soil. We debussed immediately and then each section took up all round defence until the helicopters had lifted off. We waited until a third helicopter came in – this one was a Puma – carrying a section from the Royal Engineers. Known as REST, the last two letters standing for *search team* – they had specialist equipment used to find... anything, I supposed. We remained where we were in the damp grass as their sergeant and ours discussed the operation, following which we stood and in loose formation moved towards the sight of the killing.

The car which had brought the unfortunate copper to this spot lay to one side, burnt out. I could tell it had once been a Volvo estate. The poor man himself lay in a heap in a small patch of tarmac upon which I supposed had once stood a building of some description. From a distance he was just a pile of clothes and not a man who had gone to the pub with his mates, watched football, learned to drive, fallen in love. Everything he had been was gone and everything he hoped to be was impossible now, yet he still looked like a bundle of discarded clothing from my vantage point, and I was glad that his face was not visible to me for I wanted my nightmares to be impersonal things.

That his face remained unseen fitted in perfectly with my plans for a return to civilian life, and I was gratified to feel no sense of ghoulish curiosity. This was someone else's encounter with the grim reaper, but it was close enough for me.

We were organised by the RE sergeant and given lines to walk and to search, although he was doubtful that we would find anything untoward; the IRA were exceptionally cautious these days and rarely left any incriminating evidence lying about. We began to pace the length of the waste ground as the Sappers assembled and tested their own equipment. Traffic roared by on our left, the dual carriageway only yards distant, and cattle grazed in near silence to our right. Two worlds, one pastoral and the other mechanical, existed side by side, with us and our unpleasant job somewhere in the middle.

The RE sergeant's pessimism was well-founded – there was nothing left behind to incriminate the murderers, but we paced the entire length and breadth of that piece of ground undaunted by mud, puddles, thorns and thistles. I'm sure we all wanted to find something, to be the one who found the evidence that put someone away for life, but there was nothing at all, just us, the traffic, the cows and the rain.

And the body of the dead policeman.

Before we left, I spotted Alan staring much too close to the scene of the crime, staring down at the deceased copper. With annoyance he was called away by our sergeant and within a few minutes the helicopters returned to take us back to base. I wasn't sure how I felt or even how I was supposed to feel. I didn't grieve because I didn't know the man in question, and this happened in the days before we were expected to feign sorrow for the passing of people we didn't know. We were still very British with our emotions back then.

***

The journey back was uneventful, but I took the time to study my new companions. Alan sat next to me, his face a lugubrious mask. I wondered if he was thinking about the dead man whose cadaver he had so plainly needed to study. What part of him had been prompted to drink in the details of the policeman's dead form? Was he thinking about his own death at the time, planning ahead, his curiosity piqued? *What exactly did a dead person look like?* It was certainly odd. Alan seemed incurious about almost everything except this. Perhaps this was his way of piecing together the horror of war, clutching at this one event as a way of rationalising his feelings and providing him with what he thought was a suitable memory to take home. Who knew how his mind worked?

On my other side sat Stoker, a veteran of one previous tour about which he said nothing. Stoker smiled often and spoke rarely. I had the impression that he was the best-liked man in the section. Married with a young son, he was next in line for a promotion should one come along. He was our unofficial 3ic. Beyond him I could make out the form of Chip, the only other soldier on his first tour. He had the advantage of having known the others for almost a year before being sent here, so although he was new to Northern Ireland, he wasn't new to Spencer and the rest. Chip wore his hair crew cut, showing off a skull which was almost a perfect sphere.

We were soon over the city. The centre, built up around the City Hall, was a US-style grid of streets and I knew that we were almost home – well, back at our base. The search we'd just carried out had seemed like a waste of time, but no doubt it was a matter of procedure following a murder. Smoke, mirrors, red herrings, one-way streets, dead ends; that was our war.

***

For the first time someone displayed emotion. It was almost a relief to find that a member of the congregation seemed to care about Alan's passing. For a man who had lived an emotionally sterile life to have engendered feelings in another human was nothing short of a miracle. When Alan laughed it was more like a tic than an expression of mirth, and when he looked sad it was nothing more than an extension of his natural facial languor. He was capable of a certain waspish annoyance and unmanly tetchiness like that of a spoilt child but otherwise he displayed the warmth of a Blue Circle cement bag. Now, I know that none of this was his fault.

It was his mother who sobbed but there was something about the scene which, although desperately sad, made me think that her grief was a complex thing, coloured by having lost a son she never really knew. I don't think anyone knew him. I don't see how they could have for there was nothing *to* know and for his mother, the chance to explore her son's emotions and to make some sort of bond with him was gone forever. But that was just my interpretation. It must have been hard to love someone who could only ever make a show of loving you in return. It would have been baffling and frustrating. It was unrequited love. To love and to receive ambivalence in return would be hard on anyone, but especially for a mother.

On the other hand, I could have been misreading the whole thing. Alan's dad dutifully put an arm around his wife's shoulders and pulled her close. The clergyman, untouched by grief, droned on, referring to the biography of a man he knew not.

It was all a bit of a worry. Alan wouldn't be going to heaven unless God really stretched his definition of what it meant to be a Christian to its absolute limits. The existence of God would have been too much for Alan's brain, and without that there was no way he could have made the correct spiritual preparations for the afterlife. That is not to say that I had or was even planning to make those preparations myself, but at least I had the option, and of course there was always Catholicism as a last resort; deathbed conversions sound like a great idea to me, the ultimate expression of sitting on the fence. For all I knew Hitler, Stalin and Jimmy Savile were all sitting in heaven looking down on Gandhi and David Ben Gurion burning in hell.

But none of this helped poor Alan, unless God's mercy extended to saving a soul whose limitations were hardly self-imposed. It wasn't his fault he didn't believe in God or in anything else.

Alan's mum grieved in a very British way, reserved and disciplined. This was not for show. When did I become so cynical? *Of course* it wasn't for show! That was her son in the box, not some stranger. Dad was playing his part too as the strong patriarch offering support to the mother of his child. I wanted to be touched but I was unmoved. Was there something wrong with me? I wasn't in the mood for a funeral and once again my thoughts turned towards my own problems.

For some time after leaving the army I took on one crap job after another, hoping that my situation would improve. I suppose it did, but it took time. Eventually I was able to move into a flat rather than a bedsit and my wages allowed me to eat a little better and buy new clothes. I am not claiming poverty but had almost no disposable income and far fewer prospects than I had realised. Three years in the infantry gave me a small fund of interesting stories to tell at dinner parties, but few skills that could be employed in civilian life. Plus, I never went to any dinner parties, although you had probably guessed that.

I thought about applying to university or polytechnic, finally putting my six 'O' levels to some use, but the urge passed. Besides I didn't relish the prospect of having *even less* money, with no cast iron guarantee of a well-paid job at the end of my three years.

I hankered after a job which required me to wear a suit or at least a shirt and tie, and eventually I became a civil servant, giving public money away to the needy, the underprivileged and the lazy. I was disappointed to find that a suit wasn't really required, especially since I bought myself one from M&S for my new job. The plain fact was that I sat in an office with a hundred other bods, inputting data, assessing claims and then pressing a button which produced an order book for the lucky winner – and they were nearly all winners. The job was dispiriting and frustrating. Worse than that, it was boring.

I had always thought that I could cope with boredom, after all it was one of a soldier's constant enemies, and yet the boredom of civil servitude was on a greater scale than anything I had faced thus far in my life. The army at least offered a *variety* of boring things to do, and very often exotic travel was involved. The civil service offered only one sort of boredom and it was always experienced in exactly the same place. In fact, it was waiting for me every morning, sitting expectantly at my desk like a paperweight or an amusing letter opener shaped like a Tuscan sword or a rubber stamp...

It wasn't long before I yearned for military life once again.

The Big Night Out

Debbie, I learned, was from Holywood, a town situated between Belfast and Bangor, but it was in the latter that I met her. She was waiting for me at the bus station as agreed and the minibus driver dropped me off before taking the rest of the lads further down the street. Spen shouted at me as I slammed the sliding door shut, reminding me that I was a *jammy bastard*. As I looked at Debbie, who was now approaching, I knew he was right. I could hardly believe my luck. The minibus pulled away but only got a few hundred yards before it was halted at the security gates. I had agreed to meet the lads at a pub called The Windsor – chosen for the patriotic connotations of its name – but I was in no hurry.

'How are ya, soldier boy?', she asked. I was a little taken aback at her familiarity and by the fact that she chose to mention my profession in a public place. This was after all, Northern Ireland where a large proportion of the population despised British soldiers and where a proportion of those would happily murder one given the chance. 'Don't look so worried', she assured me. 'This is Bangor. We're safe as houses.'

I had no reason to doubt her. Local knowledge was everything; she had it, I did not.

Abashed and suddenly apprehensive, not of danger but of making a mess of this date, I smiled and then leaned forward to kiss her cheek.

'I've been looking forward to this', I said.

'Me too. It must be awful cooped up in camp. I get to go home every night at least.'

We began walking slowly down the street, past the RUC station which I noticed was less heavily fortified than its Belfast equivalent. Debbie took my arm as if we had known each other for years and beamed up at me. Out of uniform I noticed how slim she was, how feminine. I couldn't recall having seen anyone quite so attractive in my life and this view was not wholly brought about by my male-only confinement. I was a reasonably good-looking bloke, but really nothing special. Debbie was simply stunning.

The evening air was cool but the rain had stopped, and when I commented on this, Debbie assured me that this was a good sign. It wasn't long before we came to the security gates, now unmanned.

'The vehicle gates are locked', explained Debbie as we made our way through. 'And all the shops have shutters pulled down.'

We were not alone; a hesitant trickle of week-day revellers were making their way towards the town's most popular bars.

'Bangor doesn't get much trouble', she explained. 'That's why you lot are allowed to come here. It got blown up a few times in the early days but not much since then.'

At the bottom of the street, we paused to look out to sea. Pink luminous clouds drifted across the distant shoreline and Debbie chose to give me a quick geography lesson.

'That's Bangor Bay', she said pointing ahead. 'Beyond that is Belfast Lough and across there is County Antrim.'

'And where is Belfast?', I asked. Debbie pulled the collar of her jacket up. I held her close.

'That way', she said pointing to the left. 'You can't see it from here.'

'If that is County Antrim, which county is this?'

'Down. County Down.'

I wondered at what point we were going to head into a pub, but the truth was I was perfectly happy just being with Debbie. We didn't have to drink...

We turned right, past a short row of shops, and then right again until we were on another long shopping street.

'This is where the pubs are', she announced. 'I take it you'd like a drink?'

'I don't mind. It's what you do when you start going out with someone, isn't it?'

The first bar was sticky-carpet noisy, thick with cigarette smoke and the ebullient cheer of the Ulsterman. It was clearly a great place for a night out. I hated it and when I looked at Debbie I could see that she did too.

'Somewhere else?', she asked above the din. I nodded and we withdrew, unnoticed by the regulars.

'I'm not that into pubs', she admitted when we emerged onto the street. 'Sometimes I go out with the lot from work, but I don't like drinking all that much.' I envied her the choice she had in the matter. In the army *not* liking alcohol marked you out as a deviant, someone to avoid at all costs. Proof of this essential truth could be found in the unlamented fact that Alan had not come with us tonight, preferring to remain in camp and perform rituals with his Ninja sword. Or so I was told by Spud. I wasn't sure if it – Ninja sword – was a euphemism or not.

'We'll go somewhere else', I said. 'I'd rather go somewhere we can talk.' We carried on walking up the street and Debbie pointed across the road to another pub. I thought she was going to suggest we went inside, although it really didn't look like the sort of place two young people might frequent, but instead she said, 'that is where the first female police officer was killed in the troubles.'

I was shocked and my mind raced back to the lonely corpse of the murdered police officer who had so fascinated Alan. I gave my head a slight shake to dispel this image and we walked on without further comment.

We made it to the top of the street without a drink having touched our lips and Debbie suddenly asked if I was hungry.

'We could get chips and then sit on the wall, looking out to sea', she added. With the mention of food my stomach gave a slight involuntary rumble. The night was

116

working out quite differently to my expectations. It was better. Much better.

'Chips sound good. Simple pleasures, eh?'

'Is that okay? Did you have your heart set on having a drink? It must be hard being cooped up all the time.'

I thought about this before I answered.

'It's fine. I think I assumed we'd be drinking but I'm not even slightly bothered.' I wasn't sure whether to say the next thing that came into my head, but the words came out anyway. 'I'm enjoying the company. I like being with you.'

'I like being with you too', she said. We stopped and kissed. I couldn't think of a time when I had been happier. The others were getting rat-arsed and I was with this beautiful woman. Maybe there was a God. But my near ecstasy was a fragile thing and nearly swept away when I thought about the impossibility of our situation. Debbie had her career in the police, and I had three years of military service to complete. Twenty-eight months to be exact. We couldn't actually be together for more than this single night.

'What's wrong?', she asked, sensing my mood. I was on my guard at once, lest I say something soppy.

'Nothing. Well actually, I would like this night to last forever.'

Debbie laughed.

'What song is that?', she said nudging me in the ribs.

'No, I really would like this night to last forever.'

The chips came in a greasy ball, but we tucked in as if we were feasting on the finest cuisine. I had been convinced that when Debbie had asked for 'two chips' that that was precisely what we would get – two single chips. But instead we got two portions.

'You just don't *spikka da lingo*, yet', she said. I conceded the point and we ate in silence, sipping on cans of diet coke. I enjoyed feeling the warmth of her body next to mine, the tang of the vinegar on the chips and the smell of the sea. I wished that we could meet up and do this once a week. I knew that the lads would expect me to try to get Debbie into bed, but this had never been on the cards, and they would feign disappointment that we had eaten a simple meal like two contented lovers gazing out over the ink-black seascape.

For the first time I realised that this was what I wanted from life; simplicity, good company, to be relaxed and content. I had no ambition other than that. I could think of nothing I would rather be doing and no one I'd rather be with.

Our meals complete, I scrunched up the papers and sat with them grasped in my lap as if absorbing the last of the heat they had to offer. We sat for a minute in silence until Debbie asked me about myself. I told her, simply and without embellishment, that I had lived near London, been in care for most of my life, done okay at school but joined the army at eighteen. I was nineteen now – still a teenager.

Then, quite naturally, she told me about herself. She was twenty and had joined the police straight from school when most of her mates had gone off to university, either in England or Scotland. She didn't think that she'd be in the police for the entire thirty years required to earn a pension. She regretted not taking a year out to see the world but there had been no funds available for such an adventure.

We chatted until it got too cold and then she suggested that we go to her house.

'My Mum and Dad's house by the way', she said, meaning, I supposed, that we would not be falling into bed together.

'I'd better find Spen and see if that is okay. The passion wagon is due to pick us up about midnight.'

***

We found Rockets and Chip in another pub and I told them of our plans. Chip looked completely wasted but Rockets still possessed a functioning brain and was able to absorb the information I relayed to him, although he was unsure if such a deviation from procedure was permitted.

'She's in the police', I said, reasonably.

'I know', he said and hiccupped. 'Just do it. You're only young once.'

A taxi took us to Holywood, a mere eight miles down the Belfast Road. We held hands as the car sped along the almost empty road and I closed my eyes briefly, feeling tired despite my happiness. There existed a lose triumvirate of 'things' required for a good night out in the army, this being some variation on, 'a drink, a fight

119

and a shag'. I knew enough to know that achieving all three was a rarity and here I was, still wet behind the ears and having achieved none of them. *What sort of heartless killing machine was I? Call myself a British soldier?*

Yet I couldn't have been happier.

It was only nine forty-five when the Nissan Bluebird taxicab dropped us off. Or twenty-one, forty-five hours, if you prefer. We paid and walked slowly up the drive, pausing just short of the door as Debbie spun me round to face her and planted a huge smacker on my lips. We kissed again and I let my free hand creep inside her blouse. She didn't resist, but I found the fact that I could see the flickering light of the TV against the curtains and hear the sound of the *Family Misfortunes* studio audience laughing at some moment of hilarity, slightly off-putting.

'We'd better get inside before you have my bra undone', she said. I was suddenly filled with lust, but I dutifully followed her inside where she introduced me to her family consisting of Mum, Dad and little brother.

Dad stood and shook me warmly by the hand, and her mum scurried off to the kitchen to make hot drinks, shouting through to her daughter asking if I wanted coffee or tea. It was assumed that I *must* want one or the other. Her Dad beckoned that I should sit and pointed at the most uncomfortable looking, painfully upright chair in the room. I duly sat on the unyielding vinyl seat, feeling it move beneath my buttocks as I settled.

I sensed that something was wrong at once and feared some sort of *faux pas*. Perhaps in Northern Irish culture the proffered seat was to be declined or maybe I should have ensured that Debbie was seated first. Whatever, the tension broke a moment later when Dad, little brother and, with reluctance, Debbie, all burst into laughter. Her mum joined in from the kitchen and at once I knew that I was the butt of a joke.

'Sorry about this', explained Debbie taking me by the elbow and indicating that I should stand. I stood as she explained further. 'This is my dad's little joke. He always gets new visitors to sit on Uncle Brenda's commode chair'. She rolled her eyes.

'Ahh', I said. I understood. Well, I partly understood. '*Uncle* Brenda?'

'He's Uncle Brian really. Family joke. You know the sort of thing. He's not even an uncle really, just one of dad's stupid friends'. Debbie indicated another chair for me to sit in.

'He's not stupid', said her dad.

'He is dad. He's in the loony bin.'

'What's wrong with this one?', I asked suspiciously as I sat.

'Nothing', she assured me. As I took my place, she plonked herself down on the arm of the chair. 'That's it for now. You have been subjected to all of our jokes now'.

It was warm in the room. A coal fire blazed in the grate and I attempted to remove my jacket. Debbie stood again, removing her own coat and then taking mine, which she hung up in the hallway, just before her Mum returned with a tray of hot drinks and digestive biscuits.

She was a good-looking woman in her early forties, and I could see where her daughter got her beauty and grace from.

'I see he got you with the commode', she said passing me a cup of tea. 'I have wanted to throw the bloody thing away for months now. Brian is in a home. He never visits. I think his nibs is keeping it for his old age'. She pointed at her husband as she said this.

Debbie's dad switched the TV off and the shiny host with his blow-jobbed hair disappeared into a speck before my eyes.

'So, you're a soldier, eh?', he said. Little brother looked on, apparently interested in my profession. I replied that I was, and we got into a brief conversation about the army before his interest waned. I drank my tea which was strong, sweet and hot, but not much to my liking. I could tell that Debbie's father was pining for his evening TV schedule and it was a relief when she suggested that we retire to her bedroom *to listen to some music.*

'See ya later, son', he said but I heard the television snap back on the minute I left the room and followed his daughter upstairs.

'Sorry about this', she said as she led me inside. 'It's looked like this since I was thirteen or something. I really need to get my own place'.

The room was tidy enough – perhaps it was RUC discipline which instilled tidiness – but there were vestiges of the little girl poking out from unexpected places. A red plastic tub of teddies was hastily kicked back under the bed and a cupboard door swung shut but only after I had spied a child's Snow White dress on a hanger.

'My mum blubs every time I say that I have to move out', explained Debbie.

'That's one of the advantages of being in care', I said with unintentional forced cheeriness. 'No one much cares when you move on.' Which wasn't strictly true. Some of the families I had lived with became attached to me and I to them.

'Poor you', said Debbie reaching for my hand. We sat on her bed.

'I didn't mean that to sound like it did', I said. 'I was a very happy child really.'

She looked at me as though I was simply putting a brave face on things.

'Honestly. I was well looked after.'

'But having no Mum and Dad...'

'I *had* parents', I insisted. 'They had problems enough without me coming along...' I had spent my life making excuses for them. I leaned over and kissed her.

'I had better put some music on', she said. 'To cover up the noise. What would you like on?' I was trying to figure out what sort of noise we might be making but I diverted my attention for long enough to peruse her record collection. It was an interesting selection, starting with Shakin' Stevens and moving along through various top artists of the day such as Madonna and Level 42. I hated it all.

'Shakin' Stevens', I said as a joke.

'You want to shag to *This Old House*?'

My mouth dropped open and then I laughed, presuming that she was joking.

***

Debbie dropped me off in her Toyota Corolla after a last lingering kiss and I made my way to the guardroom expecting to be in deep shit for arriving back late.

The guard commander looked me up and down before speaking. Then he looked at the clock which said 12.40.

'Sign in at midnight', he said. 'That way the sergeant major won't turn you into a pumpkin tomorrow morning.'

I took his advice and thanked him. Before I left, he stopped me.

'You're not even pissed. Where have you been?'

'I was with a girl.'

'So, you're the one', he said in mock awe, paraphrasing a line from the film *Top Gun* which was doing the rounds in the camp on pirate video.

I laughed but deep down I had to admit, I *was* the one.

Which all ended the next day when I got up and it was business as usual.

Some of the lads looked rather green around the gills, but the army was an unsympathetic organisation and a day's work had to be done regardless of the previous night's exertions. The clouds had dispersed for once and the sun shone down on us as it might do upon the righteous. Our foot patrol would take us into the heart of the city, and the aim was for eight soldiers to be a presence and really nothing more. As usual we could stop and question any suspects, but as often as not we wouldn't recognise them for what they were.

Back in base there was a board of photographs for us to peruse and a list of different models of car and their registrations, all intelligence relating to the local players, but I found it hard to retain this sort of information in my head. Some of the players regularly changed their appearance, growing beards, shaving them off again – and that was just the women. As for their cars, we would radio in the fact that we had seen them but there was never any point in searching them. The players never carried anything incriminating until the very moment of their planned attack. Someone else, an 'apprentice terrorist', probably, brought the weapons to the starting point and then took them away again once the attack was complete. Catching the actual terrorist in possession of an incriminating article had become almost impossible.

Belfast was a Victorian city and had once been prosperous – at the height of empire to be precise – when it produced linen, rope and ships, most of which didn't sink, the Titanic being the famous exception. The Protestants and Catholics had rubbed along okay; if you were a working-class Protestant your life was just as hard and uncomfortable as that of a working-class Catholic. The religious difference was only really invoked when the local politicians needed to create division and dissent. In the 1920s, when Northern Ireland had been established as its own separate nation within the UK, the new country's Catholics had, by and large, accepted their lot. There were rumblings of discontent, but life went on as normal.

It was the civil rights movement in the USA which changed things, making the Catholics unhappy with their situation, causing them to protest and giving the IRA a chance to infiltrate their numbers and create mayhem in the cause of civil rights. The rest was history – recent history – and what had been mere discord evidenced in rioting, became war. The army came to keep the peace. Rioting gave way to gun battles with the police and army, but these proved to be a poor means of taking the war to the hated *Brits*. Neighbours turned against neighbours and people who had once held no strong views on the subject of nationalism now found themselves bitterly entrenched as Republicans who wanted a united Ireland, or Loyalists, desperate to remain British. There was very little middle ground and as one atrocity gave way to another, whatever middle ground might have existed shrank away to nothing. The voice of reason got in a taxi and left *post haste*.

And that was still the situation as we patrolled down Arbour Street to the city centre. The houses, the people and the air were grey with menace and hatred. Anger was a currency, a living, malignant force that ran through every aspect of life. Communities had become ghettoes, hatred had become a language and distrust had become the glue that bound the people to their enclaves and to each other.

I didn't take sides. For one thing I found the whole thing too confusing in those distant days, and for another, picking a side would have made little difference to me and the job I had to perform. As ever, my role seemed to be a passive one; was I there to prove the rule of law or to give our enemies someone to attack, thus perpetuating the *status quo*? I thought about it too much. I thought about everything too much, and the truth is there are times when an enquiring mind is absolutely no use at all. There were no answers to the questions I had, but luckily I had the presence of mind to not really ask in the hope of receiving an answer.

But what would happen if we packed up and went home? A civil war? Perhaps our presence merely postponed the inevitable. Perhaps a civil war was what that little country needed to clear the air and start again.

And yet, despite the menace and the hatred, I liked the place. It was without pretence. When you walked past a gable wall with the letters FTQ daubed artlessly in black you knew where you stood with the locals. Similarly, when you encountered the artwork depicting the famous IRA hunger striker Bobby Sands, who always looked like a cross between George Best and Jesus Christ, you knew how the locals felt about having a Brit plodding down their street.

We came to a junction and crouched into cover as life went on around us. As usual a group of boys gathered to watch us. No doubt they had a pile of stones and bottles to throw but for the meantime they just watched with malign intent. I wondered briefly why none of them were at school before it dawned on me that it was Sunday; the days of the week had ceased to

127

matter. It was only then that I noticed the cars filled with churchgoers in their finery. God *would* be pleased.

The eight of us managed to cross the junction without incident and then maintained our patrol, heading for the city centre which would be completely dead; these were the days before Sunday opening. I had ceased to think of people as enemies or friends. They were just people again. This was just part of the UK. *We* were the only peculiarity.

Was the IRA at large today, or did God expect them to rest too? Were the others active – the UVF, the UDA or any other splinter group? We had to be even-handed and seen to be even-handed, but the truth was that these other terrorist organisations were some way down our list of priorities simply because they believed themselves to be on our side. Rarely, if ever, did they mount an attack against the security forces. The police did act against them as they would any other terrorist and had we searched a UVF man say, and found evidence of a crime, past, present or future, we would have arrested him as we would have done his Republican equivalent... but the situation did not seem to arise. I was genuinely on no one's side. Maybe the Queen's.

We stopped again when Spen spotted something up ahead and I found myself crouching behind a litter bin which stank of cigarette ash and dog piss. My rifle was loosely in my shoulder, battle sights up, not cocked. We never carried our rifles cocked. I looked around but mainly I kept my eyes peeled for whatever Spen had seen. He called something through on the radio and as he was waiting for a response, he called me forward urgently.

'What is it?', I asked him. His gaze was fixed ahead.

'Something on those roof tops', he said. 'Someone.'
I looked intently but saw nothing. 'Keep watching.
They're not there all the time… look!'

He was right. Two figures, no more than dark blobs
against the sky were moving about on the roof of an old
public building. It had fallen into disrepair and even at
this distance I could make out smashed windows and
boarded up doors. The lower section was daubed with
the usual slogans, but I quickly brought my gaze back to
the roof where two figures were clearly up to something.

'They're doing something, Spen. Taking something
down or…'

'Stealing the lead?'

'I suppose.' I wasn't actually sure why someone
would steal something like that. I didn't know that you
even found it on roofs anyway. Obviously *now* I know
that it is valuable and can be sold on, but I just agreed
with Spen, not wishing to appear stupid. As we
continued to watch, a blue Transit van pulled up outside
and another two men got out. We watched them until
they disappeared from view down the back of the
building. Spen was on the radio again putting forward his
new theory and suggesting that police should be called. I
couldn't hear the reply.

'Roger. We'll move a bit closer but keep out of sight
if we can, out.' To me he said, 'tell the others that we are
moving in on that building, but we are keeping a low
profile until the RUC turn up.'

'Right.' I moved down the line and passed the message to Dinger, Chip, Spud and the others. Alan asked which building I was referring to, so I pointed. He nodded as if he had just landed from another planet and was gradually storing up some useful knowledge about Earth. The message passed, we stood and slowly moved in as if we were creeping through the jungle. I was listening out for the RUC, wondering if they would have their sirens on to cut through the traffic even though this would inadvertently warn our lead thieves of their approach.

I had always marvelled at TV cops who shouted a warning so that their suspects had plenty of time to get away. Why didn't they get closer and then shout? It was done in the name of TV drama of course, but here I was in the thick of a drama of my own.

Every now and again I spotted one or both of the figures as they scrambled about on the roof, but they clearly had not seen us, and the blue van was still in place, presumably waiting to be loaded. I suppose that we all tried to keep a look out for snipers or for anything suspicious but, speaking for myself, my attention was almost wholly drawn to the men on the roof. Okay, so they weren't terrorists necessarily, but they *were* criminals. I was never going to get a better chance to apprehend a criminal than now, or to at least be in on the arrest when and if it occurred. We were maybe one hundred yards short of the building when we stopped and Spen summoned his faithful deputy forwards.

Spud, as a lance corporal, was in charge of the second brick in the section which could work independently of Spen when the need arose. That was the strange nature of this war we fought; our destinies were controlled not by sergeants and lieutenants but by corporals and lance corporals, lads who had done badly at school, only excelling at the related pursuits of football and truancy. Our platoon commander, a lieutenant, didn't lead us over the top. We didn't get a pep talk from the wise old sergeant. Out here in this bandit-infested urban jungle, Spen and Spud called the shots.

If you combined their ages, they were still younger than someone's dad and yet they wielded tremendous power, which they had to use wisely. Even more strangely of course was the fact that, in their absence, I could open fire of my own accord, so long as I gave a warning and could later justify my actions. If pushed to do so, I wondered how I might react. It was all far from clear cut, but at the back of mind I recalled the words of a colour sergeant who had been part of our training team in Ballykinler camp.

'Every decision is one which you might have to back up in court.'

It was a sobering reminder. We had to fight according to the rules, but our enemies did not. We had to take prisoners if possible… our enemies did not.

Spen was unhappy with our disposition and the reasons were plain enough; we had a massive and complex junction between us and our target. If we had to close in quickly then the traffic – which was still light – would be a barrier. Spen instructed Spud to take his men across the road, keeping distant but with the building in view at all times. We watched them go and take up positions before we moved.

With a gesture from Spen we stood and cut back on ourselves so that a short alleyway provided us with cover and helped us to cross one section of the junction. It felt odd to be so few in numbers, just four of us in a hostile world, looking out for one another. The alley was full of broken glass and dog shit, bins and the smell of piss, human or otherwise. It was no worse than any alleyway anywhere else in Britain, but there was an unmistakable tension in the air, greater than that generated by a fear of stepping in canine excrement. We followed a row of yard doors, each overlooked by a rear window. Briefly, a woman in middle age appeared, naked to the waist, and stood watching us. Her heavy breasts drooped like failing balloons. She had enormous nipples. She was in no hurry to cover up or to move from our vision.

'Fuckin' hell', said Spen, shaking his head.

We carried on walking, pausing at the end of the alley with the main junction in full view now and the building over to our right but still in sight. Spen spoke into the radio, telling the other brick of our location. I heard Spud's terse reply.

'Okay, we wait here until the police turn up. We only move if we think they're getting away. I've told the Ops room what we're doing and they're okay with it.'

We crouched in the stinking shadows and watched the traffic. Sunday morning Toyotas and Nissans proliferated taking the God-fearing of both sides to their respective churches. A metallic green Renault, held together with rust, stopped maybe thirty yards from us. We were instantly alert, but the situation was not what we assumed it to be. The car had merely broken down – or died might be a better description – and its disgusted owner, clad in denim and tweed, climbed out. He walked a few paces, muttering to himself, then returned, hefted a kick at the quivering French car before turning away again. The kick released a cloud of powdery rust which fell to the ground like orange snow.

Not long after that little cameo had played itself out, we heard the sound of police sirens and we tensed once more, ready for action, whatever that action might be. Two heads poked over the roofline and then disappeared.

'I think they're on the move', said Spen. He stood but pushed himself farther into the shadows. As we watched there was an indistinct flurry of activity around the van, but the police were nowhere to be seen. I was eager to go but Spen hesitated. The sirens were closer now but how much closer I could not say. Their discordant rattle rebounded off a hundred walls and shopfronts as they shot through the city.

I counted three figures at the van, which left one unaccounted for, unless he had slipped behind the wheel when the building had been lost to view as we moved through the alley. It was obvious that Spen wanted to leave this to the cops but equally obvious that they might not get here in time. Behind me, Alan muttered something, but I couldn't make out the words and decided not to ask what he had said; there was no time to assimilate his rambling answer. I was intent on the scene before me.

Spen sent a message to the other brick,

'Foxtrot Three-One Bravo, this is Foxtrot Three-One Alpha. You are to move out of cover and halt the traffic coming up Hawick Street. The police should be coming through so make sure they can get past that junction. If you see a blue transit you are to detain it. I am going round the back of the building, over.'

The radio crackled with Spud's reply, but they were out of sight, so I didn't see them carry out their instructions. In my head I tried to make a map of the traffic, but the details were too vague.

'Let's go', said Spen, suddenly and we sprinted towards the van. As we ran Spen cocked his rifle and I followed suit. I heard Alan and Stoker do the same.

Our feet pounded hollowly on the dank streets, but we were close before any of the robbers even noticed us. At once one of them jumped behind the wheel. Two others began running.

There was confusion. Alan was in front of the van now. Two people had shouted the standard warning, 'Army. Stop or I fire.' One of these had to be Alan. His rifle was pointed at the cab and the driver was struggling to make the old Ford start. Alan shouted again.

Spen had shouted and one of the running men had stopped. I watched briefly as he went forward and knocked the man to his knees. The siren was closer.

'Stoker, cuff this twat', said Spen. To me he said, 'let's get him.'

We began running after the third man, but it was preying on my mind that somewhere lurked a fourth who was unaccounted for. The man ran hard, his fists pumping. I shouted a warning, but he just kept running. I knew I wasn't allowed to shoot him, but I fancied my chances if I did. Beside me, Spen stopped and sent a breathless message into the radio. I slowed momentarily but he urged me forwards.

I kept running. He was using the other brick as a cut-off and I hoped they would appear in front quite soon before my lungs exploded. I shouted again, hardly able to form the words. Some way behind me I heard a shot, and my blood ran cold, but I kept going. The shot had the effect of slowing the runner slightly, but I could hear how ragged and laboured his breath was becoming. I was encumbered by a flak jacket, webbing and rifle. In any other circumstance there was no way I could have kept up, but I was still fit from basic training. Fitter than him as it turned out. I began to close the gap.

And then ahead of me Chip and Spud appeared. They pointed their rifles, shouted the warning as I nearly collapsed onto the street. Finally, my prey desisted.

'Fuck's sake. Fuckin' wankers', he said. This, I thought, summed up the situation nicely. He wore his curly hair in a sort of sub-mullet style. His seventies rally jacket – his robbing kit – was worn and dirty.

Spud made him kneel and then he was roughly searched. A few seconds later the RUC turned up and took our details. The scrote was taken away by the police who were none too gentle with him. He was practically thrown into the back of the Land Rover and I heard Spud chuckle. My breath was coming back to me now, but my head was spinning through the exertion.

'You okay?', asked Spud.

'Knackered', I said. 'Did you hear the shot?'

'Yep. Spen sent a contact report through the radio. I reckon Alan shot himself in the foot', he joked. The truth was less amusing.

***

According to the clergyman, Alan had been a loving son and brother. I could hardly bear to listen. His description of my erstwhile comrade couldn't have been more superficial. It was like listening to someone read from *The Manual of the Deceased*. He just didn't know Alan.

But then, who did?

As he droned on it was the image of Alan standing bewildered near that big junction in Belfast that came into my mind. He was the only one of us who had fired a shot in… well, not in anger because he never got angry but in mild dismay certainly.

He was carted off to be interviewed and we discussed his situation in his absence.

He had looked so forlorn as he stood there. I was reminded of a child who'd done something bad, something they had warned would happen and which they had been unable to avoid. Alan *was* childish, or childlike. I hate to use the word *simple* but that is how he seemed.

The vicar was talking about the bible now, saying that we should draw comfort from the word of God in these troubled times. It sounded like a mug's game to me, but I was a guest in his house, so I refrained from having an outburst decrying the futility of religion, or the fact that it was the worst form of slavery and a bloody waste of time for all concerned.

Also, I didn't think of it at the time.

As we stood for the next dreary song, I still had Alan's troubled face etched in my mind.

**

A second RUC Land Rover had pitched up at the other end the street next to the rear entrance of the building. The Transit was still there, now sporting a nice, crazed bullet hole in the windscreen. The driver had been lucky – Alan had missed him… but not by much. The only casualty was his underwear. He was being led away, as were two other men – boys really.

'Where'd he come from?', I asked pointing to the fourth man.

'Hiding', said Stoker. 'But we found him. Obviously.'

None of the thieves were armed and none of them were players. I suspected that they were seventeen or eighteen at the most. They had been caught red-handed but how that would translate into a sentence from court was anyone's guess. A bigger worry was what would happen to Alan. His defence would have to be that the van was being used as a weapon – that made it legitimate for him to open fire. But there was a snag as I was to find out. The van had been moving at about one mile per hour when Alan opened fire. It had been a battle of wills, the driver hoping to force Alan to move without actually injuring him and Alan hoping to make the driver stop by using his body as a barrier.

Unfortunately for the driver Alan also had his rifle and this made the contest an unequal one. I trusted that he had missed on purpose, but no doubt the lad's barrister would say otherwise. It all came back to making decisions you could justify in court.

What would Alan say in court? He wasn't a great speaker...

He came back with us that afternoon. Our NCOs had to visit the battalion intelligence officer who had driven in specially. I had never met him before, but Captain Norman made quite an impression. He was in civvies and bareheaded revealing what I presume was a double comb-over with oily sprigs of hair pulled from some point above his ears to meet in the middle of his shiny pink head. His hair was a wonder, so artfully arrayed and quite marvellous. The one thing it didn't do was disguise his baldness; his scalp shone through like the tender flesh of a baboon's arse. I think he was used to people staring. He almost defied them to do so.

When the captain had finished with Spud and Spen, he took Alan to one side for gentle questioning. The two spent little time together and for about twenty minutes we were all reunited in the room, listening to AC/DC and chatting as though nothing untoward had happened. But then the sergeant-major came looking for Alan and took him away. We didn't see him again for almost three days, in which time we learned that he was being questioned by the Military Police and the RUC, either alternately or together.

For those three days we became a section of seven men, and although it was possible to patrol a man short, we were put on other duties, which no one enjoyed in the slightest. It made us realise how good it was to get out of camp and to be our own bosses, away from the brass. Now we were trapped.

The NCOs took shifts in the Ops room, but the privates got various crappy jobs (GDs, or general duties) that would have been coming our way at some point anyway. On the first day I got spud bashing, having to fill a huge, wheeled bucket with hand-peeled potatoes. I wasn't pleased at first but the room I was put in was warm and dry and I could hear the radio in the kitchen. Crotus made my lunch and tea and brought them to me during my short breaks. He was complimentary about the standard of my peeling which left me feeling oddly cheered.

The next day I was on 'pan bash' which involved scraping coagulated custard from various huge containers. I discovered that custard grips tenaciously to metal. It is more like glue than food in these circumstances. Egg also sticks to metal, as does milk! The secret is to burn the foods being prepared, something at which Crotus was expert. The key weapon in the battle against burned on food was wire wool. The army possessed tons of wire wool – huge great spools of it in closely-guarded dumps scattered around the country, linked by miniature gauge railway lines that shunted stores of the stuff to where it was needed most. Somewhere in Britain there is an enormous factory churning out mile after mile of wire wool, huge whirling spools of the stuff, cut by industrious Chinamen and loaded onto trucks bound for every corner of the globe.

On D-Day, platoons of men waded ashore through withering gunfire laden with tough cotton rucksacks filled with the stuff, specially waterproofed to survive its possible immersion in the brine. At Dunkirk the stricken troops saved the BEF's stock of wire wool by passing it out to sea man by weary man, hand to hand and into the eager grasp of volunteers in their little ships. Nowadays it was brought in by helicopter.

It was tremendous stuff – an army staple with incredible cack-gathering properties that rendered it useless in next to no time as the gaps between the slender wire strands became filled with ex-food and turned into a gleaming shiny thing of incredible smoothness. At the same time pieces of wire would detach themselves from the main body and work their way into the unfortunate user's skin to remain lodged there for the rest of his life, causing merry hell at airport security when he would light up like Robbie the Robot.

My third day was spent at the plate wash, where I would wash, rinse and sterilise in accordance with Queen's Regulations. It was there that I learned another of life's incredible lessons – never let a black bin bag get more than half full with slops. Now, learning from one's mistakes is a great thing, but generally only in retrospect. Faced with a splitting bag from which a noxious ooze of leftovers was creeping like clammy lava, my thirst for knowledge was at a low ebb. My predicament was not helped by the fact that a small audience comprising *people who knew better than me* had formed. None of them, wishing to keep their uniform clean, wanted to help, although plenty of advice and abuse was on offer.

As a small lake of edible gunk formed at my feet, peas and beans bobbing in frothy tomato sauce, I struggled to hold the sides of the bin bag together and drag it so a place of safety.

'Fuckinell mate', remarked one kindly soul. It didn't help. Another tear appeared from which a piece of bread began to escape. I was repulsed by the sight and smells of things which minutes earlier might have looked appetising or at least edible. The food had become like vomit, certainly in status if not appearance.

'Wanna hand?', said another soldier as he scraped his leftovers into the replacement bag.

'Yes please', I said as I patched up the latest split with my hand.

'Well, tough shit.'

Eventually another bag was brought out and I managed to manhandle the full bag into the empty one giving me a double-skinned slop transportation system. With the hasty application of a mop the mess was cleaned up and further disaster was averted. I was chastened by the experience, however. It was a grim reminder of our powerlessness over the forces of nature. Or something like that.

For God, the Queen and Mrs Thatcher

I was glad when Alan returned and we were put back on patrol. He said nothing about his experiences, but I was never sure if this was because of advice he had been given, or because of shame, or because he simply did not know what to say. He was as enigmatic as ever, although the word enigmatic is usually used to describe someone about whom we *want* to know more. This was not the case with Alan. Sadly, no one really wanted to know what was going on in his head, perhaps suspecting that there wasn't much or that it was too dark to comprehend.

Nevertheless, it was a relief to get back to normal. Or *routine* might be a better word, for there is very little normal about wandering the streets with seven other men all armed with rifles. It felt good to get up in the morning and prepare for the weather and the possible danger, rather than thinking about the dastardly kitchen tasks which might be pressed upon one. I felt like a soldier again.

I was only doing what a hundred thousand other soldiers had done before me, but at times it felt important. It felt like war, which someone had once described as ninety-nine percent boredom and one percent action, even though the one percent rarely occurred. By that I mean that we had less than one percent action. Both the tension and the streets remained unchanged. The grey clouds stayed grey. We looked for phantoms and found none. We stopped, questioned, searched and scratched our heads.

My feet ached from all the walking we did and the cold seeped into my bones, suffusing them with ice. Now and again, we were told to look out for a particular person or a particular car, but we never seemed to encounter much that could be construed as suspicious. We took our share of abuse and the occasional brick lofted in our direction, but these were matters of routine. I got used to my place in the section. I was the third man along. I knew who was in front and who was behind. I knew what to do when we set up a VCP or when we stopped a pedestrian for questioning. I knew everything I needed to know.

Soon even the streets began to look familiar. There were only two exits/entrances to the base and to leave we could turn left or right, so there were definite limits to the view as we set off on patrol. Further afield, the possibilities opened up a bit but even then I got to know the graffiti, the abandoned/terminally parked cars and the bits of wasteland that served as battlefields for junior terrorists. I got to know the pubs and that strange Belfast phenomenon – the club.

When I say *club*, I mean a sort of fortified speakeasy. These dotted the city and admittance could only be gained by personal recommendation or some such. There were clubs in Protestant areas and clubs in

Catholic areas, and only members of the appropriate religion would ever visit the club. I don't know how sinister these places were in reality, but they had little external appeal, looking as if they might survive a nuclear attack. Well maybe not, but they were certainly bulletproof.

Another peculiarity of the city was the black taxi service which was reputedly run by the IRA to raise funds to buy weapons from their friends in America. I was never sure about the exact truth of this – maybe no one was –and we never stopped these taxis unless we had good reason to be suspicious. As ever, we played by the rules.

Between patrols or duties we tried to relax, but it was a boring existence. Army bases aren't nice places, and those that had been sandwiched into strategic corners of the city had the additional problem of being cramped. It meant that we all had to get along; for it to be otherwise would have been disastrous. We had more room than the crew of a submarine, and much greater access to fresh air, but we still lived cheek by jowl. Everyone rubbed along with everyone else for the sake of sanity. As I said before, we could go to the gym, or for a run, and on occasion we had organised PT in which the latter was foisted upon us. Other than that, there was a snooker table and a ping pong league, or as Stoker called it *pong-ping*. He claimed to have invented another derivation of the game with just one player which he called simply *pong*.

He was an interesting character, Stoker. I had assumed from his name that he had some navy connection but in fact his moniker derived from the fact that he had been born in Stoke. He was respected but I was never sure why.

I was still untouchable at pitch and toss. It got to the point where no one would play me, knowing that they would lose. Maybe one day I would be a world champion. I pictured myself in Las Vegas...

Watching TV was popular but for us a great off-duty treat was to watch a video. We gorged on the *Star Wars* trilogy although I personally wasn't much of a fan. There was a *Star Trek* video doing the rounds, but I think I missed that one. We watched *Ghostbusters*, *The Bitch*, which was rubbish, and a few Clint Eastwood films. We watched *A Nightmare on Elm Street* in the middle of the afternoon but with the curtains pulled and the lights off. Were we scared? I wouldn't like to say. I recall watching *Poltergeist* and being particularly shocked at the scene where the eponymous spook piles up the kitchen chairs.

There were other films, but the titles and content have faded from my memory, and this was the era of *Platoon*, *Full Metal Jacket* and *Hamburger Hill*. The first of these was released while we were still in Belfast and the other two shortly afterwards. I mention them not because we were fighting a war which was in any way similar to Vietnam, but because they influenced a generation of British soldiers... and not in a good way. It was towards the end of our tour that we got to see *Platoon* and its depiction of the US Army's failings in Vietnam. It was not flattering. I realise of course that it was only a film, a piece of popular culture and not an historical document, but nevertheless I suspect the portrayal of those times is accurate enough. We were rightly gripped by the tensions that existed within the platoon, which were at times greater than the collective tension felt by the close proximity of the enemy. The soldiers we liked the best were the drug-taking rebels rather than the orthodox, disciplined soldiers. We liked Staff Sergeant Barnes because he was tough and ruthless. We liked Elias because he was an NCO who looked after his men. We didn't like Lieutenant Wolfe because he was weak and because his NCOs only played lip service to his orders and nothing more.

And yet it showed an army in disarray, on the point of disintegrating as an effective force. This was quite unlike our own. Our admiration for these fictional but highly believable soldiers was severely misplaced to say the least. That they would be using drugs when so close to the front line was horrifying, more horrifying than the fact that they used them at all. I suppose that we could recognise the entertainment value of the film and its realistic depiction of that terrible war, but I don't think that any of us wanted to emulate those GIs. After all, we were professional soldiers, not conscripts. We had chosen the army, not the other way round. We took pride in what we did, regardless of how much we complained about it.

Rockets always had a stash of food which he shared with us on these occasions. Such was his generosity I was sure that he couldn't possibly have paid for the goods he distributed, but no one questioned the integrity of his charitable acts. He had Pot Noodles, cans of Coke, Mars bars, crisps, nuts, Yorkies, wine gums, not just individual packets but entire cartons of the things. Furthermore, no one ever saw them arrive - they just appeared under his bed.

'I get it', said Stoker one day. 'This is stuff that should be going to a bar, but you have an arrangement with the delivery chap that some of it comes your way for a much-reduced price.' He smiled and pointed at Rockets, certain that he had his man banged to rights.

Rockets' cherubic face expressed hurt.

'This is all top-grade stuff', he replied.

'I'm not disputing that, Rockets. All I am saying is that it fell off the back of a lorry. It's free enterprise. Mrs Thatcher would love it.'

I watched this exchange with interest. I was still trying to figure out the pecking order within the section and this sort of thing gave me clues. I already knew that Spen and Spud were at the top and that I was at the bottom. Alan was next to me. Beneath Spud was Stoker but that left three men unaccounted for, these being Chips, Rockets and Dinger. They seemed like eternal privates insofar as I couldn't imagine any of them staying on the army longer than they had to, but the army needed men like this as much as it needed its lifers.

Alan was watching the exchange between Rockets and Stoker. At one point he opened his mouth to speak and I cringed until, wisely, he closed it again. Rockets and Stoker were enjoying a bit of banter and Alan could not banter. He had the humour and sensitivity of a turbot. For him to comment on proceedings would have been awkward and embarrassing.

'Free enterprise had nothing to do with it,anyway', replied Rockets. 'I don't sell you the stuff, do I? I give it away. Besides pubs don't sell wine gums and stuff like that.'

'Okay. So where does it come from?'

'A contact.'

'Contact, wait out', quipped Dinger.

'So, if you give the stuff away then why do you bother?'

Rockets said nothing but Stoker was not ready to let the matter drop.

'It's just theft anyway', he said with a smirk and then laid his head on his pillow waiting for the reaction.

'All property is theft', said Chip. It was the most intellectual comment he had ever made in his entire life. 'Shakespeare', he added, wrongly.

'I wandered lonely as a cloud', said Dinger. 'That's Shakespeare.'

'Bloody hell', said Stoker. 'I'm surrounded by savages.'

***

During our time in Northern Ireland, we experienced both types of local weather – wet and dry – and it was one of the latter types of day when the big Wessex helicopter came to take Foxtrot Three One Alpha out to a patch of forest between the city and the town of Templepatrick, which was close to the airport.

We had been well-briefed on our job, so much so that I could barely remember a fraction of what I had been told. If I had wanted a bit of time away from the base then this was a perfect opportunity for me – we'd be gone for four days. Not that the officers and senior NCOs played a big part in my day-to-day life, but we would be well clear of them, self-sufficient for four days. The briefing was a mix of the factual and the preposterous. We were shown a surprisingly good model of the area we would be moving into, with miniature barns, houses, trees, a road and a bridge, all of which had presumably come from a Hornby train diorama modelling set or similar. The effect was spoilt a little by the fact that the sergeant briefing us repeatedly referred to the gorse bushes in and amongst which we were supposed to secrete ourselves, as *gorge bushings*. Spen and I exchanged a look and for that second I knew we were on the same wavelength – we were in the presence of a grade 'A' spanner.

The model had undulating hills which surrounded the isolated farmhouse and a particular *gorge bushing* had been selected for us to move into. Like an estate agent, the sergeant described the many advantages it offered us, notably a good, uninterrupted view of the house we were keeping under surveillance, plenty of room, an *en suite* bathroom and the fact that it was sited amidst other similar *bushings*. The latter consideration stemmed from the fact that using isolated cover went against widely accepted military doctrine insofar as any returned fire could be pinpointed to one location if that was the only place in which soldiers could be hidden. The problem was unlikely to occur but still, the precaution was wisely taken.

The reason for the surveillance operation was the fact that the IRA had been threatening to shoot down aircraft as they passed overhead, either landing or taking off from the airport. A proportion of this aviation traffic came from the RAF, not that shooting down a civilian airliner would have mattered to the IRA of course. It was rumoured that they had in their possession some Russian made SAM 7 missiles, short-range, man-portable devices for bringing down relatively slow-moving targets. Naturally, the possession of such weapons would lead to their immediate and devastating deployment and for them to be effective the firer had to get himself close to the flight path of the target aircraft. An obvious target would have been a military helicopter, but a better target would be a passenger-carrying jet or even one of the RAF's large Hercules transports which shared a runway with the civil airport at Aldergrove.

Hence our operation. How anyone came by this type of intelligence was a mystery to me, but I was fairly sure that somebody had to put themselves in great danger to get close enough to the men who planned for the IRA. This was high level stuff. It could be their biggest coup if they managed it. We were shown photographs of the men we were looking for and the cars that might be turning up. We were given details of the weapon itself and what it could do if used properly. No one seemed to know if they – the IRA – *could* use it properly. It had been suggested that they received training on Russian-made weapons from the Libyans, but if true, this had not always yielded the results they had hoped for. There was a story, quite possibly apocryphal, that they had once attacked the base in which I was now stationed using an RPG 7 which they fired from inside a car. The RPG was an anti-tank weapon and the rocket it fired issued a huge blast as it was launched. This blast is normally free to escape into the air behind the firer but inside the confines of a car... there were no survivors.

That's if the story was true, which I hoped it was. It proved that we were not just *morally* better than our foes but better trained too.

'So, you should be flattered that they are using you for this', said the sergeant. 'But remember you are there to watch and to pass on information. someone else will do the er… shooting if it proves necessary.'

Spen asked who that might be, presumably thinking it was a job for the special forces.

The sergeant replied with another verbal gaff.

'Normarily it would be the SAS, but in this case, it will be the Parachute Regiment. They have some guys trained for this type of thing.'

Spen nodded. I looked over at him thinking that I knew him well enough now to guess what might be going through his mind. He confirmed my theory outside.

'Fucking Paras. Get all the glory jobs. Anyone could have done what they did in the Falklands. Anyone. And as for that dickhead – what sort of word is *normarily*?'

We got our stuff together and then Spen gave us our own briefing. None of us apart from him had done a surveillance op before but he quickly passed on everything he knew.

'It's not rocket science', he assured us. 'Bring a book', he advised. I looked at Alan and Chip and suspected that they didn't read, especially not Alan. Chip had the anxious look of the corner boy about him as if he were constantly waiting to get found out for some crime or other. I could picture him in school being a right pain in the arse for his teachers. But for all that he was always okay to me, a bit like a long-suffering big brother, the type who couldn't quite bring themselves to tell you that you were actually *not too bad* once they got to know you. I could tell that he didn't like Alan for he always gravitated towards Spen. In a sense he worshipped his NCO and sometimes, without even realising, he emulated his words and gestures, as if doing so gave *both* men greater authority. I knew that if we had to pair up for some reason then I would be stuck with Alan.

We left our normal webbing behind and signed out Bergen rucksacks from the CQMS. We brought just a basic wash kit each, bottles of water, our rations which would be eaten cold, change of clothing, sleeping bags and ponchos with which we could make basic bashas. We supplemented our rations with extra food bought from the Chogie Wallah or the Naafi. Spen had a Nikon camera and film, plus a night vision aid.

Most importantly however, we also brought bags to crap in and bottles to piss in. The point of this measure was to remove any trace of our presence after we had gone.

I didn't find it hard to imagine a substandard quality plastic bag splitting open inside my Bergen, allowing a sludge of festering faeces to spill forth. Undoubtedly, I would be alerted by the smell.

Apart from that we had our normal scales of ammunition, and as we sat on the cricket pitch waiting for helicopter to come, I actually felt quite relieved to be getting away from base for a little while. I had produced my own chuff chart by this stage, not counting down the number of days until I left the army, for there were far too many of them, but instead the days until I left Northern Ireland, which seemed like a more wieldy figure. This little trip out was as good a way of removing four days as any. It was four days less until we returned to our base in Germany and then went on leave.

Having come straight from training, I had never visited our camp, so I didn't know if going back there was a good thing or not. I also wasn't sure where I would spend my leave. Maybe I could return to Northern Ireland and have a week with Debbie, although I couldn't imagine the army agreeing to that.

Debbie's first letter had arrived the previous day and, like soldiers throughout history, I had this carefully folded and placed in an inside pocket of my combat jacket. I had read it about six times already and would read it again and again, taking careful note of the little 'x's at the bottom, of which there were six. I took this as a sign that she liked me a lot – six 'x's worth anyway.

She was keen on the idea of us meeting up again, but short on specifics. I think we both recognised the part that sheer luck had played in our previous meeting. For those circumstances to come again might be a miracle, but knowing that I was in her thoughts helped maintain my morale. I could picture myself reading her letter as I crouched in the gloom of a *gorge bushing* with a dreamy smile on my face, and it occurred to me that I could almost be a soldier from any generation – the Tommy in the trench, or the jungle, or the desert, reading by the flickering, carcinogenic light of a Benghazi burner.

It was all very *Apocalypse Now* as we waited, then heard, then saw the big helicopter coming in. Soldiers and helicopters went together, certainly in the minds of those who thought about what might be associated with a career in the army. Our helicopter had an underslung load in a cargo net and the CQMS and his storeman, known as his 'dog', waited nearby for a delivery of God only knew what. The CQMS marshalled the helicopter with a series of practised gestures until it was in a hover above the cricket pitch, and then flapping his arms like a flightless bird, he slowly brought it down until the net touched the ground, all the time keeping his gaze fixed on the pilot's face. The fuselage came down another few feet and then the storeman ran underneath to release to load. The noise and the downdraught gave the impression of a localised hurricane being visited upon us.

Unfortunately for the CQMS's dog he forgot the one cardinal rule of this procedure, which was to earth the helicopter before touching it. This could be done with a spike on a wire which would divert the built-up static electricity safely into the ground. Without this precaution being taken, the built-up static electricity merely exited through his body, flinging him into the air like a discarded soft toy from a pram. From behind, I saw Spen's shoulders convulse in laughter. I glanced over at the CQMS whose head was in his hands with despair at the schoolboy error they had made. Meanwhile the helicopter remained in the hover and the storeman continued to lie prostrate.

As the CQMS took over unhooking the load, the hapless 'dog' came to and began crawling away. The load now detached, the helicopter drifted away to land on a slightly different part of the cricket pitch and, at a signal from the loadmaster, we clambered aboard avoiding the hot exhausts. No sooner were we inside than the Wessex lifted off, climbing as quickly as it could to lessen the opportunities of being shot down by the IRA.

The city was the same grey grid it had always been, a pattern of roads leading from one place of drudgery to another. The cars and buses shuffled along on their pointless journeys but I, looking down on them like an angel, could take time to wonder why they bothered. Why did the commuters commute, why did the buses fill with people and disgorge them again? If people had to work at all then why not work close to home and cut out all this wasted effort? In my darker moments I had pause to think that life was essentially pointless and that our efforts eventually mean nothing.

Our education and experience gets locked up in our heads and then goes with us to the grave. No one cares and we are soon forgotten about. Ghosts, if they exist, are manifestations of unfulfilled dreams. I am constantly surprised that we can move for the ethereal mass of disappointment that engulfs our world. Even the greatest figures in history have only managed to harmlessly flick the world on its great axis, causing not so much as a wobble.

Nothing really matters. Anyone can see. Nothing really matters…to me.

But it is true.

A cure for cancer? It just means that a few million microbes on a small planet, in a galaxy lost amongst billions of other galaxies, survive to die later than nature had intended. So, what was the point?

This morning I had arisen, washed, shaved and eaten, and now here I was flitting across the slumscape of a small regional city to then sit in a bush for four days. What did it matter? We gave importance to things that had no bearing on life.

That's how I think when I am tired, when fatigue takes a grip. Our weeks were long, and our time off filled with numerous tasks that fell under the heading of *personal admin*. The army made it so simply because there was so little light relief to be had. *Keep 'em busy*.

The red brick, back-to-backs gave way to the pebble-dashed estates, new ghettoes for old, a transference of squalor, squalor for a new generation. Society requires something which resembles poverty so that the rest of us can feel good about ourselves. We need reminders that we have escaped, or avoided, a fate worse than the one we currently endure. Things could always be worse. We only need to look at our perpetual, self-sustaining underclass. Sperm and eggs are in plentiful supply, and readily fuse to help the underclass to thrive.

Below, a football ground, empty and cold, stripped of passion. Even the twenty-two men whose aimless pursuit of air encased in leather had forsaken their grassy fortress for the time being. A hospital, a police station, both symbols of the state; two or three schools, breeding grounds of juvenile discontent; all slipped past in the down rush of air that kept us aloft. Altitude made me feel superior to those ordinary mortals who struggled heavily on earth, and even though I knew that someday

I would struggle with them, collecting trolleys for Tesco, delivering soft drinks from the back of a van, or filling in forms for some office or other, I had enough wit to savour the moment when someone took me for a ride in a helicopter! My life would become humdrum, but not today...

I knew there were upturned faces down there, but distance had shrunk them to invisibility. From this vantage point the edges of the city became clear. Houses gave way to grass and trees. Factories and shops fell away as if suddenly going out of fashion, to be replaced by farms with their irregular patterns of greens and browns, man-made and functional but clearly connected to nature. The roads became winding bands of grey, cutting through the countryside, connecting the local towns to the capital like so many umbilical cords. Here and there, plain, white farmhouses punctuated the greenness. I could make out farm machinery labouring in the fields like modern day oxen. If I craned my neck and looked backwards, I could see the water which separated us from the mainland. How different things were just a few miles distant.

The noise of the great engine made speech impossible. I looked over at Spen who yawned as if flight was the most boring thing imaginable. Next to him Alan's face was a blank. He could have been a waxwork or some realistic dummy with the batteries removed. Nothing was going on in his brain. No inventive wheels turned, churning out thoughts or dreams. Nothing whimsical cantered through his mind. There was nothing. He was the hollow man.

***

I thought about that flight as I sat there in church and wondered if something had already snapped inside him by that point. He gave so little away that it was almost impossible to say how he felt. Had the experience of interrogation with the RUC and RMP somehow crushed the shallow spirit which possessed him? Had the closeness of that near moment of violence – his rifle, his finger on the trigger pointed at the non-enemy – had that snapped some sensory circuit in his brain? The wiring was already wrong. Had it got worse? Had a fuse blown in his brain?

His mum stood and, supported by her husband who I supposed was Alan's Dad, she made her shaky way to a dais from which she would say a few kind words about her son. She wore a sombre dress, something plain and a bit cheap looking. She was not a habitual dress-wearer I suppose, and this was no fashion outing for sure. I didn't know what she looked like normally but she certainly seemed washed out by grief, the colour drawn from her skin, her cheeks sunken and her eyes rimmed by black rings. There was nothing worse than to outlive a child, and to wonder if you could somehow have prevented his death could only have been another cruel twist of a fateful knife. Alan's Dad was perhaps coping better; maybe he was just more adept at disguising his grief.

Did he even miss his son? Terrible as it may sound, there was little to like. Love was one thing, liking was another. Maybe he knew that his son would eventually kill himself. Maybe he thought it was for the best.

There was a hiatus as Mum shuffled the thin sheaf of papers in her trembling hands and tried to compose herself for the task she had ahead, which was in a sense the final act of Alan's existence; when she said goodbye he was gone for good.

She opened her mouth to speak but there was silence, and then she emitted a croak, her voice failing her, her emotions closing in on her vocal cords, strangling them like a garotte. She shook her head in frustration and tried again, before shoving the notes at her husband and sitting down.

His delivery was as toneless as hers might have been impassioned, and I wondered if he had been prescribed some zombie-fying medication which robbed him of feeling. The words were surprisingly bland, talking of love and loss, worry, despair. It was clichéd but that didn't matter. They told a story that needed to be told and used the language people expected to hear. Bland. Alan had been bland. It was perhaps fitting that his life could be recounted as a series of colourless events. There was no blame, no recrimination. Alan had met the only fate that fitted. His inner darkness had suffused the church and the clouds outside. As his father spoke, the rain began.

Boeings, Fokkers and Shorts

Obviously, the helicopter was not going to drop us right into the area from which our observation was going to take place; several tons of hot noisy metal did not lend itself to stealth, so instead it would drop us approximately two miles away and give us the opportunity to move into cover as we saw fit, and according to our own timetable. I felt only a slight tremor of unease as we descended rapidly. The Wessex was a nimble machine in the hands of its RAF crew, and they brought it down with seeming ease, pulling back at the last minute to land as if on a yielding bed of marshmallow. The great side door was open already and we wasted no time disembarking, sprinting away from the huge rotating disc and then falling into all-round defence. A second later the Wessex lifted off again and clattered away into the distance.

The local IRA – the ones we hoped to be watching – would have heard and possibly seen the helicopter, but such was our proximity to RAF Aldergrove and the civil airport that the comings and goings of any sort of aircraft created no real spark of interest or suspicion. The military were part of the little country's fabric after so many years. I learned later that the phrase used to describe the situation and our part in maintaining the status quo was *an acceptable level of violence*. It is the sort of thing that comes to haunt politicians when their critics round on them, and yet at the time it fitted perfectly. What else could we have? There was no end in sight and no political solution acceptable to both parties. There was no possible compromise.

We waited. We waited until the dew had soaked into our uniforms and we had begun to expire through sheer coldness. I watched the world from behind a clump of grass, heard the wind through the distant trees and the roar of occasional passenger flights overhead. We waited until my entire body ached and I felt as if I might not be able to stand should the order to do so ever come.

But Spen was taking no chances, preferring to know that we were not under observation before moving off. It occurred to me that the weapon intended to bring down an aeroplane could equally blow us to hell in our stupid bush should the IRA see us taking up residence. We'd stand no chance. Spen's caution was probably a good thing.

'Right', he said finally, lifting his frozen body into a crouch. We followed his lead, rising from the earth like the undead. We mentally shook ourselves down and then fell into a loose formation as we headed for our new home, Spen in the lead, then Alan, Chip and finally me as tail-end Charlie. Every few paces I turned to look behind me, checking for enemies who might shoot us in the backs, but each time there was nobody, nothing, except the invisible swirling air and the encroaching fog of darkness. The grass was long and damp. It grabbed at our ankles as we passed through, slender green fingers that coiled onto our black boot leather and threatened us with calamity.

161

The rain began to fall now as big heavy droplets, chilled by the air on their long descent, but I knew that I would remain in good health because... well, I was never sure why I kept so well. Nowadays, I get a cold just by watching an advertisement for Beechams on the TV, but then it was different. I was resilient to ill-health.

It was obviously important that we were not spotted as we entered our hide. Spen kept a good look out, as did we all, and took his time. There were no houses, paths or public areas between us and the bushes, which helped, but there was a procedure in case we were spotted, which was simply to skirt round the hide and then come back to it later from a different direction. However, it would be dark soon in any case.

I wondered about Alan's deployment. Was this Spen's way of rehabilitating his errant private, making sure that his confidence didn't sag? Spen could be tough and unforgiving. He was foul-mouthed, like any soldier I suppose – the genuine rough diamond – and yet he never said anything against Alan, as if realising that the man was vulnerable and troubled. These traits must have registered with me to some extent, but I never really thought about them until later.

That's life though. You don't always appreciate what you've got at the time. Sometimes you have to be down and kicked before you remember how good things once were and how loyal your friends. It is easy to think of this natural reappraisal as simply looking at things through rose-tinted glasses – we all do it – but now and again the tint is deserved, the memories genuine. But it is true to say that Spen never acted unkindly towards Alan, or anybody else.

I was never sure if Spen actually liked me, emotionally constipated as he was, but he certainly never put me down or poked fun. From the earliest times he seemed to trust me, and tiny bits of responsibility came my way, boosting my confidence and making me feel accepted.

He could have left Alan behind, thinking him a liability, but instead he brought him along, keeping faith with the section's odd man out. It was an act of kindness. Was it wasted on Alan? I don't think so. He felt something. He knew when he had done something wrong and he knew when he had done something right. Thinking about him now, he was big child in many ways. Or maybe a dog in human form, easily pleased by a kind word or a pat from his master.

We stopped at the brow of a hill, arranging ourselves in all-round defence as per SOPs, soaking up the still sounds of the countryside and yet more of the earth's moisture. We waited for some time and I, thin and uninsulated against the cold, began to shiver. Spen turned to look at me, bemused.

Just when I thought I could hear the grass grow and the birds rustling their bedding ready for a night's sleep, we stood once more, re-emerging like mud men. In slow procession we began our final approach, but only got as far as a large hollow in the ground leading to the final hilltop beyond which our target stood. Thinking back to the model we had looked at, this feature had been diminished by scale, flattened out, and yet in reality it offered considerable cover, or, depending on your view, obscured the target from our sight.

We crouched again and Spen drew us close.

'You two stay here. Me and Chip are going for a look over the…' He couldn't think of the word and made a sort of swan's neck gesture with his forearm to indicate that they would be checking out the lie of the land from the top of the hill. The word he was looking for might have been *brow* – the *brow* of the hill – but I said nothing. Alan and I nodded and the other two moved away in a crouch before getting on their bellies to crawl. They were back two minutes later.

'Right, I've seen it. We are going to be a bit exposed at first, so we are going to crawl in, one at a time. If they see us, we might as well pack up and go home.' We followed him to a vantage point from where we could observe the farmhouse, the outbuilding and the surrounding land which we had studied on the model, and at once it all fell into place. The sun was falling below the hills, sending shards of orange light into the sky like a drowning man's last attempt at rescue. A Boeing jet took off and headed for America. I felt a moment of longing and thought about taking Debbie away to some sunny spot when this was all finished with. I was cheered by the thought that I would actually have the money for such an enterprise; there was little opportunity to spend your wages cooped up in a small base with just a Chogies and a NAAFI shop.

Of necessity, we crawled in one at a time and Spen went first because it was he who had to select the precise spot from which our observation would take place. After a short time, his face poked out and he beckoned the next man to join him, this being Chip. When Chip had gone, it was Alan's turn and then mine.

It wasn't much of a bush really. Inside it was damp, dark and not very roomy. We didn't have much remaining light to get ourselves sorted out, and torches were forbidden because they would give away our position. This was our home for up to four days. We would be cold, wet, bored, uncomfortable and possibly hungry. All of this is fairly standard for a soldier in the field, but that doesn't mean we wouldn't have preferred a warm bed and hot meals.

Our equipment was barely adequate for the job we had to perform. The sleeping bags, although down-filled, were old and tatty. Over the years they had lost many feathers, so the insulation they offered was patchy or non-existent. Worse than that was our reliance on the dreaded poncho from which we were supposed to fashion a waterproof shelter called a basha, which resembled a primitive tent. But in our little jungle world there was no room to make such a dwelling and so we would sleep rolled up in our ponchos instead, hoping for a fine night, rather than a torrential downpour. Soldiers nowadays have Gore-Tex bivvy bags which they can simply climb into with their sleeping bags, but no one had invented anything like that, and even if they had the army probably wouldn't have bought them for us.

Our uniforms were rubbish too and we still relied on the woolly pully jumper to keep us warm. In addition, we had our 'Chinese fighting suits', consisting of a quilted gilet and zippy trousers which could be put on under your normal combats. They actually unzipped into two sections for this purpose but if you attached these sections wrongly you ended up with a garment that had six-inch legs and a remainder that went up past your arm pits.

There were some compensations to be had. For four days we didn't have to wash or shave, although we drew the line at not brushing our teeth. The reason for this was that the smell of soap carries too well and might alert our enemies to our presence. Another advantage was that we would catch up on our missing sleep. Back in camp, if you weren't watching TV, eating, reading or going to the toilet, then all that was left was sleep. But the main thing was that we would be left alone.

Spen called us in close and we crawled over the cold muddy ground to get near him. He pointed to the house, perhaps two hundred metres distant, and spoke in hushed tones.

'There it is. We're looking for, and logging, any activity. Cars coming and going. Lights going on. Strange faces. Anything like that. If we see someone with a missile, or something that might be a missile, then we act quickly. If it's you on watch then you wake me immediately.' Three heads nodded in the gloom. We already knew this but Spen didn't want any screw ups. 'As far as anyone knows the missiles aren't in the house yet, so we don't want to be calling for the cavalry until we know that they are.' This consideration visibly weighed on Spen. Perhaps he saw himself as the linchpin of a major operation.

Perhaps he was right.

We drank and had a cold meal from our rations before settling in for the night. I'd made a conscious decision to get to sleep at about seven o'clock, but I was still awake by eleven. I think I had just finally dozed off when Spen woke me to start my observation. My eyes were heavy with sleep, my brain already addled. For a moment or two I couldn't understand how I had come to be in this stupid bush in the middle of the night and in the rain.

'You're up', said Spen in a forced whisper.

When I took up my post, I was surprised to see the target house lit up, and I had to remind myself that it was we who were in hiding and not the inhabitants. They weren't hiding from us – the reverse was true – they benefitted from a show of normality even if the goings on inside were far from normal. This was a family home belonging to the McGraths, Catholics with jobs, aspirations, children, and a desire to kill as many British people as they could possibly manage. If the planned IRA operation took place, their role would actually be a passive one, after which they would be portrayed as unwilling stooges to the Republican plot, although we all knew that this was simply a subterfuge. They were willingly giving the terrorists access to their house.

Mr McGrath was a schoolteacher. Tall, grey with terribly crooked teeth, he nevertheless revelled in his capacity as a pillar of the local community, never mentioning his support for terrorism to anyone but a few selected 'friends'. His wife was a farm manager and both children were at high school. Apart from minor details like their involvement in a plot to bring down a packed airliner and cause the deaths of hundreds of people, they were extraordinarily ordinary. The extent of his wife's complicity was not fully understood, but McGrath himself, a so-called refugee from Belfast, was a dyed in the wool supporter. That he would involve his family in this manner of death-dealing was seen by us as bad form. For him it might have been perfectly natural. Maybe he thought it was fitting that his children understood the nature of the Republican struggle and were part of it.

But for now, everything was normal. I supposed that what went on behind locked doors and drawn curtains was typical of any family home and, as I watched, the house lights were extinguished one by one. I was able to distinguish the bathroom lights from the rest – they flicked on and off regularly in a pattern which coincided with the use of the various bedroom lights. Half an hour into my watch the house was in darkness. There was nothing to report. At 00:45 the bathroom light flicked on for about one minute and then went out again, after which there was only darkness.

The night noises were just amplified version of those heard during the day: the wind blowing through the valley, the distant motorway traffic and its constant roar. Nearby, small animals moved restlessly, and an owl hooted. I could see bats in aerial dogfights with unseen foes and hear one of my comrades snoring gently. There didn't seem to be much that I could really do about that but there was chance that the noise might carry on the wind.

From a haphazard framework of branches, I could pick out a patch of sky, bereft of stars but filled instead with huge grey clouds that floated past the moon, itself just a sickle blade of light. Light rain fell and a twisting ball of mist formed around the house and the farmyard. By 01:35 I was seeing secretive figures making their way between the outbuildings. I could hear their whispered conversations and sense their tension. The problem for me was this: they weren't there at all. My mind was filling the black void with what I expected to see, and as I peered through the mist it was filling in the blanks for me. Twenty-three minutes later I was shaking Alan awake.

***

When dawn broke, we were all frozen and wet. And tired. I hoped that the day would be mild and that we would dry out a little. I planned to sleep after breakfast and set about opening a packet of hardtack biscuits onto which I would spread some compo ration 'cheese, processed' (or *cheese possessed* as it was more commonly known), but I found the fact that Alan was having a crap into a bag not two feet from me somewhat off-putting. From this angle, and because I was within olfactory range, it was clear that he required a change of diet; this major faecal event was not going well for him. Or for the rest of us.

It put me off my food. You had to accept the rough and tumble of army life, for instance the times when you wanted to get an early night but were accosted by one happy drunk after another as they staggered back into the barracks after a night on the town. Or the barrage of abuse you casually accepted resulting from some minor misdemeanour or other. But to have Alan's autistic arse so close to my dinner as it expelled some unwanted leftovers into a carrier bag was too much. Spen must have sensed my mood, either that or he had reservations of his own, for he said, 'Alan go and shite somewhere else for fuck's sake', in his usual forced whisper. If Alan looked hurt or embarrassed by this reprimand, I couldn't say – I wasn't looking at his face – but he managed to bunny hop away from us, crapping as he did so. I am still troubled by that image today.

During the day, Spen took the lion's share of the observation duties, but I still managed a two-hour stint from midday onwards, during which I was able to watch Mrs McGrath return home for lunch in her Mitsubishi 4x4. We had been told about the car, and it was quite distinctive with two tone paintwork like some 1960's Austin 1100. It was the sort of thing she probably needed because of the work she did and not just as a fashion accessory as might be the case today. She was a plain woman with grey hair and carried a bit too much weight. I would say she was dowdy. Mind you her husband was no looker, so that all fitted. We hadn't seen photos of the children, but I could imagine them being fairly plain too.

Despite that her level of complicity was unknown, I still had to log her movement in relation to the house, particularly if she was seen to bring in a long parcel labelled 'missile', but on this occasion she was empty handed. I heard a door slam and a dog bark. I heard the radio playing. She stayed for only twenty minutes and then left again. For the remainder of my shift nothing happened. That was the thing about ops: like so many duties or tasks in the army they comprised long periods of inactivity and boredom punctuated by some variation on boredom and inactivity. There were worse jobs though, and I still didn't pine for the bustle of base life.

Like the rest of us, with the exception of Alan, Spen spent his off-duty hours either reading or sleeping. His book was a huge, dog-eared paperback by Clive Cussler, typical squaddie fayre. We liked adventure and danger, supposedly the business that we ourselves were in. Perhaps it was the fact that we had so little of either that made us seek it out in the form of the printed word, or maybe we liked to transfer ourselves into the protagonists' shoes, thinking that we could have done better or at least as well in such dire circumstances.

How any of these fictional characters actually survived was amazing. They managed to extricate themselves from every kind of peril including being bound with wire, anchor chain and duct tape. Pinned to a chair, next to a bomb or left in a burning building or a room filling with water, they always managed to escape from their bonds in the nick of time. I was pretty sure I couldn't manage it.

Of course, the reason we were here was to help foil a plot to bring down an aeroplane, and it was only logical that a number of planes flew over us at about two thousand feet, the limit of the missiles which might be brought into use. I had no idea about such matters, but the closer the firer was to the target then the greater his chances of success. That much was obvious. I presumed that the aircraft which flew over were mostly Boeings, but I recognised a few Fokkers and even one or two Shorts which had been built in Belfast. The military aircraft – the Hercules and whatever helicopters came in and out – were absent. I'm sure they were still flying, but they didn't come over our heads.

Chip had a book too. I had never seen him read before and he looked like a man who was far from engrossed in his reading material. His face was mildly contorted as if the words were trying to escape on their brief journey to his brain. Perhaps he was dyslexic. In those days, relatively few people were diagnosed as such, compared with today when it seems like every other person you meet suffers from it. Was Chip a more resilient type, was he used to managing, just getting on with life? Maybe he was just crap at reading – that too is possible.

Alan wiled away his time by staring at the sky, or what tattered pieces he could see through the ragged canopy of green. His face had a blank quality to it which somehow communicated suppressed turmoil rather than serenity. Perhaps, with the passing of time, I am just ascribing these facets to him. Since I know his eventual fate, am I trying to see the signs associated with that dismal ending to his life's story? I'll never know.

My memories will only become more confused and mixed up with the passage of time, until eventually my recollections will sound like insane ramblings. No one will care what happened to us. They already don't care.

I do know that McGrath senior arrived home before his children, at 16:15. His kids were dropped off at the end of the lane by the school bus at about 16:30. Mrs McGrath arrived in her 4x4 at about 18:30. Did her husband have the tea on the table? Who knows? What sort of family was it? How could you hold down two responsible positions and have two normal well-adjusted children (if they were that, of course) and live the life as an urban guerrilla at the same time?

This domestic pattern was repeated each day and each night, as it would be in any similar family. The McGraths were distinctly middle-class in fact. He drove a new-ish Subaru, she drove her functional but recent 4x4. The house was large and looked well-maintained as if they had known a degree of prosperity for most of their lives. From all this, they didn't strike me as typical freedom fighters and I began to wonder if we had made a mistake. Revolution would normally foment in the ghettoes and the slums or come from some sort of peasant uprising amongst the serfs, tired of being downtrodden, poor and without rights. But none of this was true of the McGraths, who were clearly prospering under the terrible yoke of Britishness. What possessed them to become accomplices to an act of terror?

The obvious conclusion to reach was that they were being coerced into these actions, but we had been told quite specifically that that was not the case. McGrath was willingly letting the IRA use his house as a base for this atrocity. His wife must have known what was happening, which isn't the same as giving permission of course, and as for the children? Well, they were old enough to understand what was happening.

Daddy who is that man?

Ah, that man is the plumber come to fix the leaky tap in the bathroom.

Well, why has he just shot down an airliner with a Russian made surface-to-air missile?

But it was all so normal.

Until the end of day three.

***

The congregation of mourners seemed diminished as they stood next to the grave. Proximity and the relative confinement of the church had added bulk to the gathering, but the reverse was true once they took up station next to the oblong hole in the ground into which Alan's body would be lowered.

The grave digger lurked a respectful distance away, but the men whose job it was to lower the coffin into the ground remained close at hand. Dressed sombrely in greys and blacks, they blended in well. I decided, as I stood there with a bunch of complete strangers, that these men had been chosen for their lugubrious nature, their sorrowful gait and their hangdog features. They were all in their fifties at least. I couldn't picture them being young or happy or filled with hope, but maybe that was because I couldn't remember myself having been any of those things. Perhaps they were a right bunch of party animals, but I couldn't see it.

I wondered if they had day jobs in the manner of retained firemen, with their dark suits hanging up next to a side of beef in the butcher's shop, or laid out flat in the boot of a taxi, or in an Asda carrier bag next to the till. Were they ready to spring into action at a moment's notice? They had to be doing something when they weren't burying people. I wondered how I might get into their line of work, for the way things were going I was soon to be searching for a new career myself. I hadn't given much thought to a career in *funeral management* but soon I wasn't likely to be in position to rule anything out.

The clergyman had taken his droning voice outside and he was saying a prayer now as his big white dress thing – a cassock? – billowed in the stiff breeze like a sheet. I was in no mood to listen to a man dressed as a ghost, suddenly anti-everything, angry about life and about people being left to kill themselves, and about me standing on the edge of my own personal abyss after having served my country. Blah, blah, blah. My thoughts raged on, flashing round my head. I was assailed by my own demons. Surely there was something better than this for people like me and Alan? Surely someone should step in and say, *no, you have done enough. Have a rest and we will look after you.*

But it was all bloody nonsense of course and I knew it even before the temporary storm clouds had dispersed. I hadn't fought in the Battle of Britain or gone over the top at Passchendaele. I hadn't breached a minefield at El Alamein or fought off the Chinese hordes in Korea. But then again, I would have done, had that been required. It wasn't my fault that the only war I was given to fight was the low-key conflict being waged in this previously forgotten corner of the UK. I felt my blood rise again.

But it was all hopeless. Everything was pointless. Alan's wooden box with its cheap handles was being lowered into the ground. It was a stark enough reminder. You could say what you liked, have your dreams, achieve them, destroy them. You could love or hate. You could have a family or go without one. You could strive for the greatest of goals. You could make people happy or sad. A select few, either by design or by some cosmic accident, might change the world. But when your time came, you were stuffed in a box and dumped in the ground and that was a fact of life. Or rather it wasn't. It was a fact of death.

I knew I'd feel better later in the day, but a graveside was not the place to start seeking redemption or hope. I hadn't given up on life as Alan so obviously had, but standing here now, I got his point. Finally, I felt a sense of loss. He was in there, in that box. Dreary, dull, empty Alan. There was nothing inside him and soon every trace of his insubstantial life would be gone. I was glad that I hadn't been called upon to speak at the service. What could I have said? Or more accurately, what could I have truthfully said that wouldn't have hurt his mum and dad's feelings and tainted their memories of him?

***

I wasn't keeping watch when it happened, but I was soon drawn in nevertheless. Alan spotted the Transit van lurching up the rutted path that led to the McGrath homestead. He immediately woke Spen who sent a hasty message through to the Ops room. Of itself, the van's arrival signified nothing, and yet it was hard to conclude that it wasn't part of the bigger plot to bring down an aeroplane. Of course, we were all a bit charged after two days of total inaction, desperate that this should be the vehicle delivering the missiles.

It was just an ordinary white Ford Transit, like a hundred thousand others. It might have been delivering a new sofa or a rabbit hutch, but we were *sure*. I peered over Spen's shoulder briefly but there was little to see so I made do with listening in to his description of events as he passed them on to our leaders back in Belfast. I imagined quite an audience gathering in the Ops room, the air crackling with tension, expectation and cigarette smoke. Funny to think that it all hinged on Spen, an ordinary lad from London, whose hair was slightly too long and who looked more like a cast member from Oliver Twist than a soldier.

'Two men, early thirties, have left the van and are going inside the house via the front door. They haven't knocked, just gone straight in. The van's engine is off, and the lights are off too. They haven't taken anything inside with them, over.'

Odd that they hadn't knocked. The house genuinely belonged to the McGraths; some manners would have been appropriate. It made me think that his relationship with the terrorists was not as cosy as we had been told, otherwise they might have been a little bit more respectful. If he was operating under duress then they would feel no compunction about simply blundering into his house as they had apparently done. I continued to listen to Spen's commentary on events, like the audience of a bizarre radio show.

'There are lights going on in the living room but still no one is returning to the van, over.' I heard a faint response from the radio. This was followed by a prolonged silence, during which we sat ready for action. Alan slipped past me and moments later he was pissing into a bottle. His place was taken by Chip who squeezed in next to Spen to get a better look. I felt the damp from the ground soaking through the seat of my trousers and was reminded of my general discomfort. By this point I smelled fairly ripe and, although I had continued to brush my teeth twice a day, my mouth hardly felt fresh. I hadn't removed my boots since arriving and nor had I shaved. My face was coated in cam cream and stubble. I must have looked like a coal miner.

I ran a hand through my hair and regretted doing so at once. It was thick with grease. It was scant comfort to remind myself that we were all in the same boat. Time passed and the excitement subsided. Uppermost in my mind was the fact that I stank, was cold, hungry and uncomfortable. I was beginning to dream of civilian life. I would contrive to spend my time ensconced in an armchair, in a warm house with hot food and hot showers on tap, if you'll forgive the pun. An end to my discomfort seemed unattainable for now.

Spen turned to us and spoke quietly.

'That's it. We wait', he said.

'Have they got the missile?', asked Alan. He blinked slowly.

'Who knows?', replied Spen, patiently. A lesser man might have scolded his underling for asking such a dopey question; how could he know if the missile was in the van? But Spen had a kindly side to him. Alan needed him more than he needed Alan.

The night drew in. I supposed that Spen could have called in the special forces guys now, or possibly that call was for the Ops room to make – I'm not sure – but there was a chance that the van contained nothing incriminating. We needed to be sure. It wasn't a question of sending in the cavalry and asking questions later, everything we did had to withstand scrutiny in court if necessary.

The troops in Northern Ireland encountered the enemy every day. The RUC knew all the terrorists' addresses. But it wasn't a question of simply getting rid of our foes as one might on a conventional battlefield. We were fighting on Crown lands in the midst of innocent people who needed to be kept safe. We constantly trod on eggshells.

With a sigh, I lowered myself onto the wet ground once again, curling up next to my rifle but not quite cuddling it. My boots were two freezing muddy lumps. My combat trousers were constantly damp, and the moisture had wicked through my Chinese fighting suit trousers to chafe my skin. I guessed that I was either rotting away or that I was warding off such a state simply because the cold weather made microbial reproduction impossible. I shivered constantly but seemed to perspire at the same time, adding another layer of cold moisture to my skin. Alan had finished pissing now but the smell of urine lingered. I could see the same feelings of unhappiness on his face.

***

I slept fitfully for about an hour and then sat up, not feeling refreshed in any way. Fatigue had become a perpetual state of being. My sleep was coming in fragments, but these portions did not add up to a restful whole. I think that a warm meal would have helped, or even a hot drink. Knowing that I would have easy access to these things soon was not quite enough.

It was too dark to read, so I ate a packet of boiled sweets from my rations and tried to keep warm. I felt pretty miserable. My mind was blank when I heard a crunching noise and turned to see Alan tucking into the contents of a Pot Noodle. His hand repeatedly dipped into the white plastic tub like a mechanical claw at a fair ground – the sort of thing that never has enough strength to pick up a soft toy weighing three ounces.

'Aren't you supposed to put hot water on that?', I hissed in the darkness.

'You can eat it dry', he claimed. Spen flashed us an angry look, his face an off-white blur in the gloom.

'Fuck up', he said.

I had a vision – a vision with sound really – of Alan's Pot Noodle performing some kind of chemical transformation in his stomach once it began mixing with stomach acids and enzymes and all the other gloopy weirdnesses that his intestines would produce. It might start to bubble up and expand, giving off spicy gases, taking up three times the volume of its dry self, pushing relentlessly at the walls of his gut, making things spill from either end. Alan's rustic ablutions were already problematical, and the consumption of a dry Pot Noodle could spell disaster for all of us. He might even explode.

Chip beckoned me forwards. He and Spen were backing out of the viewing area.

'Your stag', he said. Spen tapped my arm.

'Anything at all, let me know', he said.

The moisture trapped between my skin and my clothing was cold and clammy. I felt as if the heat had been entirely leached from my body, but I knew that this could not be true – I would be dead had that happened. Nothing lifted my spirits: not the promise of a warm bed and warm food, not my soggy letter from Debbie, not even the knowledge that there were people in the world living in more miserable conditions than me.

Well, that's not entirely true. The thought of Debbie did cheer me rather, but it never did so for long because my happiness was always supplanted by the fear that our relationship would not survive the accident of geography that blighted it. She had her career in Northern Ireland. I had mine in Germany. The truth was this: her career was more important than mine. I would do my three years in the army, but she probably had a job for life if she wanted it.

Sadness fell on my shoulders like a leaden weight. I tried to dispel my feelings of unhappiness with the thought that something would work out for us, but it did no good. Nor did thinking, *'it is better to have loved and lost than never to have loved at all.'* I might have been able to cheer myself up had I not been so bloody cold.

A couple of miles to my right – or was it to the east? – I could make out the blinking lights of airliners lifting into the sky. Depending on the wind I could hear the whining turbofans and jets too, but very little air traffic came over our heads, which made me wonder if the IRA's plan was rather flawed. What if no target presented itself?

The house was illuminated like any other. The same irregular pattern was repeated as happened every night, with trips to the bathroom, or to the kitchen. In the latter, I watched as Mrs McGrath washed the dishes; domestic bliss with a mass-murder edge to it. Was anyone leading a more extraordinary life than that family? What did the children make of it all?

So, someday soon they would be getting home from work or school, perhaps bringing the shopping in and putting it away in the cupboards, putting the tea in the oven and, oh yes, shooting down an airliner packed with holiday makers and fat businessmen with hotel coffee on their ties. *All in a day's work.*

The dogs barked distantly and the motorway traffic maintained its perpetual roar. We had watched the van since its arrival and no one had been out to visit it yet. I wasn't sure what this signified, but it made me think that they weren't innocently delivering a new sofa or some flat-pack furniture for Mr McGrath to curse over as he rounded out the Phillip's head screws, hammered things in crookedly and assembled it in entirely the wrong order. Were the two missile men sitting in front of the TV while they waited? Why didn't they put the van out of sight?

These thoughts and others chased around in my brain like puppies let loose, but a fresh downpour soon dampened both my spirits and uniform anew. A few lazy bolts of lightning flashed their warning across the sky, and the rain drummed on the van roof and on the corrugated top of a farm building which I knew was there but which I could not currently see. I began to hope that something would happen simply to bring this little operation to an end. That done, we could return to our base, which in my mind had now taken on the aspect of a warm cosy place to stay instead of a spartan horror of concrete and barbed wire.

My watch was drawing to a close when something finally happened. I immediately summoned Spen, who slithered into place next to me. There was enough light from the moon and from the house to see by, but he took up the night vision scope and peered through it. I told him I had seen a figure emerge from the house and make his way to the van. I had heard the side door open and slam shut but had not seen the figure emerge again.

'He's still in there?'

I nodded and replied in the affirmative, hoping to be believed.

'You're sure?'

'Sure, Spen.'

He picked up the radio handset and sent a brief sitrep through to the Ops room. As he did so, the figure stepped down from the van's interior and came briefly into view. He strode round to the driver's door, pulled it open and started the van's engine. A moment later he was joined by the other man and a moment after that the van was performing a five-point turn prior to leaving the farm. From beginning to end it took no more than a minute and now the van was bumping off down the track once again. Spen relayed the whole thing to the Ops room but that was that.

'Now what?', I asked quietly.

'I don't know. We wait until our lords and masters get back to us.'

'Do you think the missiles are inside? Do you think we missed it?'

'I don't see how we could have.' He looked at his watch and stood me down. 'Go and get Chip', he said.

***

I slept well that night despite being awakened for my two-hour stag and despite being cocooned in a wet sleeping bag inside a wet poncho which gathered pools of water during the night. I dreamed of Debbie and of being in a pub with her. It was a good enough dream although Alan made a number of disturbing appearances, the precise nature of which I couldn't recall when I awoke. I was in good spirits. I had become inured to the cold and was well rested, but the main thing was that this was our last day in the field. Literally in the field.

We would stay until teatime, possibly being relieved by another team, or possibly just being extracted – no decision had yet been made. I ate an oatmeal block and drank a can of coke. Meanwhile Alan had yet another crap. The rest of us must have been constipated but Alan's bowels were in demonstrably perfect working order. I was even getting used to that. To have a man's ugly white arse, divesting itself of… ugh. No, I can't talk about it.

When I had finished my very unsatisfying breakfast, I removed the magazine from my rifle and pulled the barrel through before rubbing the weapon down with an oily rag. I thought about Debbie and as I did so, a stupid smile formed on my grimy face. I caught Spen looking at me as if I'd gone mad.

'It'll never work out, you know', he said. I sighed and pulled a face which suggested that I wasn't too bothered either way. In fact, his words stung me because they would probably prove to be true. It was naïve to think that an enduring romance could blossom in such hopeless circumstances. An image of her with another man flashed through my mind and I felt crushed at once.

However, my emotional turmoil did not last long as another van was spotted coming down the path. This time we all sensed that this was *the one*. The household was awake, but no one had left for work or school yet. I squeezed in next to Chip for a look and saw Mrs McGrath in her work clothes making breakfast for her family, pouring tea or coffee and making toast. All very normal. The van was a smaller thing, a Renault or a

Peugeot in dark blue and about the size of a hatchback. Its wipers sloshed from side to side, making a grating noise which came to us easily through the morning air.

When it pulled up in front of the house only the passenger got out, the driver taking the vehicle round the back, a move which would make things difficult for us since it was now out of sight. Spen and Chip exchanged a glance and I thought I understood its meaning: what now? All the planning might be wasted because of a simple oversight. We needed to see the weapons before we did anything further. Now, however, we couldn't see whether or not they were being taken inside or if they had been brought at all. It hadn't even occurred to me that this might happen, and nor had it occurred to anyone else it seemed. We certainly didn't have a contingency for this.

'Hello zero, this is Foxtrot Three-One Alpha, over.'

There was no answer and Spen tried again. And again. With a muttered curse he moved the radio slightly and tried again. Still nothing. That was the thing about radios. They were not one hundred percent reliable and often failed just when you needed them most. The problem could be any one of a dozen things such a dead spots, interference, bad luck or some sort of unquantifiable bastardy. Whatever it was, Spen needed orders or advice and he wasn't going to get any.

'Fuck it', he said. 'We need to see what is going on.'

'If they have bothered to drive it round the back', I said. 'Then they must be unloading the missiles. Or intending to.' When I thought about this great wisdom much later, I realised that there were a number of legitimate reasons for taking the van round the back, one being that the farm buildings were situated there. If they were dropping off farm supplies of some sort, then logically they would drive as close to the barns as they could. However, Spen agreed.

'This is fucked up', he said. 'If they do try anything then we can't get in touch with the Paras to intercept them.'

I knew at once where this was leading, and I was glad that *he* was being paid to make the decisions and not me. It was clear that he thought we could do at least as good a job as anyone and if we couldn't get in touch with our officers then he would have to act on his own authority. But as with anything in this blighted land he might have to later justify his actions, particularly if we made a hash of it. I could see this argument going through his mind almost like the teletype at the bottom of the football scores. He was quickly weighing up the options although this did not take long, such was their paucity.

'Chip, me and you are going across to the other side. Alan, you and him' – he meant me – 'are staying here'. You are going to keep on at zero and let them know what's happening if you get through.'

Alan blinked.

'What if we need to get in touch with you?', he asked.

Spen smiled.

'That's easy, Alan. You can't.'

**

It wasn't a simple journey to make undetected. The ground fell away on all sides and the house with its outbuildings sat in a bowl which must have flooded regularly. Spen and Chip slithered up the bank behind our hide and crested the high ground on their bellies. From that point they skirted the bowl in a crouch only appearing again when they got to the other side.

'There they are', said Alan pointing. I got a whiff of bad breath; he was taking the whole lack of hygiene agenda a stage further than the rest of us by not brushing his teeth, although for our enemies the smell of his breath might have been easier to detect than the smell of toothpaste.

I watched as the heads of our two comrades appeared over the rim of earth that surrounded the house. Spen was wearing a woolly hat, the sort of thing that is called a beanie hat nowadays, and Chip was bareheaded. Their blackened faces made them look like the Black and White Minstrels from the TV, which in different circumstances might have been comical. As it was, I failed to see the funny side, because I was stuck here with Alan and had to think what we'd do if things went awry, which was very likely. Alan had probably been in the army for longer than Chip, but it was apparent that he was never going to be Spen's number two in situations like this. But for me to be left in Alan's charge felt plain wrong for a number of reasons, not least because I felt that I possibly possessed more common sense than he did and that consequently I might make better decisions when pushed. I really wasn't sure how Alan might react if our missile men made an escape in our direction and we were called upon to react.

The radio was in our possession, and when I thought of it, it was obvious that Spen should have taken it with him. It might actually have worked in a different location and neither Alan nor I were all that expert at using it anyway.

Spen and Chip remained in place, observing, not moving. Presumably nothing was happening with the van, so there was nothing to do but wait.

We waited and waited. It began to rain and then stopped. Aeroplanes came and went. None were shot down.

Of course, we still didn't know if the missiles were actually *in situ* or had even been brought in the van.

I kept watch for about an hour and then lost interest. Alan took over. He was good at doing nothing, his brain dormant when required. He was untroubled by imagination, guilt or carnal thoughts. He was an empty vessel which, contrary to the popular adage, made very little noise. Alan's preferred state was to be in some sort of semi-trance, which he could reach with remarkable ease. It was useful when he was required to perform a mundane task but not when a touch of dynamism was required. Alan was a plodder, the plodderiest of plodders. Our situation might change quickly, whereas Alan's thought processes would not, which might put us at a disadvantage.

It was surprising but true: relatively few aircraft ever actually flew directly over the house. We didn't know if our enemies were waiting for a particular flight, or if they just intended to shoot down the biggest plane they could see. I tensed when a Boeing in blue and white livery flew over, gazing at its retracting undercarriage and thinking of the mayhem that a missile strike would cause. Apart from anything else, the downed aeroplane might actually land on top of Alan and me. But it passed over and continued on its way bound for... I didn't know where.

When I looked over, I could tell that Spen and Chip had experienced similar concerns. I wondered if we should try the radio again and put that thought to Alan, who I supposed was my *de facto* boss. His eyes opened wide as if in terror.

'Errrr, do you know what to say?', he asked. I had assumed that *he* did but clearly not.

'I'll just do a radio check', I said confidently. My voice procedure was of the most basic kind, and I had not once used the radio in my time in Northern Ireland.

Alan nodded. I considered this to be consent and so I lifted the handset with a show of confidence but feeling like a boy given a man's job. I was worried that someone of great importance might be listening to my call and that I might make a complete balls of it. Supposing the commanding officer happened to be there, and I got my words wrong? How stupid would I look and how much trouble would Spen be in?

'Hello Zero, this is Foxtrot Three-One Alpha, radio check over.' The words out there in the ether, I was hoping there would be no response and that my message would drift away in space to be picked up in a thousand years by some alien who might scratch his scaly green head in puzzlement. Instead came the reply, 'Zero, okay over.'

FUCK with capital letters. Now I had to follow up with something intelligent. There were so many ways to fuck this up. I had heard a story about someone who had had to use the phonetic letters X-Ray Foxtrot in a radio message but had got tongue tied at the crucial moment and instead said X-Trot Foxray. Apocryphal story or not, the words stuck in my head and I had to fight them back.

'Foxtrot Three-One Alpha, we have split into two groups to get a better look at the van which has just turned up, over.' I was relieved to have uttered the words correctly.

'Roger. Any sign of the missile, over?', I was asked. There was no need for code since the radios automatically scrambled our transmissions. I didn't realise that having established communications with base I could drop my callsign and so I primed myself for the next message.

'Foxtrot Three-One Alpha, not that we know of, over.'

'Can *you* see the van, over?', I was asked and immediately I knew that *they knew* this was not Corporal Spencer talking. I had to think fast.

'I am just moving round there now', I said and then added, 'over'.

'Roger. Keep us informed, out.'

That was that, but Alan was looking at me. I felt sure that he was going to argue with me but instead he said, 'we both need to get over there, don't we? We can't do anything here.'

'Yep. Correct. Let's leave the stuff but bring the radio.' We couldn't bring all the Bergens, sleeping bags, ponchos etc.

Together, we slipped out of cover and began scrambling up the bank as stealthily as we could. I had the feeling that I was saving Spen's arse, but I wanted to do it in such a way that he didn't get charged. The problem was the fact that he had omitted to take the radio. Without it the operation could easily fail for want of proper communications.

Alan and I stumbled along through the slippery grass behind the ridge that surrounded the house. I had the radio on my back, but apart from that we carried only our rifles. Should anyone now stumble across our hide they would find a small stack of Bergan rucksacks, sleeping bags and several bottles of urine.

We avoided skylining but this also prevented us from keeping Spen and Chip in our vision. I hoped that Spen would approve of my decision to move. In reality I don't think we had any choice. We ran in a crouch, our booted feet thudding across the ground, which sounded hollow as if we were running over so many graves. We were both young and fit, not out of breath. We could have run like this for miles but before too long we were flat on our bellies as two things happened, one a consequence of the other.

Firstly, we heard the sound of an aeroplane coming our way. I turned to watch, and something clicked in my brain – an unusual piece of intuition, an educated guess – whatever it was it has never happened since. I knew this was the plane they were going to shoot down.

I scrambled to the top of the ridge and saw the missile being taken from the van and hurriedly prepared. I could see the panic on Spen's normally irascible face. The airliner was still distant but moving fast as it lifted into the sky.

'Zero, the missile is being aimed at an airliner!', I gasped but there was no response. I delivered the same message again checking that the pressel switch was depressed as I spoke. It was. Alan and I had hit upon another dead spot but there was no time to try again.

Spen was urgently signalling me to radio through but I shrugged helplessly. I wasn't sure if he understood. Below us the two terrorists were carrying on with their hasty preparations, quite unaware of our presence. They were almost casual in their movements as though they did this sort of thing every day. The plane was closer, and I turned to see its white fuselage and wings and the ugly black scars into which its wheels were retracting. The time to do something was now. My heart was pounding.

'Let's go', I said. I scrambled to my feet and began running, cocking my rifle as I did so and hoping that it would fire after several days' exposure to the elements. Behind me I heard Alan's feet pounding the earth and together we stormed down the hill. Finally, the terrorists saw us. I heard them shout a useless warning as one leaned into the van to retrieve his Armalite rifle, whilst the other took aim with the missile. Everything was very confused from that point onwards; a shot was fired with no effect, and then another hit its mark. felling the missile firer. As he fell, his missile was discharged, hitting the side of an agricultural trailer, the sort of thing that took potatoes to market.

The missile did not explode. Meanwhile, Alan and I were closing the gap. I managed to shout, 'Army. Stop or I fire!' It came out as a breathless shout, almost a sob, but did nothing to deter the remaining IRA man who levelled his rifle at Alan. But before he managed to pull the trigger, Alan fired on the run, missing wildly, but putting the man off his aim and probably causing him to soil his Republican underpants. Soiled or not, he managed to loose off a round, and we heard the fizz of the projectile as it whizzed past our heads. We were about one hundred yards distant when Alan fired another round, missing again, but this time not by very much. Whatever, it had the desired effect, for the second man dropped his rifle and put his hands in the air. With four of us closing in he had never stood a chance.

***

It was ironic that the man whose bullet had felled the missile firer was also the one who saved his life by administering a field dressing. I listened with detached amazement as he chastised his patient through the rough and ready procedure he administered.

'You fucking IRA cunt', he said. 'I hope I am only saving your life so that you can die in agony at a later date.' I had to hand it to Chip – he had imagination. 'But you'll be going to jail if you live and I wouldn't be surprised if some of those other prisoners didn't fuck your lily-white arse the minute you get in there. It must be hard going without women for all those years. You'll be the closest thing they'll have seen to a women for fuckin' years.' He paused and spoke dreamily as he roughly wrapped the tape of a field dressing round the man's chest. He had his prisoner/patient sitting upright. The man was groaning in agony, his jacket front slick with blood. 'Yep. My guess is that it's shower time when they get you. A game of hide the soap. You know what I mean? It'll be painful and embarrassing to start with, but you'll get used to it.' He carried on in this vein for the entire time, never tiring of the torture he inflicted.

Alan led the other man away so that he was out of earshot. Spen was on the radio by now calling in an ambulance, police, WIS and SOCO. I looked over at Chip as he finished applying the dressing. I was astonished when he let go of his patient whose damaged torso fell backwards onto the hard earth. I winced as his body thudded. The man let out a cry. Chip stood.

'Oops', he said. I thought he was going to kick the injured man but instead he walked away as if nothing had happened. The prisoner shot me a pain-wracked glimpse as if hoping for sympathy. Unfortunately for him there was no bloody chance of that. Had it been down to me I would have let him bleed to death, although on reflection and without the blood of battle thudding through my arteries I could see the sense of Chip's actions; we now had a prisoner to interrogate, and a wounded man might be easier to explain away than a dead one.

The plane was long gone, and I wondered if the passengers would ever know of their close call.

Spen came and stood next to me.

'You know, we did something great today', I told him.

He pursed his lips and nodded.

'Maybe', he said. 'Maybe not.'

He looked distressed. Spen pulled his woollen hat from his head with resignation and then ran a hand through his long tangle of sandy hair.

'What's up?', I asked.

'We nearly fucked this up.' His attention was taken by the group of men who were approaching from our left – the Paras whose job it had been to intercept the terrorists. They would be pissed off. 'Oh fucking great', said Spen.

The Paras stopped when they were ten yards from us and then began examining the area for signs of battle.

One of them, a colour sergeant, detached himself from the group and came over to Spen.

'You in charge?', he asked. There was no particular tone to his voice, no accusation.

'Yes', said Spen glancing at the soldier's rank badges and adding, 'Colour.'

'What happened?'

'We ran out of time, really. They only took the missile out when the plane was about to pass over us. I suppose everyone thought we would have more time to act.'

The colour sergeant nodded and walked off. Spen came over to me. 'We need to get our story straight. In fact, we don't. I'll just say what happened. I should have taken the radio with me. I just forgot. What can I say?'

This should have been his moment of glory, but he was crestfallen instead. I felt sorry for him.

'Let's just make it look like it happened on purpose. We did the job didn't we?'

'We're going to get quizzed on this. It will get too complicated if we start making up a story. They'll get us one at a time and we'll never be able to stick to the same thing. It's easier if I come clean.'

We Got the Blues

He was right of course. As usual, everything had to be legal and above board. The McGraths complained that the men had been attacked on their land, claiming innocence. The complaints fell on deaf ears and the parents were both arrested. The missile firer spent two weeks in hospital under guard. He survived and was charged, although he managed to complain about his rough handling during Chip's medical treatment. Little attention was paid, especially since Chip had saved his life.

Spen was challenged about the fact that he had failed to take the radio and, as good as his word, he took responsibility. Since the operation had been a success he was not punished for his mistake. Alan, Chip and I were given an avuncular clap on the shoulder and that was that. Because the plane had *not* been shot down, we were responsible for a non-event and non-events brought with them no reward. It was hard to see how we could have acted differently. Even if Spen had brought the radio with him, there would have been little chance of bringing the Paras in on time to prevent the missile being fired. When I had time to think it all through, I came to the conclusion that it was a stupid plan in any case. Why did it have to be the Paras anyway?

The other thing was that we had no control over the presence of radio dead spots and the other thing was that it was not our fault that no one had thought about the fact that the van might move to the far side of the house, out of our line of vision. The whole thing was a balls-up from which we had managed to secure a decent result. But balls-ups don't bring with them shiny rewards. There would be no medals for us. And that was a fact of life.

***

We were pleased enough with our efforts but after a day's rest it was back to normal. The thwarted attack was eventually mentioned in the news as some sort of police statement or something of that nature, but no details were ever given. I'm sure that the men responsible went to prison for a few years. I never heard what became of the McGraths, but I suppose the children ended up in care. I still think of that peculiar time now and when I do I feel the cold afresh, as if someone has wheeled me into a fridge without my knowledge or consent. I remember the lights going on and off and trying to figure out who was where in the house at any given moment. But as for our reward? Nothing.

I had been slightly shocked when I looked at my appearance in a mirror, thinking that my beard was more impressive and bushier than I had expected. Washing the cam cream and dirt from my face seemed to thin it out rather and I was left with a face full of pale stubble only one step removed from bum fluff. It had to go anyway; the Queen's soldiers are clean shaven. As I shaved and then showered, I felt temporarily revived. The feeling didn't last and, after a fry-up at the cookhouse, I took to my bed and fell fast asleep. Dinger, Stoker, Spud and

Rockets respected our need to rest, and crept about like mice. This only happened because one of the sleeping men happened to be the boss, Spen. Had it been just me in need of sleep they wouldn't have bothered, for who was I after all? Nevertheless, I fell instantly asleep as the others watched Star Wars with the volume respectfully reduced almost to zero.

The next day was spent washing kit and on general admin, after which we would be put back on normal ops, but I was pleased to receive a letter which turned out to be card from Debbie, who had somehow realised that it was my birthday; quite an achievement because I had actually forgotten about it myself. The card was an expensive one – the sort that plays Happy Birthday when you open it up. I was immensely cheered; birthdays had never meant much to me without having a Mum and Dad to buy me presents or to pretend they were happy that I had been born, (which clearly was not the case, since they had given me away). But for someone – anyone – to remember was oddly touching, especially in the midst of the grim place in which I temporarily resided. I looked at the card over and over again, at the picture of a cake and candles on the front and then at the writing inside, counting the number of kisses. There were four by the way.

There was another reason why I was glad to have it in my possession, that being that her letter had fallen apart during my time spent in the OP. It had turned to an inky grey mush, soaked through as I was by the torrents that fell upon our little rustic hideaway. I knew that I was probably investing the card with greater meaning than was actually intended, but nevertheless I found it strangely comforting to have. It represented love and sanity in a lunatic world. Out there was someone who cared about me, and for me that was a strangely unfamiliar feeling. It was a nice feeling, comforting. I liked it even if it only made me fret all the more, knowing that our relationship would almost certainly never come to anything. Maybe it really was *better to have loved and lost than never to have loved at all.*

I smiled as I imagined Chip crediting the wrong poet/writer/playwright with those sage words. I presumed they had been written by Shakespeare. He would have said it was from the Bible or *Mein Kampf...*

The card remained tucked into a crack on the frame of my bunk for the rest of the tour, although some wise-ass did rip the little tune-playing device out and throw it onto the roof of our hut, before returning the otherwise intact card to its normal place. It was still playing when we left, weeks later. Opening the door was elevated to a grand occasion by a few notes of that celebratory refrain dancing into our ears.

***

Seven weeks of our tour remained, when I finally bought a personal stereo and ten pre-recorded tapes from another soldier who was being returned to Germany for compassionate reasons; I think his daughter was ill. Anyway, he was glad to offload any bits of extraneous kit for rock bottom prices. Suddenly I was bang up to date with the latest (1980s) technology at my fingertips, and all for fifteen quid including some tapes from The Eagles, Madness and Elvis Presley. Nothing wrong with any of those artists, they were just not my cup of cocoa. But it was nice to clamp the headphones onto my head, close my eyes and drift off to sleep each night. *Simple pleasures.*

Patrols began again and as usual I was assailed by doubts as to the effect we were having. Were we *actually* making this little country any safer by pounding the streets? Maybe we were, maybe we weren't but it was hard to quantify, so we just got on with it. After the initial blast of hyper-alertness each patrol tended to become something of a slog, and the idea of being perpetually vigilant became quite foreign. Had we been shot at daily, things would have been different – helping us to remain focussed on the task – but that isn't a complaint now, and nor was it then.

Our main enemy was complacency, and we could easily have come unstuck had a terrorist decided to fire on us. No plan survives contact with the enemy and I had no doubt that this would hold true if one of us got hit by a 5.56 bullet from an Armalite rifle. We would take cover, send a contact report, locate the enemy, return fire if any of those things were possible. We might not do them in the right order though. If encounters with the enemy been a regular occurrence then we would have acted differently, been more prepared.

Had we been fighting a conventional war, patrols would have been mounted *knowing* that an enemy was nearby. In fact, the enemy and the need to gather information about them would have been the whole point of staging the patrol, but we didn't have that dubious luxury. The best we could hope for was to avoid stumbling into a terrorist trap.

The streets and the houses somehow mirrored the skies, which remained fixedly grey throughout our days there. We moved like ghosts through lands where the predominant emotion was hatred. It is safe to say that no one dared to like us or to give us the benefit of the doubt, certainly not in the drab near-ghettoes in which we operated. We were a lost cause to these people. If we were lucky we were ignored, and generally speaking that is what happened; anything else took effort and the locals were worn down by their burden of relentless hostility.

By now, being greeted by the tune of Happy Birthday each time we stepped out of our hut was losing its lustre. No one was ever feeling particularly happy. The routine began to pall, the restrictions became too... restrictive.

The days stretched into weeks, and the weeks seemed to go on for ever. The comfortable routine was becoming boring and we longed for the one percent to break the monotony, just some minor incident that would send our pulses racing but which spilt none of our blood. Perhaps we had been in receipt of our excitement ration for this tour, having caught our missile men. That was no mean achievement, no matter how you looked at it but it was most definitely in the past.

There was no real break from the tedium, no way to release the tension since we'd already had our night out in that great Ulster fleshpot – Bangor. If our tedium had even come in different forms... But day in day out, we patrolled, gathered int, reported to the Ops room and then did our basic admin before grabbing some sleep. And so on it went in a relentless cycle of foot patrols.

I wrote a letter to Debbie but didn't hear back from her. Undaunted, I wrote again, and again there was no reply. Was I dismayed? Yes, frankly I was. On the other hand, it was no great shock. What had I expected? In my head I ended our fragile relationship but in my heart I kept hoping for a letter from her and made excuses on her behalf. She was busy with overtime or had gone on holiday. But I knew the truth; our 'fling' had run its course.

As for the rest of the section, they had problems of their own. Spen was still fretting about the OP and the fact that he hadn't taken the radio with him when we split into two groups. In his mind we were denied the full credit we deserved simply because of that omission. He was frustrated and I could tell he wanted to make amends somehow.

Chip seemed down in the dumps too, and if I knew him better I would have been able to ask why, or even *if,* that was so. Maybe we were just succumbing to an in-theatre malaise.

Even the irrepressible Stoker, wit and raconteur of note, seemed jaded. Always laconic, he seemed just downhearted now as if the fascination of army life was ending in a way which he had not foreseen and which he could not comprehend. I suppose he seemed puzzled by his presence in this utterly hostile world. *How had he ended up living in a concrete fortress in the middle of Belfast?* We could all ask *that* question.

Stoker was the only man I knew of who had a poster of Margaret Thatcher. What does that tell you? I don't know either.

Spud was a little bit withdrawn too, as were Rockets and Dinger. However, with Dinger, the most startling thing was that his hair had grown and was turning curly in a most un-military way. I was surprised that he got away with it. Had I known him better or been closer to him, I would have commented upon his sub-Afro. But they were the men of Foxtrot Three-One Bravo and I really didn't know them as well as I knew Spen and Chip. They weren't a total mystery to me but the bonds between men of the same brick were just a little tighter than those of the section as a whole.

Naturally enough, the person whose demeanour I think about most from that time is Alan. Now that his ultimate fate is known, I can't help but look back on those times to see if the signs were there, signs that something was wrong. But he was an enigma. We knew almost nothing about him, and perhaps there was almost nothing to know. He never talked about his family, he didn't have a girlfriend and he never spoke of any plans for the future, either in or out of the army.

He continued to look down his nose at me, glad to have someone below him in the pecking order as he saw it. I wasn't sure if that remained the case, but it didn't matter to me either way and I actually didn't want to hurt his feelings by suggesting that Spen had more faith and trust in me than in him.

Was he cracking up? Was there something happening inside that he simply couldn't find the words to describe? Did he need to talk to someone but didn't know who to trust or how to begin the conversation? Was he unknowingly going under, the attendant emotions masked by his lack of self-awareness? I could ask these questions now but back then I wasn't looking for any sort of answers. Well, to be honest, the questions weren't even occurring to me. I was nineteen and living my own life.

When you are nineteen or twenty you think you are immortal and that bad things only happen to other people. I had my own hopes and dreams for the next (civilian) phase of my life, but these didn't extend beyond the age of forty. Laughable. I'm now well past forty but have never even come close to matching my actual situation with my modest aspirations. Is that the same for everyone or all but a chosen few?

So, as ever, Alan was a presence in our lives. He ate with us. Patrolled with us. He cleaned his rifle when we cleaned ours. He would sit and watch the videos we would watch and listen to the radio when we did. He slept when we slept and joined in with the snoring chorus we created every night. He even laughed at our jokes, although I am sure he didn't truly understand them or find them funny half the time. But for all that, he was just there. Alan was a presence. Just a presence. None of us knew him at all and it became clear that the parts of his brain that dealt with emotions and so on were not firing properly. He was an extremely life-like mannequin.

How to Start a Riot

When my little chart was showing just fourteen days left, my mood picked up. My great romance with Debbie had finished, although her card's electronic heart continued to play on the roof of our hut and when we had occasion to visit the police station she was nowhere to be seen.

We would be entitled to some leave when the tour finished, but I was in a quandary about that since I had nowhere to go really. I had no home other than the block. The army was my home!

But with two weeks left I could look forward to *something else* without having to give too much thought to the realities of my situation. I could spend my leave in the barrack block I had never seen and have days out exploring Germany. That sounded like a terrible idea. Our base in Belfast seemed more homely than some unseen garrison on the bleak German plain. I didn't know for sure that the German plain was bleak, but in my imaginings from that time it certainly was. So, I got on with the job in hand which was to make Northern Ireland a safe place to live in, one with an *acceptable level of violence*.

But when I have alluded to the mundane-ness of our patrolling I have only done so to allow a description of the defining point in all our lives, the moment which the eight of us (seven now) remember with the greatest clarity and with the greatest residual shock and fear. We all met at some sort of emotional turning point which coloured our lives from then on in. We became united in that shared experience in a way that transcended mere camaraderie. It was something which would become the focal point for any future conversations if we ever happened to meet up again, which as yet, we never have.

It began innocently enough with a dull patrol, through the dull, menacing streets. Clouds hung like ghosts, threatening a downpour. We wore berets and waterproof jackets over our uniform but beneath our webbing. Based on past experience none of us expected anything much to happen and for seven hours out of eight nothing did. We trudged up the hill and down the hill in a manner befitting the heirs to the Grand Old Duke of York's soldiers. We stopped a few cars, searched a single-decker bus and ran a few registration numbers through the radio (using a system called 'Vengeful', which I didn't understand) to discover that they were unconnected to any form of violent or illegal activity. We crossed road junctions in perfect formation and kept a keen eye out for trouble. Or sixteen keen eyes to be more accurate.

We habitually stayed together as eight on a patrol, but on this occasion, we split up, having seen some suspicious activity ahead. Suspicious? What does the word even mean? Anything can seem suspicious if you look at it with a jaundiced eye. Things that were suspicious to us were probably commonplace and ordinary to a civilian. The locals knew what went on in their shops and houses and on their streets. Some of it was illegal but most of it was mundane.

But as outsiders we lacked their depth of knowledge and their acute understanding of how things worked. A gang of young men hanging about on a street corner was probably just that – you could find them in any town or any city in the UK. But for us they might be a terrorist cell… which of course they never were. Our enemies did not meet up and plan their war on street corners. They were much smarter than that. They knew how to make things much more difficult for the intelligence services and RUC.

There were five of them this time, dressed in the uniform of the disaffected youth – jeans, T-shirts and bomber jackets of varying states of disrepair. Their hair was worn long, a style which wasn't punk, new wave or heavy metal, but just generically untidy. Even at a distance I could make out the alpha male. He wasn't the tallest or the broadest, but he stood slightly apart and had the attention of his followers who laughed at his jokes and nodded when they were expected to agree. Again, he could have been any young man in his late teenage years, but this was Belfast where some young men spent their time doing bad things. He looked over first and clocked us coming cautiously down the street, quite unhurried as we approached the end of our patrol. His entourage followed suit and a few choice comments were exchanged, although we were too far away to hear the precise words used to describe us. These boys were Catholics. They despised us with the casual hatred bred into their type. I sometimes wondered if they could really explain why they hated us.

Spen tapped the butt of his rifle to get our attention and the signal was passed down through the section until we were all aware of the hazard he had spotted. His pace slowed as we closed in and Spen's caution took us all in its grasp. He sensed that something was wrong, and we trusted his judgement whilst recognising that it was an imperfect tool. Spen was our leader and we would follow...

'Spud, take your lot across there and down to the road. We'll keep on slowly and meet you down there. Something funny going on', he said. Without a word, Lance Corporal Murphy took Foxtrot Three-One Bravo down a back street which ran parallel with the main road to which we were headed. At the end he would turn right and take his men down an alley to join the road. The gang looked at us insouciantly, observing in disdain as we split into two groups, although what significance they ascribed to this I could not say. Did Spen have a sixth sense? Whether he did or did not we were bound to follow.

'Hello Zero, this is Foxtrot Three-One Alpha, we have a gang of youths at the end of Talbot Street. I have sent Foxtrot Three-One Bravo down another road just to get the jump on them, over.'

The answer, which I couldn't hear, would have been, 'Zero, roger out.'

Overhead a boxy little aeroplane cut a noisy swathe through the air, but we barely paid attention to it. There was a certain amount of tension as we continued our approach. We might easily be heading into some sort of confrontation... truth be told we might be causing it. I don't know what made me think that, perhaps just the realisation that gangs of boys or young men hung about together and that it didn't necessarily mean anything. Our actions might be seen as harassment. Not that we had that intention – I was not sure what our intention was – but Spen obviously had an idea.

We were about a hundred and fifty yards short of them now. The main drag opened up to us as we edged out of the narrow confines of Talbot Street. As ever this could have been Liverpool or Birmingham, any city at all, but we had to remember that Belfast was a dangerous place, especially for men wearing the green uniforms of Mrs Thatcher's Army.

Distantly a car scudded past – a pale blue Austin Allegro – and this was followed by red Vauxhall Chevette. Then there was silence. The boys, who had been laughing and joking as they drew on their rebellious cigarettes, made no sound as if aware of the role they had to play in the unfolding drama. When I think back on it now, I wonder what would have happened had we just come upon them and walked past, or if we had arrived after they had vacated the area. Still, that didn't happen. Something else happened instead.

We were about one hundred yards off when two of the lads broke away, turning to our left – their right – while the rest remained in place. As this happened another person joined the original group, an older man in his thirties wearing glasses and a combat jacket. His cut-price urban guerrilla look was completed with jeans and black boots. I thought that his presence might signify something, perhaps an escalation of a dangerous situation but that didn't make sense because these were the days before mobile phones; no one could have got in touch to tell him that he was required. Therefore it was all a coincidence. All the same...

We carried on, dodging the dog shit land mines that littered the pavement. One of the younger lads threw his cigarette butt into a nearby garden as if doing so spoke of his hatred for us. They remained in place, keen to show they were not cowed by our presence. This was their patch, their turf. We were the outsiders, the hated enemy. They knew their way around much better than us. The only advantage we had was considerable firepower, but that was an advantage in relatively few situations. If they decided to give us grief, we couldn't shoot them no matter how tempting that might be. You can't shoot someone because they call you a name...

I still didn't understand Spen's intentions. I glanced behind me to Alan and Chip but neither gave much away.

I looked down at the rifle in my hands and suddenly felt grave uncertainty for the first time since I had arrived in Northern Ireland. It was a peculiar sensation.

'What are you up to lads?', asked Spen as we drew level with them. Predictably none of them spoke. I wasn't sure if they were actually obliged to or not. Did the law state that they had to answer a soldier's questions? I had no idea.

One of their number with long hair and frown, spat on the ground in a sort of challenge. *What were we going to do about that?* We couldn't ask him to clean it up and yet it was a clear indication of his feelings. He was representing the view they all took. He was their leader.

The tense silence continued, and I wondered how we could move the situation on. If they made no response, did we just walk away? Did we ask for ID? I mean, who carried ID? Apart from soldiers that is, and they only carried it because it was a chargeable offence not to.

'Just hangin' about?', he asked again. The young men turned their backs to him, but the older man looked directly at Spen and smirked.

'ID please', said Spen, reasonably. I worried that the man would simply refuse to identify himself; I wasn't sure what happened next, but I knew we couldn't just lift people without justification. What were these lads actually doing wrong? If they were hanging about, spitting and looking unpleasant in Birmingham or Burnley what would anyone do about it? Precisely nothing.

Needless to say, no form of ID was forthcoming.

Spen tried another tack, asking the older man for his name. The man smiled and said he was called John.

'John what?'

'John Smith', he said. Spen nodded and smiled. There were a number of problems with this answer but if Spen was discomfited in any way he didn't show it. The first problem was that the answer was unlikely to be true and the second was how to prove that this was the case.

As Spen was deliberating the other brick turned up, some fifty yards down the road. Spen sent them a terse radio message to stay put and immediately the lads took up defensive positions behind walls.

'That's a very common name in England but not so common over here', he said to the man. The man smirked and the others followed his lead. I could see that Spud was now having a similar conversation with the two lads who had walked off. I still wasn't sure where all this was leading. If *John Smith* insisted that he was really John Smith then so what?

'So, is it a crime now to be called that?' The voice was thick with Belfast menace, like the last words you heard before getting a bullet in the brain.

'Not at all, sir. I'm just surprised. And who are these lads?', he asked.

'Would you believe me if I said they were called John Smith too?'

One of the other John Smiths laughed.

'It would be a hell of a coincidence, I have to admit', conceded Spen. His tone was friendly but both protagonists knew that there was nothing friendly in this exchange. At best it was the precursor to something *un*friendly. In this strange game we played with our foes and their supporters, one thing had become clear; no one really bothered with smart talk. When asked for their identity, people, regardless of their religion or political view, simply gave it to us, and that included known terrorists.

We might make a note of the fact that we had stumbled upon them and questioned them, and this information would go to the intelligence boys who could piece together the movements of a known player perhaps, but lying to us was pointless. They would always be found out and then they *would* be in trouble.

213

And it was this knowledge which led me to believe that we were being sucked into something bigger than a routine P-check. By this stage a few front doors had opened and one or two of the local unemployed scumbags had decided it was time to put their slippers on and investigate for themselves. It wasn't a mob but the ingredients for one were slowly drawing together like a gathering of the clans. I remember feeling distinctly worried. Spud and his lads were getting into a bit of a quarrel too, but I couldn't hear the words being exchanged.

The impasse was broken when a car pulled up – a Mark 4 Cortina with a pale blue vinyl roof. The driver was the spitting image of the older man being questioned: a mass of black curly hair atop an unshaven face. With some difficulty he leaned across and wound down the passenger window.

There was a brief comedy moment which reminded me of the famous scene from Dad's Army in which a German prisoner asked Private Pike for his name. Mainwaring rapidly intervenes with the classic line, 'don't tell him your name, Pike.'

This time around it was our new vehicle-bound companion who fed us the comedy line.

'What's up Seamie?', he asked. It was Spen's turn to smirk but Seamie, who was no longer plain old John Smith, rolled his eyes in annoyance.

'These boys have nothin' better to do than to harass innocent people', he said to the driver. The word *harass* came up frequently in our dealings with the Republicans we met. The driver, presumably incensed, pulled over and got out of his car. His presence gave us one advantage, we now had a VRN to pin on this little gang and once put through Vengeful we would have a way of ascertaining the possible intent of the men we were dealing with.

Spen backed off as he read the number plate into the mike and Chip took a step forward to prevent the driver listening in.

'You do realise that there is no law against standing on the street, don't ya?', said the new arrival. He was medium height but broad shouldered. A considerable gut hung over the waistband of his cheap jeans. He was pugnacious but out of shape. It wasn't hard to picture him as some sort of ale-house rebel, ready to support a cause or jump to the defence of the innocent once he had a few jars in him. He was the embodiment of rent-a-mob, the gormless foot soldier of a hundred revolutions.

'Just back off a minute, pal', said Chip.

'Back off? I fuckin' live here. You're the one who needs to back off.' The man was angry. Spen was talking to the Ops room. Chip kept a poker face and I felt Alan moved a little bit closer to me as if he could find succour. A few more people had gathered, women and men, all ages and all states of scruffiness, mostly unemployable, all angry and disillusioned with life. They stood nearby or leaned across the garden fences, all seemingly ready for a fight.

No one would want to miss this. It was the big fight, the chance to hit back at the hated Brits; I just wished that it wasn't us. I shot a glance at Spud who now had his own voluble crowd to deal with. I heard him shout and raise his hands as if he was being overwhelmed. He and his men edged backwards until Dinger and Stoker were out of sight once again being forced – gently so far – back down the alley from which they had just emerged.

'You're the ones who need to back off', said the man again. This time he jabbed a finger in Spen's direction, shouting over Chip's shoulder. Above the growing cacophony I heard Spen ask for police support as he described the situation. From across the road, I heard someone shout, 'Brits out!' an oft heard sentiment from those terrible days. By this stage I think there were about twenty-five people involved not including us. Seven or eight were haranguing Spud and his men and the rest were observing or throwing occasional insults at us. The anger had come from nowhere, but it was real enough. I felt a genuine sense of danger. What would we have done had they tried to overpower us? It is one thing to have a rifle but quite another to use it against unarmed civilians.

Shooting unarmed civilians, even those with evil intent, would be a massive coup for the IRA, sparking riots and insurrection of the sort which had typified the early part of the Troubles and put this tiny country on the map for all the wrong reasons. There would be questions in Parliament, in the US Senate. We – eight British soldiers – would be hung out to dry.

The numbers continued to grow as did the level and intensity of anger being displayed. Spen was finished on the radio now and trying to talk to the man who we now thought of as the ringleader. Spen was calm but the man was in a belligerent mood, increasingly so, and feeling courageous now that he had an audience behind him bellowing their support. The numbers increased as more people spilled from their houses like ants disturbed in their nests.

The worst sign was that some of the originals were going back inside to exchange their slippers for boots and shoes, which I took as a sort of escalation; they were readying themselves for action. You can't really fight for freedom wearing a pair of carpet slippers.

Spen turned to us and spoke.

'We're staying put and waiting for the coppers now', he said. His tone was even but I could see mounting alarm in his eyes as the situation continued to deteriorate. Another car pulled in close to us – a Datsun Bluebird, with rust streaks on its faded purple flanks – and four men got out dressed in combat jackets, jeans and black boots. They looked like they should have been armed. Another car pulled in further up the street and four more similarly clad men climbed out, the mob assembling with terrifying rapidity.

This pattern was repeated several times in the next few minutes as yet more agitators appeared on foot from the street and other streets nearby with varying degrees of intent. Those in makeshift uniforms were the ones which worried me most. I could imagine them having rolled up balaclavas in their pockets, ready to don like some sort of cut-price superhero should one be needed. *Behold it is Terror Man!*

The mob wasn't quite baying for our blood and nothing had yet been thrown at us, but the potential was definitely there. In a sense their passivity made things more awkward for us because they weren't doing enough to warrant a warning shot being fired. We simply had to wait for the RUC to come, or even our own QRF who were just a few streets away in our base.

And then things changed. Something was thrown in our direction; a stone which hit no one but skittered along the pavement. Even our new chum Seamie was put out, for it had only missed him by inches and he looked around for the culprit, an angry scowl in his face. But the stone was a message and Seamie understood that better than the rest of us because he began to move away taking the young lads with him. He was still shouting abuse at us. We were *Brit wankers* and all the rest of it – water off an English duck's back. The mood changed and I checked that the men in the combat jackets hadn't put on their balaclavas. The tension become different in some indefinable sense, but things were getting worse.

Another couple of cars turned up, one at either end of the street and these slewed to halt and reversed themselves into positions through which no further traffic could pass. They were trying to block us in. Spen sent two messages in quick succession – the first to base informing them of this new development and the second to Spud.

'Foxtrot Three-One Bravo, this is Foxtrot Three-One Alpha make your way to my location now, over.' I just heard Spud's acknowledgement over the cacophony and turned my head to see him attempt to take his brick in our direction. Like blood platelets forming a clot, the crowd seemed to congeal around the other brick. In horror I watched as they were engulfed, but my attention was drawn to the shower of stones and half bricks that fell amongst us, landing in the sterile puddle that had formed around us where once had been the baying mob.

I heard Alan cry out and when I looked it was apparent that he had been half knocked to the ground and blood was pouring from the side of his head.

At once Chip took Alan's beret and clamped it firmly to his head with a protective hand. Another salvo fell, one of the stones catching me on the shin just above the cuff of my boot. Pain scythed through my being, but I let nothing show on my face. I heard a stone hit the barrel of Chip's SLR and then another ragged volley of masonry came our way as if it had been secreted in readiness for this assault. Perhaps it had.

I couldn't see the other brick at all now, although the angry crowd that surrounded them was moving towards us, presumably with our men in the middle. In those days we carried our rifles attached to our wrists with the sling so that they could not be taken from, or used against us, therefore I knew that it would be difficult to snatch a weapon away from the grasp of a soldier in Three-One Bravo. Nevertheless, they were in considerable danger of being overpowered. More stones began to fall, and the jeers and abuse continued, rising to a crescendo with each new downpour of masonry.

We were nothing more than the entertainment for the crowd. Their blood was up, their hatred distilled into a toxic brew that bubbled in their Republican veins. On another day they might have been too busy, or too depressed to hate us, but not today.

I heard a rifle being cocked, looked at Spen, who nodded and then followed suit. I heard Chip doing the same, but Alan was busy trying to staunch the flow of blood from his wound. Another shout went up for our preparations had not gone unnoticed.

'Gonna shoot us are ya?', called someone from across the street. He was an enormous man in a white vest and track suit bottoms, the uniform of the archetypal slob. I was reminded of Jabba the Hutt. 'Fuckin' Brit bastards. Why don't youse fuck away off back home?'

Spen shouted a warning – the usual challenge but his words were met with another sporadic shower of stones. The other mob – the one surrounding Spud and his men – was moving towards us, taunting and jostling Foxtrot Three-One Bravo as it did so. It took great restraint to simply keep walking. I heard from them later that they had been spat upon over and over.

More stones landed and this time all four of us took a hit. A huge cheer went up. Distantly I heard sirens and hoped that help was coming. Spen swore and swiped blood from a cut across his cheek. The two disparate crowds were closing in on each other now as two amorphous, pulsating multi-cellular entities seen under a microscope. The noise level made speech impossible, but the message delivered by a hundred voices was indistinct, aurally blurred.

The sirens sounded closer now but there was a danger that the RUC might not actually be able to deal with the problem. For just a second I spotted an army helicopter and knew that the situation was being monitored at least.

Finally, the two crowds became one and they split away from Spud and his men, who looked considerably shaken after their experiences. Now we were one cohesive unit once again, wounded but still capable of defending ourselves. The threat was such that I personally thought we should have opened fire, but at whom? Every action we took would be examined in minute detail at court and that presumably was the point – to provoke us into making the wrong decision. It wasn't hard for me to picture the eight of us standing in court together explaining why we shot some old crone with false teeth, moustache, curlers and paisley pattern headscarf, just because she called us a load of Brit bastards.

Of course, it wasn't the abuse which was the problem. It was the bricks and stones and the threat of being lynched by a mob who knew the limitations of our possible retaliation.

Still, Spud and the rest looked relieved to be back with us. They too had cocked their rifles. Into the widening gap was thrown a selection of objects designed to injure us. We all, with the exception of Rockets, carried some form of cut or abrasion and the situation was just getting worse. We began walking in rough formation – like all-round defence but on the move – towards our base but the mob came with us, taunting, shouting abuse, spitting and throwing stones. Now and again one of them would lunge at us as if they were going to steal a rifle and this new trick caught on with great rapidity until it seemed as if everyone on the inner circle was doing likewise.

I had only to slip off the safety catch and pull the trigger to dispatch one of these people to hell, but the image of us all in the dock was at the forefront of my mind. We had enough ammunition to shoot the whole lot but even then I didn't exactly fancy our chances; we could still be overpowered. The siren was closer now and

I prayed to a God in whom I had never believed that he would rescue us forthwith.

Finally, as we approached one of the abandoned cars used to block the street – it was a large Vauxhall saloon, obviously stolen – the first of a new type of weapon fell amongst us. The petrol bomb, somewhat timorously thrown, erupted in flame the minute it smashed on the tarmac. It had the effect of dispersing the crowd who had obviously not been expecting it any more than we were. As one we ran into the gap which had opened up, but the crowd immediately closed in around us again. They seemed angrier than ever, as though *we* had thrown the petrol bomb – ironic really since we were the only ones showing any type of restraint. We were a bit closer to camp though. The air stank of unbreathable fumes.

A shot was fired, and we crouched even as we edged forwards, covered by the mob. But it soon became clear that the shot was a friendly one directed at the crowd with the intention of making them disperse. A terse message was delivered via a megaphone, telling the mob that they had to disperse. They didn't do so. I caught a glimpse of two grey-painted RUC Land Rovers and two olive green Army ones belonging to the QRF. I knew we would be okay now that the numbers had evened up a bit, and yet there still existed a mass of angry bodies to wade through until we joined up with them. My conviction was somewhat dented when I heard more shots being fired and then screams going up from the crowd – a crowd whom I no longer regarded as human.

This was a primitive horde and nothing more. It was astonishing how quickly we could shed our humanity when the perceived need existed. You could say that these people were troublemakers and yet, when it suited them, they must have been fully functioning members of society capable of working, paying taxes and bringing up children. But for now, I would rather have been surrounded by wolves.

To our right I could make out a new disturbance, really a disturbance within a disturbance, and realised that our rescuers were trying to forge a way through, or create a channel through which we could escape. The mob didn't like this impertinence. What sounded like a thousand beer-fuelled voices rose to the heavens in protest. It was an inhuman sound, redolent of the jungle or some wild landscape untouched my man, rather than the urban sprawl of a British industrial city.

The QRF pushed through with difficulty, being jostled on both sides. *Jostled* isn't strong enough a word. They were shoved, thumped, pushed, spat upon. The trick as far as I could tell was for them to enable us to get out without become trapped themselves. Once they had forged into the outer edge of the mob they began to push outwards and we joined them in this effort, seeing that escape was close. The police joined the fray but somewhere a megaphone still implored the mob to behave in a civilised manner, which was obviously a bloody waste of time.

We became part of a surge, like a free-for-all rugby scrum, pushing for freedom, twenty men, soldiers and police engaged in one great effort. Punches rained down on us amid great warm gobs of saliva. Someone aimed a kick at my groin, missed and fell over. The mob trampled on his angry little head. A hand snatched at my rifle taking hold of the stock in an attempt to wrench it free from my grasp. I pulled the rifle back, hauling at it against a show of considerable strength until the wrongdoer was next to me, his face almost in mine. He tried to aim a head butt at me, but the gloved hand of another soldier pulled violently at his neck, almost snapping his ugly head clean off his shoulders. He relinquished his grip and we continued to push through, through a seething human jungle that stank of last night's beer and this morning's sweat. I could see the Land Rovers now.

Spen, one step ahead of me, stood to one side pushing his men through to safety as more RUC arrived and quickly set up a cordon, the other side of which represented safety. We were at a choke point now, the place where one of the cars had been left to block the street, but Spen grabbed us singly and propelled us out of that cauldron of hate. I went first, then Alan, then Chip. Next in quick succession Dinger, Rockets, with blood pouring down his face, almost blinded in fact, Stoker and finally Spud. Throughout this evacuation blows rained down on poor Spen as he got his men to safety, but he stood his ground with quiet heroism. We took to the safety of the RUC line and watched as the QRF guys made their own escape. At once the crowd withdrew to stone-throwing range and the riot which had been brewing for all that time suddenly began in earnest.

I found that I was shaking but laughing too, laughing in sheer relief at having escaped. Adrenaline was coursing through my blood vessels and I felt quite giddy and ready to get stuck in…

Which was never going to happen. A Saracen turned up to take us back and we piled in for the short trip to base. Bricks, bottles and stones fell upon the

Saracen's armoured roof like a demonic hailstorm. The noise was deafening.

'Fuckin' ell', said someone as we lurched way from the scene. But at least we were safe. We would live to fight another day. I looked around me as we rolled about in that metal hull. The anxious faces etched with fear began to relax, the years seeming to fall away as youth returned by tiny increments. I cast a glance at Spen and gave him a thumbs up but all I got in return was a weary smile. I suppose recent events had taken their toll. He plainly felt guilty about what had happened but from my lowly perspective it was hard to see how any guilt could be laid on him.

Spud too looked rather shaken. Stoker looked over at me, smiled and shrugged. Men like Stoker lived forever, came through every scrape with their good humour intact.

Within minutes we were back at base, the huge gates swinging open magically. Never had such a dump seemed so welcoming. The sergeant major, a man who had barely featured in my life as yet, was waiting for us. He led us to the loading bay where we made our rifles safe, for once actually ejecting a round; we had all been ready to open fire.

'Get checked out by the medic and then get yourselves to the cookhouse and say I told them to make you tea or coffee. Corporal Spencer, Lance Corporal Murphy, a quick word.' We walked in one direction and our NCOs in another.

'Are they in trouble?', I asked Stoker.

'Doubt it. They just need to get their version of events while it is still fresh. Are you okay?', he asked, solicitously. I was taken aback slightly; usually no one cared about me. The army is not a 'huggy' type of organisation.

'Yeah. I'm fine.'

'I'm not' interjected Rockets. 'I think I'll definitely be requiring a change of underwear.'

The medic was one of the regimental boxers, with a nose that had been broken a thousand times and now looked like a sausage mis-shape. He and another man, his *de facto* assistant, wiped away the blood and applied dressings as required. None of us apart from Alan were too badly wounded. They organised for him to be taken for an x-ray in the military hospital in another part of the city and let the rest of us go.

Crotus was almost sympathetic to our plight and even rustled up a few biscuits from his own private collection. This kindness was peculiar, and I didn't really enjoy it because I knew that it could never last. We would soon be back in the old army, the one that didn't really care what happened to you.

Ashes to Ashes

I remained standing for a few moments as the gravedigger piled the first few spades full of earth onto the coffin. It landed dully and without ceremony, almost symbolic of the old dust to dust monologue. The door on Alan's life was slowly being shut and from this point onwards we would begin to forget all about him. A hundred years from now would anyone know anything about Alan and his pained existence? I doubted it. He didn't even have children who could have children of their own and perpetuate the memory of a brave man. No family legend would grow up around him. He was one of Mrs Thatcher's soldiers. She would be remembered but he would not. I doubted if I would fare any better of course. And yet for those few months we had been engaged in something extraordinary.

Our story was only the same as thousands of others and yet it went beyond the boundaries of normal human experience. We felt emotions that everyone feels at some time or other and yet the stimulus for these was quite extraordinary. We found ourselves in situations requiring absolute clarity of thought when that was almost impossible to achieve. In my mind, I saw Alan's face pouring with blood. I felt his apprehension communicate itself to me from beyond the grave. And that isn't just a fanciful notion – I really felt those things all over again with an intensity that sent an involuntary shudder down my spine.

I was almost alone now: just me, the birds, the gravedigger and his monotonous dollops of earth, a few hangers on with nowhere better to go and Alan's parents.

I was alive. I had a future. Alan was not and did not, and yet I struggled, perhaps unjustly, to see myself as being any more fortunate than him. My own life was a bloody mess but at least I had a life. That is what I told myself. I was stumped when I tried to think of ways to turn this particular sow's ear into a silk purse, but I felt an obligation for my dead friend to keep trying.

I wondered briefly if it was down to me to keep his memory alive. But it wasn't. That really *was* fanciful. It was never going to happen. We were all dead as dust, we just didn't know it yet. As the mourners continued to thin out, I realised that Alan's mum and dad were occasionally firing curious glances in my direction and I finally twigged that they must have known everyone present apart from me. Alan had not exactly been plagued by friends during his life and this must have been reflected in the make-up of the crowd: aunties, uncles, cousins all drafted in to swell the ranks so to speak. Strangely, my heart began to pound as they approached.

***

If ever there was a time to collect your thoughts it was during sentry duty, the reason being that there was little else to do. It was during my stint in a piss-stinking sangar that I tried to make sense of the near riot I had witnessed. I suppose what troubled me most was something that really didn't relate to me at all and it was this – what should we have done? There was a philosophical argument attached to my recollections, namely that the whole thing would not have occurred had we not been there. *Does a falling tree make a noise if there is no one there to hear it? Does a riot start if there is no one there to provoke it?*

Of course, Spen did not deliberately provoke the riot, but had we simply walked past or even completely avoided the young men who became the core of the disturbance I can't see how it would ever have occurred. Spen had every right to ask them questions and to try to establish their IDs, in fact it was his job, but if he had left them alone then they would probably have become bored and gone home to watch TV or drink cheap lager, or whatever the discontented youth of the day actually did.

I wasn't privy to the 'debrief' that he and Spud took part in and I wasn't quite sure what mood they were in when I saw them again. Chastened might be the word I would use now, although I am sure I didn't know of it then. But why were they chastened? I think we were all slightly traumatised by the mental and physical pounding we took but no one laid the blame for those events with us, the ordinary private soldiers. So that left me wondering if our NCOs – specifically Corporal Spencer – had taken the blame? I hoped not because I didn't think – and still don't – that he did anything wrong. The lads on that street corner definitely looked as if they were up to no good, so why shouldn't he challenge them?

But perhaps the real point is whether or not the mischief they intended was of the terrorist variety, and there lies the sticking point. What exactly were they up to? Where does discretion lie in this circumstance? I still don't have the answers to the questions I have posed. Maybe we should have ignored them, but equally to do so might have been seen as weakness on our part or an unwillingness to challenge what might have become anti-social behaviour. I tried to put myself in their shoes for a moment. How would I have reacted in the same circumstances, hanging around on a street corner in my own town and finding my innocence being questioned by a stranger from another country? We weren't really from another country – I know that – but from their perspective we were foreigners who had no right to be there.

We were in an impossible situation, an invidious one. We were trained killers, armed and let loose to…keep the peace. It didn't sit right. Soldiers aren't police officers and vice versa. As far as they were concerned, we were the enemy. So, what would I have done?

And that is where my analysis of the situation falls flat. I wouldn't have done anything. I would have been fascinated by their presence. I would probably have wanted to chat to them. I couldn't get myself into the minds of these people who looked like us but belonged to a different species.

So instead, I stared out of the sangar down the long dark street and watched the comings and goings of the local populace, all of which were completely innocent and much of which involved the consumption of strong alcohol. Had we been enforcing prohibition rather than an acceptable level of violence we would have been kept busy, impossibly so, but we were more concerned with bombs and bullets than streams of urine directed at gable end walls of houses. But this could have been a Saturday night in any city.

I did a quick mental calculation; it was actually Tuesday.

Tuesday? Saturday? It didn't seem to matter. They were all tanked up as they staggered home under my watchful gaze.

The traffic was sparse as befitted the late hour; mainly taxis and oddly a couple of milk floats dropping off cow juice for the breakfast drinks and cereal. Rarer even than the traffic was the sight of someone able to walk in a straight line. Now, despite the fact that this side of the camp faced a large patch of barren land that looked like a reminder of the Blitz, there were still a few houses left and outside these was the usual selection of rusty cars, ready for the scrapyard, but still in use against all mechanical odds and in the face of common sense and legality. It was these cars which provided me with the greatest surprise of my tour, leaving an indelible image of man's inhumanity to man. It was not the sort of image which lends itself to a painting of that difficult tour, which might one day be hung in the officer's mess, but it certainly had an earthy, unforgettable quality to it.

When I saw the man staggering down the street, propelled in one direction by broken wind and in the other by hiccups, I never suspected that he was about to commit the strangest crime. He might have been walking for quite some time such was the overall lack of forward momentum he displayed, and he certainly didn't look as if his hand/eye coordination was of a notably high standard. However, as he drew alongside the first of three cars – a white Austin Princess – he slowed and then stopped – giving said vehicle a long, hard look as if it had uttered an insult under its breath for which some form of retribution was required.

He moved off again but paused, or re-paused. He looked over his shoulder as if the original insult had been repeated. Having done this, he turned his head again and gazed to his front, thinking hard about some puzzling aspect of his journey home, or his life.

I was intrigued but it was clear that whatever he had in mind was not some sort of terrorist crime, just something that he wanted to do unobserved. He must have forgotten about the sangar which gave views of the entire street in both directions.

He turned but still seemed rather hesitant, in at least two minds about his next course of action. He lurched over to the long sloping bonnet of the Princess now, and then, with surprising deftness, dropped his trousers and underpants to reveal a large white arse. It was a rare two-moon night. This action had certainly narrowed the band of possible outcomes, but I was still surprised when he hesitantly perched his flabby arse over the car's bonnet and begin the arduous process of crapping. It wasn't easy. The phantom crapper was unsteady on his feet as it was, but putting himself on tiptoes to achieve the correct angle of attack for his ablutionary commando raid exacerbated the problem considerably, especially when he tried to hold his arse cheeks apart to assist with the dropping of his bomb. It began to get messy. And noisy. I winced at the barrage of gaseous explosions uttered by his normally unseen nether regions. Thankfully I was out of smelling distance.

As he strained, he began to rant under his breath, this being part of the revenge process, and I wondered what the owner of the big Austin had done to incur such an awful punishment. Would he be able to figure out who had donated his new bonnet ornament, or had he upset so many people that his suspect list would have filled a book? And, if the punishment fitted the crime then what had his crime been?

Although I was horrified at witnessing this unspeakable act, I was fascinated too. Was any part of this planned? Had he just been desperate for a crap and decided that fate had brought the contents of his large intestine and the car bonnet together? Kismet. Did he really know the owner of the car, or was this just a trick he had decided upon on the spur of the moment? Would he be embarrassed if his crime ever made it to court? Shortly before joining the army I had read in the local paper about a young man up before the beak who had broken into a restaurant, stolen a small amount of cash and then shit behind the bar, decorating his leavings with squirty cream before exiting the building into the waiting arms of the constabulary.

It was the sort of crime that followed you around for the rest of your life. You would always be the man who broke in, crapped and decorated your crap with squirty cream. Stories like that were too funny to be left untold.

When he had finished and pulled up his trousers, he examined the finished product. Satisfied that his faecal assault was complete, he rubbed his hands together and staggered off down the street, entering the third house on the left. If a witness was ever sought, I could say that I had seen it all but round here I doubted if excrement crimes were ever reported. The biggest enemy, apart from ourselves, was the RUC. To involve them was a crime against Republicanism, recognition of their right to police, a recognition of their right to exist. Supposedly the Republicans policed themselves, but how they dealt with crimes befitting a punishment *less* than kneecapping, beating, or death was unclear. What did they do if someone threw litter or was double parked?

***

We all became a little bit demob happy in the last week of our tour. The CO came round to tell us how well we had done and how we had earned our leave and so on. Prior to this I had barely clapped eyes on the man. Once we got to Germany and life returned to normal for the battalion as they faced the Communist hordes massed on the other side of the iron curtain, he would become a more familiar face, but for now he might as well have just landed from another planet. It was a strange thing, now that I thought of it, but for the last few months my boss had been Spen and no one else. It was to him I turned, and it was him I served. Day to day, I wasn't thinking about the Queen or Mrs Thatcher. I wasn't thinking about the CO, Major Raper or my own platoon commander. I was thinking and working for Spen. He was our Sergeant Barnes. When we finally got to watch Platoon, I knew that he filed that role perfectly. He made the decisions and we acted out his requirements.

We looked no further than him for a solution to all our problems and he dealt with everything that came his way without comment or emotion. I'm not sure if I really knew much about him. He was, as had once been mentioned by Rockets, *a charisma*. He meant *enigma* of course.

We had a few more patrols to do, some guard duties; it was business as usual, but things were coming to a natural end. Soon we would be handing over to the next battalion, a few of whom – tough looking Scots – had arrived already. They didn't like us. They wanted us to know that they would be taking a hard-line approach with the natives. There would be none of our namby-pamby ways being employed. They didn't say this. They just made it clear in some other subliminal way. It was bullshit of course. We all had to play by the same rules.

***

We finished with a whimper rather than a bang. When I left the hut for the last time it was still wishing me a happy birthday from the rooftop; we barely noticed the tune any longer. We had some leave and then met up again in Germany, but in a sense it was the end for Foxtrot Three-One. I was given my campaign medal by the CO in a little ceremony. I found the metal disc and its length of ribbon – green and purple – fascinating, and would often look at it wondering what I had done to deserve such an honour. It's in my sock drawer now, along with various other trinkets from the life I once lived.

Everything was different in Germany – West Germany in those days – and we had no enemy to fight, apart from the Communists from the east who hadn't actually declared war. Somehow, despite their firepower and their ideological hatred for us, they were an even more elusive foe than the IRA had been. Elusive in the sense that I couldn't quite believe they were poised to attack us at all. The sense of comradeship you feel in the army can be rather elusive too, especially when things keep changing. By *things* I mean *people*. Free from the restrictions of service in Northern Ireland, my new mates seemed to change their attitudes and behaviour, although what was actually happening was that they were returning to their normal selves, the people they really were when they had a certain degree of freedom of action.

Stoker didn't change much – he was quite a laid-back character, laconic, witty and untroubled by worry but the others…

Rockets, caught up in the moment of being a 'Northern Ireland Veteran' began drinking heavily. It wasn't as a result of those traumatic, dangerous days that he did this – at least I don't believe that to be the case. Rather I think that copious amounts of alcohol became his conduit to recount his days in that troubled land. It all became a bit 'pull up a sandbag', dull and repetitive. The stories became more elaborate, bore less relation to the truth. Within a couple of years, it might have seemed like he had fought and defeated the IRA single-handedly. He became fat and unfit, his face bloated, his nose red. The process aged him. After a while he got moved to the MT section, learning to drive a four tonner. It was a sideways move. Probably some professional intervention should have occurred – counselling on alcohol use, or something like that – but I'm not sure if the army bothered with things like that in those days. For one thing, boozing was part of the job and a man's ability to consume beer was almost as important as anything else.

As promised, he left the army in exact accordance with the number of days indicated on his chuff chart. Once he left the army I lost touch immediately because that is what happened in those days, but we had stopped being friends... if we even had been. Rockets' life went in one direction, mine in another.

Chip stayed in the army but moved off to another company, the reasons for which are lost to me. Again, we didn't fall out, but we had never been close, and so what might have been a friendship simply withered on the vine. Dinger stayed in the section but his time in the army was drawing to a close. I went to his leaving do, an event in which he got so drunk that he painted himself yellow with a tin of emulsion and an elderly brush which he unearthed from behind a box body in the MT shed. The rest of the night was spent with him in the shower being scrubbed by a series of helpful mates armed with bass brooms and fuelled by beer. What was left of his skin still bore a yellowish tinge when, rather ill, he climbed into the transport which would take him Gütersloh for his flight back to civilian life. After that, I never saw him again and never heard anything more about him. I assume he's still alive and still jaundiced in appearance.

Spud stayed in the army, got married, began drinking to excess, got divorced, left the army and ended up working in Argos, none of which sounds like a recipe for happiness. I had liked him, but I wasn't sure if I really knew him. The return to Germany changed everything. He stayed in the section and became its corporal when

Spen moved on, but he clearly had no interest in running up and down hills on the German plain. Digging holes, driving around in ancient armoured personnel carriers, being guard commander... it bored him. He was waiting around, as were we all, to fight a war which was simply never going to break out.

Spen's career never recovered and he left the army too. He wasn't quite a broken man, and indeed he had no need to feel that way, but he did feel unfairly blamed for events which got out of control. I tend to agree with him. In those awful circumstances Spen did what I would have done, and none of us ever doubted his judgement. But someone, somewhere told him that they were displeased with his leadership of the section. No disciplinary action was taken and there were no grounds for such, but he was moved to another company and then he just faded away, except in my memory.

If he rang me today and asked for my help, I would gladly give it and not just because I have nothing better to do... although that does make it easier. In the end I think that I worried about him. His spark was gone and the job he loved was no longer quite the same.

He probably should have been mentioned in dispatches for his work that day in foiling a plot to bring down an airliner.

All of which leaves just Alan and me unaccounted for. The latter stayed on in the section, as an ordinary, common or garden rifleman with no responsibility and no real prospects. The army for all its faults does offer a clear career structure but none of the routes on offer were available to poor old Alan, simply because he wasn't quite right. He could have been a lance corporal, then a corporal, then a sergeant, colour sergeant, sergeant major and so on, but it was never really on the cards, and when he asked to become a clerk instead, after five years as a rifleman, he was granted his wish, trained in the dark arts of clerical wizardry and bunged into the orderly room with a typewriter and a filing cabinet all of his own. He might have died there unnoticed had he not left the army, drifted from one crap job to another and then killed himself. It was a grim outcome.

Of course, there was Debbie too. You might wonder what became of her, but the truth is I have no idea. I suppose she'd be in her late forties now, maybe running to fat but still attractive. I could hazard a guess; say that she married another cop, had two children and then divorced before leaving the police and starting up her own bakery in Belfast. But who knows? I was just another notch in her velour headboard.

***

'Are you one of his friends from the army?', asked his dad, hopefully. I nodded and held out my hand. We shook warmly enough but when I told him my name his shake faltered, and his face looked blank. 'I don't think he mentioned you', he said, which if I am being honest made me feel a bit unloved until I remembered that Alan and I had not been friends particularly. Not enemies but not friends either. He perked up however, adding, 'but you're the only one who came today.'

'I'm sorry about what happened to him. I wish there was something I could do.' I felt that I was on safe ground here and that no sort of commitment would be required, after all what *could* I do? The man was dead. I couldn't resurrect him. I couldn't replace him. And that is why I was taken aback by the reply I got.

'Actually, there is one thing', said the father. We began walking back to the church, the seasonal rain beginning to intensify. To either side, stood rows of gravestones, a reminder of the fate that would unite us all. If you wanted evidence that life was a waste of time then you could do worse than visit a graveyard, the ultimate expression of futility. No one mattered. Even Churchill, Wellington, Nelson ended up stuck in the ground...

To my left, a huge crow cawed and then ejected a dollop of crap from its backside. It landed like a paint bomb on the tomb of Harry Stiles, born 1883, died 1917. So not *the* Harry Stiles, then...

Alan's mother was waiting for us under the porch of the church's front door. She looked cold and depressed. Why would she be anything else?

'Name it', I said. 'What can I do to help?'

Mr *Boring Alan* hesitated before he spoke, as if the idea, whatever it was, was already losing its appeal. His wife took his arm and pulled him close. I wondered if they had always been so affectionate, or had the death of their son brought them together after years of drifting apart? That was what married people did; they drifted apart then divorced or died – the funeral really had not put me in a good frame of mind...

'Audrey, this is one of Alan's army friends', he said without giving my name, which he had probably forgotten anyway. Again, we shook hands and again, I gave her my useless platitude. I didn't want to tell either

240

of them that my presence here was solely down to the fact that I was at a loose end and that I was on the verge of becoming unemployed.

'It's lovely to meet you', she said.

'I wish the circumstances were different', I said. I hoped that wasn't an oafish thing to say but she smiled politely. There were lots of things I couldn't say to them. I couldn't say that their son and I had not been friends, or that no one really liked him much. He had found a home with Spen and the boys and the former made sure that Alan was well looked after and er... tolerated. He would have it no other way. I smiled at the recollection of Spen's fatherly ways and how he gave a visual reprimand – the look – to anyone who dared take the piss out of Alan. I couldn't say that the only reason Alan put up with me was because he thought that I might be further down the pecking order than he was. As I said before, I actually doubted that this was the case; in terms of trust, he was below me. Not that it mattered. Nothing mattered now.

'Will you come for a drink?', asked dad. Mum nodded her assent. They were eager, so I agreed. I was trying to kick the booze, or at least cut down, but maybe I was due a day off. The thought of drinking had a sudden terrible appeal as if the consumption of alcohol had suddenly become my number one priority.

'Yes', I said, as if it was my duty to comply. What could be better than having a chat with two old people who were related to someone whom I hadn't particularly liked and who was now residing in the earth in a graveyard in rural England? Heaven. But I went anyway. They gave me a lift to the pub and introduced me to some of Alan's other relatives, the names of whom and the precise nature of their relationship to the dead man I forgot at once. This was before I had a drink; it would only get worse.

We sat in a booth, me nursing a pint – I didn't want to get completely hammered in their presence – Mr Boring Alan with a half and Mrs with a sherry. Her drink was a lower middle-class cliché. Did she think it made her look urbane? But I was in no mood to think ill of the poor woman. Our discourse, hesitant enough, was interrupted by a near constant procession of friends and relatives commenting on how lovely the service had been and how much Alan would be missed, both of which you could safely dismiss as bullshit. It had been a standard, by numbers, service. Vicar for hire, talking heavenly crap about someone he didn't know and assumed was going straight to hell in any case. You go to hell if you kill yourself, don't you? I think that's right. Either way it was all crap.

'So, you were in the same company?', asked dad.

'D' Company. That's right', I said. Inadvertently I made it sound like 'D' Company was better than the rest. It wasn't. It was the same as the rest. As a military unit it was, wait for it… okay. I didn't believe that our regiment was better than any other, or that our battalion was better than the other battalion in the same mob. I didn't think that 'D' company was any better than 'A', 'B' or 'C' companies. In an out and out fight I thought we could hold our own… but that was it. We were just the usual collection of misfits, cowards, heroes, criminals, lunatics, fornicators, bigots, liars, cheats. We had sworn allegiance to the Queen and the poor woman probably had no idea in whom she had trusted the nation's security. Somehow, we got the job done, and had the Russians ever attacked we would have fought bravely enough.

He smiled. Maybe Alan had talked fondly of the company.

'Alan said he didn't like it in 'D' Company.'

Or maybe not.

'Really?'

'That's why he became a clerk, I think.'

'He liked Corporal Spencer', chipped in mother. I nodded and smiled at the recollection. I wondered what Spen would look like today. Fat, bald? Dead?

'Yes. Corporal Spencer was a nice bloke. He was good to Alan. He always looked after him.'

'Were they friends?', asked mother. Father interrupted her at this point, and I realised that he had probably been a National Service man.

'It's not a question of that, Audrey. He was the corporal. Alan just had to follow orders.' She looked crestfallen – in her world the possession of friends was everything perhaps, especially when it came to her son. Even in death she wanted everything to be right for him. She wanted to know that Spen had been his friend and that they had been content in the army. She was trying to piece together a happy life for him, joining fragments into one whole like a quilt. It was for her to create a good life for him, or as much of one as she could. It was no use to him of course but perhaps she could herself die happy knowing that some part of his life had been rewarding and pleasant. I was happy to oblige.

243

'They got on really well. Corporal Spencer would be very sad if he knew. They all would', I said. Now I wished that they – my long-lost comrades – had made it to the funeral, but presumably they didn't even know that he had died.

I realised then that it would have been nice to see them again, although we might have found it difficult to find common ground so many years later. Thinking that made me think about my own mortality, my own funeral. If I dropped down dead right now, I didn't think that there was enough money in my bank account for even the most basic burial.

'So, were you in Germany with him?', asked dad.

'Yeah. We met in Northern Ireland and then Germany after that.' *What did they want to know? What did they want to talk about? I would let them take the lead.*

'I think that's when things changed for Alan', said father. Mother nodded vigorously and I immediately realised that they saw me as the person who could provide answers. From their point of view who else could they ask? If his difficulties began in the army – and I wasn't convinced that that was actually the case, I think he had been born wrong – then I was the only chance they had to find out what had happened. I felt hopelessly ill-suited to the task and yet their beseeching faces spurred me on. This was an opportunity to help someone and I would take it. *Would I have to lie?* I'd cross that particular bridge when I came to it.

'You think he changed after Northern Ireland?', I asked and at once they both nodded eagerly.

'That's when we noticed a change in him, isn't it, George?' George nodded his agreement. A man approached – he looked like he could have been Alan's Uncle – and clapped George on the shoulder. He didn't speak and then drifted off.

'The only thing is, I didn't know him before.'

'But you were there from the start? You see, he was okay when he went there.' It was Audrey who spoke. I wondered what her definition of 'okay' was. Was he okay by his own peculiar standards or was he okay compared to someone else, someone, dare I say it, normal?

'They'd been there about a week when I got sent out. They were going to send me to Germany to be part of the rear party but then Alan's section was a man down so…'

'So, you were there *most* of the time?', asked George, hopefully.

'Yeah.'

'So, what do you think changed him?', asked Audrey. I looked at her, feeling crushed with pity and then downed my drink.

'Alan kept himself to himself a lot of the time. What were the changes you noticed – you knew him much better than me?', I asked, feeling like a cod-psychiatrist.

'Well, he became withdrawn', said George.

'He wouldn't make eye contact', said Audrey. At this point George looked at her askance.

'He was always like that love. A bit anyway.'

'He got worse, though', she insisted. George was plainly sceptical.

'Mmm', was all he said. He plainly knew that his son, the apple of his eye, had been born an oddball. Mother may have been blind to that, or at least partly so. Dads were most realistic about their sons, although this was a huge chunk of supposition on my part with no basis in fact, and totally unrelated to any experience I might have – I was a childless orphan, the loneliest of the lonely. My current social life consisted of this funeral.

'He never talked much about Ireland', said George.

'He did two tours, didn't he?'

'Two, yes.'

'And how was he after the first one?', I asked, *Mister Therapist* now. His parents looked at each other blankly.

'Em, I don't really remember', said George. Audrey nodded in agreement; she didn't remember either and for a minute I wondered what the hell I was doing here. I had no special knowledge to impart.

Alan was odd. Or had been. But this was not an easy thing to say to his parents. To take the conversation further and to maybe shed some light on the reasons for his eventual death, I thought that I need them to realise that he had problems from birth. I was sure about that. Asperger's syndrome to be precise.

I excused myself and went to the bar, figuring that I was within staggering distance of home, admittedly right on the outer edges of that range. I opted for a Scotch this time, hoping that the drink would take me where I wanted (oblivion) without making me bloated and constantly in need of the toilet.

When I returned, cutting my way through a small lake of mourners each regaling themselves with memories of the dearly departed, I knew I had to carry on with my explanation of Alan's troubles. I think that they were trying to pin his death on the army or on Northern Ireland and it was only natural that they should do so. After all, if an alternative culprit can be identified then it should be exploited – *alternative* as in it was nothing to do with them. How could you live with yourself if you missed the signs that your child was suicidal? Or worse, how could you carry on if the reasons for his death were attributable to you as a parent? I didn't get the sense that they wanted compensation or that they were going to sue the army. They just wanted answers.

'I don't know if Alan saw anything in particular that would have made him change', I said. That was not the right answer. Their faces fell as if they were suddenly disappointed and I felt compelled to come up with something better.

'It definitely happened out there', said Audrey. She began rooting through her handbag for tissues or something – something she didn't really want. This was a gesture, a distraction, designed to draw me away from the sad truth that I was not providing the answers she wanted.

I could make things up. I wasn't actually averse to that. I had lied before and would do so again.

'He always seemed a bit detached', I said. 'I mean, you've already said it yourself, he kept himself to himself.'

'He was very shy', explained mum, missing the point as she probably had done all her life.

'I suppose things affect people differently', I said, thinking of the incidents we had seen or experienced. Which one of these was responsible for the trauma that finally tipped him over the edge? They looked at me expectantly and I found myself relating the story of our tour of Northern Ireland. They were both riveted – transfixed might be the word – and I was able to recount long forgotten detail. Like the time we went to the border…

The Border

As usual our transport was the reliable Wessex helicopter flown by the RAF. Two were needed for us and all our kit because we were being sent there for a week and had to take our own rations with us, which came in the form of ten-man ration boxes, six in number. Eight men for seven days equated to fifty-six days of food. Six ten-man boxes equated to sixty days. There was a cook in the base already.

The journey south took twenty uneventful minutes, during which we sat numbly in the bowels of the huge quivering beast that churned its awkward way through the air over Northern Ireland. We were headed for South Down, which meant little to me but made me think of the South Downs in Suffolk where people of my acquaintance had sometimes holidayed.

I gazed out to sea, catching glimpses of the stunning coast and long sandy beaches, both of which seemed crazily untypical of the country as a whole. Northern Ireland was all about riots, bombings and shootings, not about people taking their families to the seaside, buying ice cream and making sandcastles. The two did not go together at all. We skirted the mountains, gazed down upon the endless forest and carried on with the sea always to our left. Or port.

This was bandit country now. There were people on the ground who wanted to kill us. It still seems odd to think of it on those terms. What might have been an agrarian wonderland was actually a potential killing zone. I'm not talking about anything on the scale of Vietnam, but it was a dangerous place, nevertheless. Had it not been, of course, we wouldn't have been sent down there to guard the building of a new police station.

No one was quite sure why we had been taken from Belfast to guard the site when there were thousands of other troops much closer at hand, but we swept in and landed in the base for the briefest possible time; long enough only to pile out with our kit and rations, before the Wessex made way for its twin to do the same thing. Within maybe thirty seconds they were gone, haring back to Aldergrove, and we were left standing in puzzled silence. Immediately, we sensed the slower pace of life down here and the fact that the weather was going to be no kinder to us. The wind blew fine, cold rain in at us and our spirits sagged immediately.

'Fucking hell', said Spen as he looked around. An NCO was waving at us beckoning, inviting us to join him. We moved in, leaving our ration packs in a neat pile behind us. The boxes got soaked and became soggy useless things.

'Right lads, I'm Colour Sergeant Donaldson', said the man. He was old for a soldier, probably mid-forties. His face was bisected by a huge moustache, too large for Queen's Regs. On his shoulder a pair of para wings but this man was from the locally raised UDR – the Ulster

Defence Regiment – and spoke in a broad County Down accent. He smiled as he spoke, in the manner of the avuncular sergeant major rather than the psychotic NCO.

'I'm sort of in charge of this lovely place for the minute, so any problems come and see me. We've got bunks for you and there is a cookhouse and a TV, but this place is a fucking dump. It's wet, cold and uncomfortable. If I was an estate agent, I would refuse to sell it.' We chuckled at his humour. He probably used the same line with every bunch of cold, wet soldiers who turned up, but a little bit of humanity was often lacking in our lives. I think we warmed to Donaldson at once; he wasn't pretending that this little outpost was anything other than a total shithole.

'C'mon and I'll show youse where to put your kit and then I'll show youse around. I'm sure our cook can get some lunch on for youse.'

Our billet was an ISO container kitted out with eight bunk beds and a Calor gas heater. The walls ran with condensation and everything smelled musty.

'The worst billet in the army, lads', quipped Donaldson. 'Make yourselves at home.'

Spen looked at the colour sergeant in disbelief. Donaldson shrugged.

'It doesn't look much', he said as if he was going to complete the sentence by saying that it was better than it looked. However, he didn't say that. Instead, he said, 'and it isn't much.'

He took us for a tour.

'Okay then, the cookhouse', he pointed to what looked like an elongated garden shed. The cook was struggling to pull our sodden ration boxes inside, looking very unhappy as he did so. 'The Ops room', he said pointing to another shed from which two antennae projected. 'Four sangars', he said pointing to said buildings, each nothing more than a concrete block house reinforced with sloping sandbag walls. 'And a helipad.' When you've seen one helipad, you've seen them all.

'You've been briefed but just a reminder, you are here for the security of the builders who are putting together the new police station. You patrol and keep an eye out during the day and then just keep yourselves secure at night. That's it. Oh, and you have to keep an eye on the generator. If I'm not here you just fill her up with diesel every day and check on the oil.' We walked over to the great green beast which chugged away providing all our electricity. Donaldson was heedless to the rain. 'Check this wee gauge here', he said pointing to a *wee gauge*. If an inch of red is showing it needs more oil. The oil is over there in a drum. You just lift off this cover...', he pointed to a circular dome on top of the generator's main body, 'and pour some in until the gauge changes. Easy.'

We nodded, eager to take shelter.

We ran off to our new digs as Donaldson chatted to Spen and Spud in the Ops room.

Chip echoed all our thoughts when he said, 'what a fucking dump.'

I looked around at the spreading puddles of rain on the tarmac and found it hard to disagree. The skies were solid grey, devoid of any other colour, and I felt my high spirits begin to dissipate. High? They weren't that high to begin with, but there was something about this type of cold and damp which was worse than the other varieties of each I had so far experienced. I realised that this was cold and damp from the sea, tangy and tiring. It soaked into your bones and then radiated outwards again. We emitted cold, and when we crowded together we made each other colder.

I know that's not true but that's how it felt.

In terms of our little mission, all became clear when I took my first turn in the sangar that afternoon, climbing slippery wooden steps to the concrete fort which, as it turned out, overlooked the sea and beyond that the Irish Republic. On a sunny day it would have been beautiful, and I suppose it had some sort of brooding splendour, but I was too preoccupied with my acute discomfort to think of it that way. But for the record the Irish hills were like a mirror to those on the British side of the border sweeping down to a sea, made for smugglers to ply their crafty trade, or for terrorists to escape across, following some freedom fighting. I could picture sailing barques making their smooth, elegant passage to the coast, with exotic cargoes from... probably Liverpool, but you get the idea.

A modern-day coaster, blue and orange, angular and rusty, steamed into harbour as a fishing boat chugged its way seawards, attended by a flying posse of seabirds hoping for some scraps. Colour Sergeant Donaldson pointed out the landmarks.

'This is Carlingford Lough', he said, indicating the watery inlet. 'Across there is the Irish Republic or the heart of the Dark Empire as it is known.'

I looked at him incredulously.

'It's a joke', he said, smiling. 'Although some of our little friends do come across from that part of the world, do their stuff and scurry back.'

'Do the Irish try to stop them, Colour?', I asked, seriously.

He shrugged.

'They're supposed to. I expect that some of the time they do what they can and other times they just turn a blind eye. If you think about it some of them must be sympathetic to the cause of a united Ireland.'

'I suppose so.'

'Over there is the new police station. The IRA like to take pot shots at the workers, so we are here to try and stop them.' He looked around conspiratorially as if checking that no one else was listening in. In reality there *was* no one else. 'Waste of fucking time though. They don't stand up and identify themselves so that you get a fighting chance. They fire a shot and then they're gone. I don't think they even care if they hit anything. To be honest I think some of them must be cross-eyed. Which is a good thing. So, all you have to do is keep your eyes peeled. The normal rules of engagement apply so you have to give a warning if you are going to open fire, which is handy if they are a mile away.'

'I couldn't hit them from a mile away, Colour', I quipped.

'True. It's all bollocks isn't it?'

I laughed. Donaldson didn't seem to care much about the niceties of army life.

'This your first tour?', he asked. I nodded.

'I've been doin' this for fifteen years. Before that I was a sapper. I don't mean doin' this', he added waving his hands from side to side to indicate that he was talking about this little base. 'I mean fightin' the IRA. Bastards.' He looked out over the water as if contemplating the future of mankind.

'Well, that's about it. I'll leave you to it. Any problems just get on the blower. Some of my boys'll be around later and we'll be goin' out on patrol.' With that he was gone, and I was left staring across Carlingford Lough, not completely sure what I would do if someone did attack the workers on the nearby building site. There was nothing wrong with Donaldson's briefing except perhaps that it was too honest; we were there for show.

There was little to look at bar the waves and the clouds, and my thoughts strayed to other things such as Debbie and my life after the army, although I already knew that the two things weren't connected. I felt a pang of jealousy when I thought about her with another man already, a policeman probably, with prospects, a Ford Capri and a revolver. I watched yet another coaster head inland. From my perspective it seemed to be on a collision course with a yacht, a sleek, rich man's toy. At the point of impact, the yacht was simply subsumed by the ship and then ejected from its stern; the two had passed.

If I looked over to my right, I could watch the builders hard at work. They didn't look *that hard* at work actually and this made sense to me when I realised that they were being well-paid for their troubles. The longer they spent in danger, the more money they earned, which was a strange set of priorities really. They got me thinking about what I would do when I left the army myself, and I was reminded sickeningly of the fact that I had no skills at all apart from those I had acquired in the service of the Queen.

If anyone happened to be looking for someone who could fire an SLR or a GPMG then I was their man, but then again so would hundreds of others. But other than that, I wasn't qualified to lay a brick or mend a TV. I was a useless potential civilian.

I was able to observe my surroundings through a slot in the brickwork though, and it was when I stood away from this for a moment to inspect the barren room that I heard the tell-tale crack of a bullet as it smacked into the breeze blocks. A little cloud of grey dust eddied within the sangar.

I swore and then crawled onto the blower, grabbing it, pulling it down from the cradle and gasping out the word, 'contact!'

In a second Donaldson was on the other end.

'Keep down! Y'okay?'

'I'm okay', I said. Five seconds later he was next to me, asking again if I was okay and if I had seen anything. I felt a little bit guilty when I admitted that I hadn't.

'Sure, never worry. This is what they do. One shot and then fuck off.' He peered out, scanning the lough and the hills behind. 'You never see them. Good shootin' though. You're lucky.' He was poking around at the bullet hole in the breeze block wall with apparent interest. 'I'll leave the bullet in there and get the coppers to have a look at it. They might know which gun it was fired from and who fired it.'

'What now, Colour?', I asked.

'Nothing. Just keep going.' He smiled and added. 'And get ready to duck.'

I had been replaced by Alan by the time the RUC turned up. They took their bullet away and we never heard anything more about the incident. I asked Spen if I could have an extra medal since someone had actually bothered to shoot at me, but he gave me a withering look which I took to mean that I could not.

The only other incident of note came one day when I happened to check the oil level on the generator as we had been instructed by Donaldson. I'm not sure why I even bothered. It wasn't that I was particularly responsible or conscientious about these things, but somehow I was drawn to the big throbbing generator anyway. The rain had given up for the day, but the ground was wet, laced with puddles, and slippery. I had to clear the moisture away from the gauge that Donaldson had shown us and to my surprise it indicated that the machine needed its fix of engine oil. I could have walked away but deciding that it was time to make a mature decision for the first time in my life, I gathered together every scrap of initiative I owned (which wasn't much) and set out to add oil in the way we'd been shown.

The oil drum was heavy and oily, which was no surprise on either count, but I managed to drag it over to the generator and pour a small amount into a plastic measuring jug, the sort of thing your mum makes the custard in. That done, I removed the domed lid on the generator's main body and poured in a small quantity of oil. I waited a second or two and then checked the gauge. Nothing had changed down there and so I added a bit more, waited and checked again. Still nothing. I had no idea of the machine's oil capacity, so I repeated the above procedure a number of times until I had added a litre of oil, which seemed like a lot.

I frowned, which didn't help. The gauge had not moved, so perhaps a large quantity of oil was needed. This being my reasoning, I added another litre of oil in one big helping but once again, nothing occurred. The oil level was still low according to the gauge. If anything, it might have gone down.

I was perplexed but not deterred. Mere common sense wasn't going to stop me from successfully completing the task I had allocated myself. I decided that I would add another litre of oil and then leave it. If nothing else I had delayed the moment when the engine would seize. As the final litre glugged into the aperture and slid down into the depths of the great booming machine, I knew I had done the right thing. I wasn't a mechanic, but I had made a decision and acted decisively upon it. I stood back, looked at the dish shaped lid on the ground and knew that it was time to replace it.

What happened next, I can't explain, although many possible explanations were subsequently offered by a group of men with no particular mechanical talent whatsoever. Upon replacing the lid to the hole through which the oil had been added, a strange, sloppy, sucking noise rose from the depths of the generator. I took a step backwards for it was immediately apparent that this was not a good noise. Something was wrong. This fact was compounded when, which a huge shuddering surge, the mighty machine, all three tons of it, began to shake and rattle. The revs increased deafeningly, and the generator vibrated so violently that it began to move off its base.

A huge cloud of black smoke erupted from the exhaust, the air filled with choking, cloying gas. Day became night and I staggered backwards, my heart pounding, my eyes burning. I heard shouting but I was lost in the cloud again. The noise was incredible, I could hardly breathe, and I couldn't see anything no matter how far I moved away.

I stumbled, having tripped over some invisible object (everything was invisible) and landed painfully on my arse. My rifle fell from my grasp. When I stood, I was disorientated and tried to escape from the cloud, my lungs filling with poisons. I ran and the next thing I knew I was back at the generator once again. Through the black mists, I spotted the on/off switch and an emergency cut off and I leapt upon the latter thinking that I could save the base from being blown to pieces. I pressed.

Nothing happened.

The generator was running red hot by now and there was no doubt in my fevered mind that it was on the point of exploding. Despite the fire in my lungs, I felt suddenly heroic, having inadvertently returned to the machine and attempted to turn it off, but the feeling was short-lived because the emergency stop was obviously over-ridden by whatever I had done to the generator… It continued to rattle and growl. I could hear nothing, see nothing. My breathing was laboured, almost impossible…

I began to crawl away, staying as close to the ground as I could, finding that the air was slightly cleaner down here and that I could breathe a little bit, and as I made my way out the noise stopped as the generator finally gave up and died. The cloud of darkest black lifted in spectacular silence and thirty seconds later I was sitting on the ground, in a puddle, as black as your boot and surrounded by my friends from Foxtrot Three-One. No one spoke. I looked up as the cloud lifted into the sky. It was immense and immensely black but turning to grey as it dissipated.

'What the fuck?', asked Spud.

'What the fuck?', I replied.

***

An Army Air Corps Lynx took me to hospital in Belfast and they kept me under observation for three days during which I had no visitors, no flowers and no grapes. I rang Debbie, hoping that she might come and visit but I got her dad who said she was on duty for the next few days at least. I asked him to say I'd called but I don't know if he did so or not. I certainly never heard from her. If she couldn't be bothered to come and visit her poor wounded soldier then I guessed she had moved on. Never mind the fact that my wounds were more or less self-inflicted…

By the time I was ready to rejoin the company, our foray to South Down was nearing its end, and I was taken straight back to our base in Belfast awaiting the return of the others. The sergeant major kindly found me lots of shitty jobs to do until I was reunited with my comrades. I was in fact up to my knees in black bin bags when the Wessex dropped them off.

'You're alive then', said Spen.

'Just about.'

'We had no electric for two days', said Spud. He sounded displeased.

'I don't really know what happened', I said. Their lack of sympathy was discomfiting.

'Well, you poured oil into the fuel tank for some fucking reason. You destroyed that generator.' It was Rockets speaking. There was contempt in his voice.

'Well, never mind', said Spen. 'It was just an accident.' Presumably he had intercepted my crestfallen looks and taken pity on me. The others were less kind. Soon I was alone with my bin bags again. I felt rather miserable. Without the respect and friendship of these seven men I had nothing.

**

I ordered another drink. The party hadn't really got going but I reminded myself that it was a wake or something of the sort.

261

'He was always a kind boy. I was surprised when he joined the army', said Alan's mother. By 'kind' I think she meant odd but what mother would ever say that about her son? 'He was a bit odd, too', she added, instantly disproving my theory.

'So, you didn't see it coming?', I asked but Alan's parents looked at me with perplexity.

'See what coming?'

'That he might kill himself?'

'Well, I don't know. It would be easy to see signs that weren't really there at all. I just think that something changed in Northern Ireland.' It was Alan's father who spoke, rubbing his temples as he did so. 'I don't know what you lads got up to out there. I have often thought that in a way I didn't really know Alan. Not in those days. It was all a mystery, you know. I did my National Service in the Royal Signals, but it was all different by the time Alan joined up.'

Maybe not that different, I thought but I kept that to myself.

'Did the others like him?', asked his mum.

Of course, they didn't really. There was a friendly tolerance of his peculiar ways, but no one complained when he opted out of nights out or just spent time by himself. The advent of computer games must have been a boon for him; time spent in non-judgemental company.

'He was very quiet, but I think everyone liked him. He took a bit of getting used to', I said. The words were supposed to sound mildly comic but both parents looked very concerned. 'Not in a bad way. He was just different. He wasn't your typical squaddie. He was reserved. Not particularly wild. He wasn't a drinker or anything like that. Most of the lads liked a drink, that sort of thing. But he was someone we could rely on. He was a good soldier.' I paused. I had just told the truth – he genuinely was a good soldier – and they seemed pleased by the flattering portrait I had painted of their deceased son.

'He was always interested in science fiction', said his mum and I was temporarily stymied. Not only had I not known that, but I was lost for a means to respond. I wasn't a fan of sci-fi myself beyond watching Star Wars on VHS during our tour in Belfast. The quality had been poor which detracted from the film rather. I thought that I needed another drink. The buzz was there in my head, the mild euphoria, the ridiculous feeling of well-being in which I found myself imagining that someday my life would radically pick up despite all the evidence to the contrary. I put off getting that next drink, partly because I hoped that Alan's dad might make the offer and partly because a suitable response to mother's sci-fi statement had suddenly occurred to me.

'I remember him explaining about time travel.' Mum and dad both grinned; this was more like the man they knew. 'He managed to convince us all that it was possible.' I told them the story.

***

Dinger was staring out of the window. The heating was on and we had just returned from a patrol on which we had all got thoroughly soaked. The room was filling with steam, the windows running with condensation. A plane skimmed the roof tops, having taken off from the harbour.

Dinger said, 'fuck me, that was close.' No one made any comment. Stoker was polishing his boots and singing along to AC/DC. Spud was writing a letter and Spen had gone for a shower. Perhaps to get attention, Dinger tried another tack. 'Looks like snow', he said, which was clearly not true. The sky was heavy with rain but not snow.

'I love the snow', he said. Rockets threw a Nutty bar at him which hit the back of his head. 'Eat that', he said. Dinger picked up the confection and retired to his bed where he lay staring at the bed springs of the bunk above.

He threw a Ripple at me. 'Eat that', he said.

'Where do you get all this stuff from?', I asked. He had been given the same question many times.

'It falls off the back of a Pakistani.'

'A Pakistani lorry?'

'No, a Pakistani person.'

Alan was reading a book about unexplained mysteries and the paranormal. It was called 'Unexplained Mysteries and the Paranormal' and featured a picture of a UFO on the front cover. It was the sort of thing that an uncle bought you for Christmas.

'Good book?', asked Chip.

'Yeah. Got it in my stocking last year.' A brief silence ensued, during which we tried to figure out if

Alan was joking or not. But Alan never made jokes and that knowledge settled the matter for us.

'So, what is the greatest mystery?', asked Chip. He had been reading The Sun.

'Time travel', said Stoker.

'I think it's the Bermuda Triangle', said Dinger sitting up on one elbow. AC/DC continued to play in the background. *She's a whole lotta Rosie, a whole lotta woman...* 'All those aeroplanes and ships that just disappear.'

'Time travel isn't a mystery', said Alan. He rarely joined in with one of our great intellectual debates, much less started one.

'You can't time travel', scoffed Dinger.

'You can go back in time', said Alan. He was sitting up now, animated. This was something that interested him, and he was eager to share his knowledge.

'Can you go forwards?', I asked.

'No.'

'No? You can't go to the future?'

'The future doesn't exist', asserted Alan, sagely.

'Eh?' I think it might have been a collective *eh*?

'You can travel back through time but not forwards. The past exists but the future doesn't.'

'Where'd'you get this from, Star Trek or Doctor Who?', asked Dinger. There was no reproach in his tone.

'Yeah, what about *Back to the Future*? Marty McFly goes to the future', asserted Chip.

'Hence the title', added Stoker, with cod wisdom. 'Besides if the past exists then the future must exist also.'

'There is only the past and the present', said Alan reasonably. 'We never get to the future.'

'We're already in the future', I said. 'Compared to where we were when this conversation began.'

'But are we? Surely, we are just in the present', said Alan.

'Yeah but… It *was* the future', I said. I was starting to have my doubts. This might be an argument I would eventually lose and yet I considered myself to be Alan's intellectual superior, which wasn't hard.

'Exactly. It *was* the future but what is it now? Where has the future gone? You never get there. As soon as you get there it stops existing. You have more chance of getting to the end of the rainbow.'

I scratched my head, actually and metaphorically. This couldn't be right. I began to formulate my counter argument.

'But you can plan for the future, so there must *be* a future.'

The rest of the section looked on with interest at this gigantic battle of wits, gigantic being a relative term you understand.

'Okay', said Alan, patiently. He was quite clearly in control of this debate. He could pre-empt any argument

I might come up with. 'These things you plan for, when do you *do* them?'

'The things I plan for in the future?', I asked, thinking I was about to steal a point. I kept the note of triumphalism from my voice. I was carrying the opinion of the rest of the section here. They had entrusted their shared beliefs with me. We knew we were right, and that Alan was wrong. I had to demonstrate that that was the case.

'Yes', replied Alan, plainly.

'In the future!' There! I had laid out all my cards.

'No, you don't. You only ever do them in the present. If you plan to go to the toilet for instance, by the time you actually get around to doing it, it is the present.'

I frowned. I frowned for the whole section. I frowned for sanity and for the entire world of rational men. And women. But damn Alan, he was making a completely unbeatable argument, unbeatable by me anyway.

'So, there is no future', I said. It was a simple statement rather than a question.

'There is no future', confirmed Alan, which for him was practically the truth. Stoker shook his head. A future with no future did not appeal.

'One of my teachers said I had no future', said Dinger, sadly. 'Looks like she was right.'

Spud had yet to speak on the matter. He continued to do so now and resumed his letter writing task.

Dinger asked him if there any point writing a letter if there was no future. Spud pulled a face. As if sensing the mood, Alan spoke again, offering solace.

'But you can go back in time because that exists', he told us.

'Go on then', I said. 'Explain yourself.'

'Well, if you look at the sun you see it as it existed eight minutes ago because it takes light eight minutes to get to Earth from the sun. Therefore, you are looking back in time.'

'Bollocks', said Dinger. 'Besides you shouldn't look at the sun. It'll harm your eyes.'

'No chance of looking at the fucking sun over here anyway', said Chip.

'It's true. And if you travel faster than the speed of light you can go back to the sun and see what it looked like before that eight minutes passed.'

'It would look the same', I said.

'Yes, but you would have gone back in time.'

'So, all you have to do is go faster than the speed of light?', I asked.

Alan nodded. He looked ready to try it. He had a Mr Spock type logic and for a moment I could picture him as some sort of humanoid alien on another planet.

Dinger asked, 'so how fast does light go at?'

'One hundred and eighty-six thousand miles per second.' Alan grinned, having delivered that fact. He was very happy.

'Fuck' said Dinger. He thought for a moment. I could hear the cogs in his brain meshing at high speed. 'And it takes light eight minutes to get from the sun travelling at… whatever you just said?' Alan nodded. His eyes glistened madly as if he had finally convinced a disbelieving public of a theory's truth, which in a sense he had.

Spud had been pretending that the conversation was not his type of thing but now he took note, saying, 'so no one is ever going to be able to time travel because they won't be able to go that fast.' Back in Germany, Spud had a Ford XR3i which he claimed did one hundred and twenty on the autobahn; even that wasn't fast enough.

'Theoretically, they could but it is very fast', said Alan. A silence befitting a room of dumbfounded men fell.

'I don't think I did this at school', said Chip.

***

They enjoyed the story, Alan's mum and dad.

'He didn't do very well at school. Always a misfit. Never in trouble, just not quite… part of it', mused his dad.

'Do you think that there was something a bit…', I ran out of words.

'Something wrong with him?', asked mum defensively. She surprised me with her next statement. 'I worked at a school before I retired. Just a teaching assistant. Some of the children had autism or Asperger's and I always wondered if that was what was wrong with Alan. No one talked about that sort of thing when he was young, but I always wondered about him.' Beside her, dad was nodding vigorously.

'He was always a bit cold. In his emotions, you know? As if he could never really get to know anyone.'

'Do you think that is why this happened?', asked his mum. I really needed that drink. I stood, made my intention to go to the bar clear but paused offering a shrug and a few words which offered no solace at all.

'I think it might be connected. I don't think that any particular thing happened to him in Northern Ireland.'

I squeezed in next to a fat farmer-looking man who reeked of whisky. His bloated red nose glowed, and he burped discreetly but repeatedly into his hand. I couldn't get my drink quickly enough, but when I did I returned to the table to find my new companions gone. I looked around but there was no sign that they had ever existed. No coats hung over chairs, no handbag, no empty glasses. I wondered briefly if I had joined the wrong table, but I recognised the carpet burn on the floor (where else?) and the pillar upon which a series of sepia photographs had been hung; a family scene – all knickerbockers and enormous moustaches, two men with shotguns and a superimposed dog…

Alan's parents were gone and with them their recollections of the son who had chosen to end his life.

***

So, I'm still here, for the meantime at least, and carrying on with life. I don't have a job any longer, but I am looking for one that requires a long-retired soldier with a paunch and six 'O' levels. My search isn't going well but I live in hope, which is more than poor old Alan did.

It's a funny thing about him though. I look back on him with no fondness at all, and you would think that if I could be bothered to write a book which was largely about Alan, that I might have done so because I was desperate to preserve his memory or something equally noble.

But that just isn't so.

He just happened to be in Northern Ireland at the same time as me and he just happened to die first.

Those few months in Northern Ireland represented the only noteworthy period in my life and yet I probably didn't achieve much; I didn't change the world and I won't be remembered for anything. Still, that's life.

***